The House Above the Waves

Emma Barrett-Brown

© 2020 Emma Barrett-Brown
All Rights Reserved

The House above the Waves

First Published Independently
2022 ©Emma Barrett, Plymouth UK

This book has been sold in the agreement that it shall not, by way of trade or otherwise, be reprinted, resold, hired out or otherwise recirculated without the author's express permission. All persons, characters, events and incidents contained within this book are entirely fictitious and any similarity to real-life events is purely coincidental.

Chapter title custom font:
Griffy by Font Diner, licenced for commercial use(c) www.fontdiner.com

Printed and Bound by KDP – Kindle Direct Publishing

This book is for:

My late Mum and Dad.
Miss you both!

One

The sound of church bells rang out in a glorious peal, echoing across the village that day. The air was humid but warm, August, and the year 1848, almost ten years after the ascension of our beautiful young queen to the throne. All about me, the birds chirruped and chirped, broken up time and again by the buzz of an inquisitive bee or wasp. The church, the very same where my own mother lay still and quiet under the dirt, was bright with summer flowers: some picked locally and others purchased by the huge fortune available to those who wore the name *Carfax*. The bride too was radiant if a little faint and sorrowful of expression. She was very beautiful, her long hair – bound and half-hidden under the veil, was fair enough to gleam white in the sunshine and her eyes as bright as forget-me-nots on a summer's day. Her gown was white too, in the tradition of one about to embark upon matrimony. She was slender, tall, and her shoulders pulled back to denote the elegance for which she was known, despite that in birth she was as low as I was! She was a quiet girl, her demeanour spoke volumes of such, as did the pretty pink blush to her cheek. The very picture of purity, correctness, and restraint. Angelic, almost, but frail and wispy rather than the strength which abounds in such divine forces.

Lord, how I hated her.

The groom was of a different breed entirely to his bride. He stood stiffly with her hand clasped in his but even a million cherubs chorusing could not have brought a smile to his face.

His skin was darker in tone than one usually saw about the pale faces of the southern-English, a warm shade of caramel despite his European features. His hair was so dark it was almost black where it fell in a fine haze to his ears, just long enough to tuck behind them. His colouring denoted his heritage: *Creole* – almost a cuss word amongst the well-to-do, especially in that tiny village where prejudice ran so deep. More so, for the gossips, of how neither parent held those same dark looks – he must be adopted, people whispered, or illegitimate! I suppose though, as a young woman who loved him, I did not think very much of such things. Bastian was beautiful to me, handsome as ever a man I saw, especially that day. He was dressed as finely as his bride, in a tailored jacket with tails, fine trousers with a detailing of buttons down the side of them, and a starched shirt. A deep green cravat, and waistcoat of black finished the outfit. He was fashionable in our youth, although he never grew out his chops or moustache as was fast becoming fashion amongst the well-to-do. His expression was dark too, a grimace enough to cause the unwary observer to pity the girl for the sorrow in her eyes.

Sebastian Carfax. The man I loved.

Even if I had not been born the daughter of a mere physician, even if I had had wealth and cunning and an eye that burned with passion… or with goodness, I never could have had him then. Bastian had been betrothed since he was fourteen years old, and that unsweet union was tethered by bonds unbreakable, between men with secrets. I knew some of them, then, as I stood and held my tears inside, lips pressed and chest so tight it was painful, but there was still more I was to learn yet.

Alice Monroe, minutes away from a lifetime as Mrs Carfax, tried a tentative smile as Bastian lifted her hand and was delivered of the ring to shackle her to him. The ring-maiden was another like him, dark and mysterious, his sister and my dearest friend, Leonora. She wore a gown of green silk in the highest of fashion with her skirts widening again, as the trend of the late 1840s denoted. She too wore a false smile. She knew, just as I did, that the wedding was a sham, and that the groom was hard pressed even to utter the sacred words of matrimony to this girl he did not love. At my side, my own Papa laid a hand on my arm. If he was not a fool, and certainly he was not that, he knew the pain that I was in, knew the hurt flooding every part of my form. After all, he was the one who had inadvertently thrust us together when he'd first sent me to take lessons at the Cliff House some five years earlier.

The Cliff House, as it was known locally, or more formally as "Fiveham Hall", was a large, gated mansion some twenty-minute walk from my house. So named, or so we were told, for some old feudal lord who had governed all five hams – that is towns or villages – of the district. Fiveham was set precariously out on the jut of a cliff, overlooking the cold grey English seas with just a fence about it for safety. Positioned where it was, the sea spread all about it on three sides, turning to blue as the sun began to feebly pull us closer and closer to the summers, then fading back to darkness as the skies turned to grey. All about grew wild red valerian and the rougher, choppier loosestrife which poked up its head here and there. Beyond the house, to the northeast, the thickness of woodlands reached out to touch the sea with long twig-hands and bracken. We had but one little cove, that to the west, and there the wide and open green fuzz-covered clifftops which looked down in the swirling mass of grey waters. For as long as I could remember, this great estate had been the property of an old lady, Evelyn Paxton, and her three little dogs which were ought but small balls of barking, nipping, fluff as far as I was concerned!

Aside from Fiveham, the only other houses of note were the farms which bordered us, leading out as far as the eye could see, when it was not obstructed by the lush woodlands. None of those was so grand though, and nothing of the ilk of Cliff House stood at least until Camborne! With little other of local gentry in the area, then, it was rare to see, as I did one morning from my window at the curate's little schoolroom in the village, the sight of gentlefolk walking about. I was just eleven years old then, and in some ways that day was to splice my life in two: the *time before him*, and the time after.

I saw Bastian first. Perhaps that is an omen of fate in itself, that at first, before the others, there was him. Even then, as I watched him, I noticed the dark hue of his hair, and the richness of his tanned skin. As a younger man though, still a boy really at sixteen or so, perhaps the distinction was not quite so clean cut. He could have been European, Italian perhaps, or Spanish, to my childish eye. His naturally dark hair set off the image well of his exotic birth though, as did his dark eyes. The young man who was to become so very much to me ran out onto the grass at the edge of the semi-square of the village, grass on which I was forbidden to walk, and so my first memory of Bastian is that of my wondering if he would be in trouble for treading over the little daisies and buttercups. The brightness of those flowers was newly bloomed too, spring flowers which never lasted long in the salt breeze of our coastal village. Vibrant yellows and whites, with the odd crocus giving a glimpse of purple which contrasted superbly with the green of the wet, dewy grass. The lad bent, and there recovered a cricket ball which he showed to somebody beyond my view.

I shuffled over to look more carefully. Far more interesting to my eye was this spectacle, than the boring chalky mathematical problems which lay before me on my board. I was alone in my studies, as I so often was. There were very few children in our tiny village and those of poorer families rarely joined me at lessons with the curate – especially in crop planting season. No, for them the freedom of running wild in the fields, cutting, hoeing, weeding and sewing the various maize and corns whilst I remained stuck in my isolation. Perhaps they would not have seen it such, but to my childish ire, they were the lucky ones!

Through the window, I saw a man move into view and call the boy back to his side. For a moment, Bastian paused there by the green and the older man pointed something out to him, his hand shading his eyes as he surveyed what was before him. I heard a childish giggle float in through the window and then a young girl joined the other two, running across the grass just as Bastian had. Nora's hair is not so dark as Bastian's, and this fact remained in childhood. Her hair was still dark mahogany though, but her skin paler, more like the soft hues of a forest at sunrise. Ever the children were close in affection, and as I watched she took up his hand. She must have been eleven or so, then. Finally a fourth person walked rather than ran into my field of vision, another child. This one was fair, clean and tidy with not a hair out of place to indicate frolicking. Alice, as poised and beautiful then, as she would be some five years later, on her wedding day.

So many years later, back in the stuffy church, I allowed the memories to rush over me as I watched Alice accept the ring, and then bow her head before the vicar as he spoke of any impediments to be named. How I wished I could shout out that no, they could not be married. The groom was not in love with the bride! He had other commitments! To me! He was being forced, pushed by reasons, motives, which none but we knew. I cast my eyes then to Lord Carfax, that grizzled beast of a man with his dark hair, bushy eyebrows, and stern straight lips. His wife, Lady Carfax, sat at his side. She was as much his opposite as Bastian was to his bride. Where Carfax was bland of appearance and aging, she still seemed young, youthful enough to have been a sister, rather than a mother to the groom. Of course, she *was* twenty years her husband's junior, his arranged bride just as Alice was to their son. Lady Carfax had colouring which was atypical to her Cornish heritage, with her pale skin and fox-red locks. She was somewhat reminiscent of her grandmother, that being the by then late Dame Evelyn of Cliff House. I had met the old lady but once in my friendship with Nora and Bastian, other than my childish games of espying her from the village, but still I had mourned for her, such an impression she'd made to my fourteen-year-old self.

'*Maddi wants to meet Grandmother!*'

The echo came to my mind, of that long-ago day and again I was dragged back into reminiscence.

The images in my mind came with sensation too. Nora's sweaty and plump childish hand in mine, pulling me past her laughing mother and up the stairs. By then I was already growing to be a fixture in the house.

I had come to have lessons with the family when I was thirteen, that being perhaps a year after I had espied them from the window of the schoolroom! A shared governess and a new role as companion to the little girl there: the girl now stood by her brother as he was married. The walk up from Seaview – my father's house – to Fiveham was quite a pretty walk, even when the skies were grey and the weather cold. Still the views of the sea were spectacular, sometimes I thought more so when the wind churned up the waters, making them to grey and white devils. It was cold though, the sea breeze turning to choppy winds as they gusted over the countryside. I was wrapped in a shawl under my coat and warm gloves but still my hand was cold enough to hurt.

At first as our maid, Nell, had ushered me into that grand house I had been afraid and quiet, but it had not taken the two Carfax children with their easy ways and funny accents very long to pull my young self out of my shell. Bastian was much the quieter of the two. Not reticent at all, but certainly less boisterous than his sister. He was, I suppose, a little older than us and so showing that level of maturity one reaches when approaching early adulthood. Despite that, he still had a level of playfulness to him and was not above grappling his sister – or, later, me – and threatening us with the pond, or a pile of cow dung when we were out at play. Such are boys, but never was he a bully in his playfulness, stopping with such genuine remorse when once he made Nora cry, that I thought for a moment that he might cry too.

Nora, then, was my best and most dear of friends! She was a beauty, and even at such a young age, she knew it, as she did the privilege of her position. Their father was a Baron, after all! Titled, important, and well-known in London for his hand in the politics of the day. Bastian did not take lessons with us, already deemed too old for that I suppose and often he was tutored by a gentleman who came to the house. He went away to boarding school for a time too, but always he found us in his holidays, all of which were spent at home with us, and then off we would go to frolic and play. Those were the days I recall most, in nostalgia. Days of innocence. Nora's loud laugh, her sweet smile, Bastian's quietness, the way he used to build little ships in bottles, tugging the attached strings to open them up once they were done like a magic trick.

On the day that I was first taken to Grandmother, one of those little ships was displayed on the dresser behind the chair where the old lady sat. The old lady was rather something odd to a child like me. She had grown frail in her aged years: her grey hair loose was over her shoulders rather than tied away like most grown-up ladies, and her eyes not quite in our own world any longer. Her little dogs still sat by her feet, reminding me of the days when she'd walked them across the cove in my youth, but she did not fuss them or lift them up. She seemed smaller too, in the big chair, her hair was very long, a hint of flame-red still apparent here and there in the grey. She wore only her nightgown with a shawl draped over her shoulders for warmth. A white muslin hat covered her hair and on her nose sat a tiny pair of spectacles. The room was dim, and there was little ornamentation but for a portrait of a man on the wall, grand and framed in gold. I glanced to it, looking at a handsome face in modern enough garb of perhaps thirty years gone, and then back to the old lady.

'Ah, Leonora, dear and who is that? Alice?' the old lady squinted in our direction.

'Grandmother, this is Madeleine Chilcott,' Nora said, a little breathlessly and I realised I must be in the presence of the one person of whom my bubbly and vivacious friend was in awe. 'The doctor's daughter – do you recall? Alice has fairer hair, and Maddi here has freckles which Alice does not, see!'

I bit my lip then. I had of course heard tell of the little blond girl I'd seen when I'd first laid eye on the Carfax family, but I had yet to meet her as she still resided in London with her father then. Already, though, a pang of jealousy grew in me, and that was before I knew that she was to marry my friend, and before I knew even that I loved him!

'Ah yes,' the old lady wheezed. 'Hmm. Come here, child!' Her voice was brisk but had a hint of softness in it too. 'Let me look at you. My old eyes can barely make you out!'

Nora's hand prodded my spine and, tripping on my own feet, I stepped forward to stand by the bed. The old lady looked me over with her small beady eyes for a long moment, and then leaned over and patted the coverlet of the bed beside her chair. Feeling somewhat unconventional, I sat down there.

'Now, now… let me see… who could you be?'

'Miss Chilcott,' I repeated again, patiently. 'Maddi. I'm here for lessons with Nora.'

'Ah, yes! The doctor's daughter, is that right?'

'Yes, milady.'

'I see. Only child, are you?'

'Yes, Ma'am, Mama was a little aged for childbearing when she married Papa… or so they say.'

The old lady smirked at that, perhaps enjoying my naïve admissions. 'Was she then?' She laughed, 'Unfortunate. And so your father is left with no boy to follow him in the profession, hmm?'

'Father says I might aid him, in his work, when I am older.'

'Hardly work for a little lady! Are not girls of your status supposed to aspire to become charity-working ornaments only?'

'Maddi is no ornament,' Nora said, with a shrug, then, when I huffed, 'No, I mean not that you are not pretty, just that you are not without your own mind.' For a thirteen-year-old, I suppose the compliment was profound, although inwardly I did find myself pouting still. Even then, I knew I was bordering on plain. My face is narrow but my features in line enough not to make me look shrew-like. My hair is a dirty blond that even calling "honey" was something of an overstatement. I have wider hips and a heavy bust which was growing in even then, despite something of a trim waistline.

I was prevented, however, from a reply by the door swinging open again and Bastian's entry. Ah, how fondly I recall him then. If I was fourteen, then he must have been nearly eighteen, young still, but already a man in the making. Not overly tall, really, although already he was above me in stature. His eyes were so dark that they were unreadable, and his hair a fine mess of soft black curls about his cinnamon toned features. The candlelight of Grandmother's room softened Bastian too, casting away some of the hardness of the high cheekbones he'd inherited from his mother.

That Bastian was the favourite of his grandmother was instantly obvious by the old lady's beaming grin and discretely I moved so that he could sit with her. Even as a child, I admired the gentle way in which he held the old lady's hand as he spoke to her, sometimes repeating himself several times. Ever constant, he, throughout all we were to endure in the years to follow, his big heart the one thing which never changed.

As finally, we stood to leave, Grandmother took my hand in hers. She traced the lines there with a nail, and then looked up into my face. 'It will be worth the wait,' she said, 'In the end.'

'I don't understand you…'

'You will,' she smiled, and then curled my fingers back over my palm, I looked down at my hand and then back to her old face.

'Thank you,' I whispered, not knowing then, for what I thanked her, for the hope she had given me for later life.

All those years later, as I watched that lady's grandson step closer to his bride and kiss her lips, then I knew what that prophecy was. It was a salve for a broken heart, a hope for a future worth waiting for, even on that most terrible of days.

After the final words were spoken, and the applause of the guests, mainly just the locals, was quieted. Bastian took Alice by the hand and led her back down the aisle. I wonder now, how many others saw the tears in her eyes, her pressed lips and the frozen smile on her features. I wonder too, how many saw as her foot purposely slipped on the cobbles, making her look a little faint. I could not help a sardonic thought, that of how much of it all was calculated. Alice was one of the very best of actresses, when it came to such.

Bastian paid his new wife no heed. Instead, his deep brown eyes locked to my grey ones as he approached, a million apologies in them. He spoke not, but what could he have said before so many? I spoke not either, for how could I have? Especially in the light of my own secret, of his child growing in my belly under my gown of soft blue cotton. Not quite showing through my disguise of a higher waist just yet, but definitely there below. Bastian did not know about that yet, though, nobody did. I held his eye for the entirety, and then as he passed me, I inclined a slight nod. A silent message. Despite how my heart was breaking, it was a nod of understanding, of acknowledgement for an act he'd really had no say in. He saw it and moved as though to come to me, checked himself, and then closed his eyes for a brief moment. When he reopened them, he cast them not back to me, but to the stone floor of the church, solemn but collected once more as he left the building, leaving me behind. Still, in all I have endured in this life, I think that was one of the very worst moments I have ever faced and survived.

Two

Moving away from that heartbreak, it is easier to dwell on what came before than those awful days after that wedding. When I look back in reminiscence of childish summers, I think of all the time that I knew the Carfax children, and of when it was that I came to love each of them. Not that first day in the nursery, I don't suppose. Even when after lessons were done, Nora had pulled me by the hand to her own chamber of girlish things and had begun a game of dress-up, gifting me, with the permission of her mother, both a new hat and a pair of gloves from her own cast-offs.

'It is well to be charitable,' Lady Carfax's response, upon Nora's request to give me the items, and so a little lace fan and a set of unused cotton kerchiefs had been added to the pile. Thus was evidence of her nature of giving, but it was not when I had loved her. Perhaps then, on a cold winter's day, in my fifteenth year, when we had sat together by the frozen-over fishpond and Nora had sobbed at the fate of the little fish within, despite the reassurances of both myself and of her brother, that the pond was deep enough. The fishes and frogs were likely perfectly used to such things and living merrily below the surface. Perhaps it was then, but more so it was a thing of constancy; her bubbly nature, her way of turning every dour day into a new adventure to be seen only from the shining viewpoint of the world's greatest optimist. I know not, with Nora. That love grew slowly in the companionship and company most desired by an only child, as I was.

With Sebastian, it was different. I knew that I loved him in a sudden burst, like the stars of a million nights all shone at once and pointed down at him, chiming "*He is the one!*". That was in the summer of our third year of acquaintance, and of my sixteenth year of life.

I was still taking lessons with Nora at Cliff House, then, for those went on until my seventeenth birthday, some year later. Nora, who was a year younger, still studied too but by then Bastian had already given up his tutor and was learning the duties of his adult position – he had no interest in politics or business, but as a local squire, guardian of the land, he was gifted indeed. I suppose he must have been nineteen then, but young with it still for his constant company with us. Nora and I had sat well through Empire, History and Literature, but as our attention spans had been lost, Caroline, our sweet-tempered governess, had bade us go and "self-study" in the gardens for the last hour. We had, in good faith, attempted a joint essay on botany, but had given it up after only half a page and laid down the book. The day was another glorious one. All the summers of my childhood seem to be bright and hot, the buzz of droning flies and the scents that only the countryside can bring – not all pleasant, but a true part of the atmosphere. After that we'd explored a little in the old woods which lined the shore: hide and seek and then pebbles before stopping to sit and prattle more so down by the sea in the cove by The Cliff House. By the by, Bastian joined us, as ever he did, with pockets full of gingerbread he'd begged from the kitchens.

Oh, how sharp my memory of that day still is: the games we played, the screams as Bastian play-threatened to throw his sister into the sea and how my heart had pounded as he'd then run at me with the same intent. The Carfax children and I spent much time in those days down on the beaches: mainly the main fishermen's coves as those were deemed safer, although sometimes we used the smaller private coves about Fiveham. That day we walked down from the house the far bend at the edge of the commercial beach. There were three ways to the village from the house. The first was to take the road, a bumpy and ill-kept trail which led down to first our little charmingly-named village of Blossom Cove. To arrive at the seaside, one had to take this road until arrival at the edge of the village, go past my home, and then cut a right down the steep hill until arriving at the rocks which denoted the seaside. The other way was to walk down the drive and then make a right there, over a stile and into the fields. There to walk the cliff-paths which lined our coastline but which were treacherous in places, and slippery. This way took some ten minutes from the walk, but was often muddy, slippery terrain. The third way was the way we went that day, a route only possible at low tide, across the beach itself, over the crunchy seaweed and across the sand. Still I can hear the echo of my screams that day as Bastian caught me, picked me up and threw me over his shoulder, my long cotton skirts bunched up, straw hat to the wind and my hair falling loose its bindings.

'I have you now!' he cried. 'To the sea with you!' He hadn't done it though, not quite daring to throw me in.

'Put me down you oafish boy!' I said at last, but I was dizzy with smiling. Then we'd sat, finding a fairly flat rock to sit upon and chatter. Nora leaned up against the rocks behind us, her hands caressing the dry old soil of the cliffs we were always being told to be more wary of, whilst Bastian and I sat on either side of her. The sun in the sky was still high but dropping down now towards evening and time for me to venture home. Four o' clock, perhaps, or thereabouts.

'Well, I do declare that today has been another perfect day,' Nora said, absently playing with one of her ringlets.

'Agreed,' Bastian said. He was sitting with legs curled beneath him, already much more a man than we were ladies. His hands played with the sand, worrying at it and then absently picking up a discarded shell and fiddling with it. 'One of few remaining to me, I fear.'

Sympathy rushed. I knew all about Alice by then, of course, and despite that I had not actually met I had by then espied her several times on her visits which had begun shortly into my – and her – sixteenth year. What a thing, to me a mere commoner, to think that since he was fourteen years old, this boy had had no agency in his life. Alice was his betrothed, and the engagement, set up by his father, could not be broken for any circumstance.

'But why not?' I had asked, upon hearing of it two years earlier, 'Why must you marry like so?'

He'd shrugged, 'Matters of estate and finance,' his only reply.

I looked up at him, now grown and with the start of worry lines on his brow, and things suddenly seemed less bright and warm in our spot under the baking sun. A tiny little crab moved by my hand and I paused to watch it a moment before looking back at Bastian.

'You have some time yet, though?' I asked.

'Not so. I was told this morning, that Alice's father is returning to the Caribbean on business next year, which means the wedding must be arranged soon,' he said burying his hand in the silty sand.

'I suppose we always knew it was coming,' Nora said, 'Look on the bright side though, Bas, at least you will come to know her better now.'

'I do not think there is much more to know of her, that is the problem. Pious, quiet little mouse that she is.'

'Many think those exemplary traits to have in a wife,' I commented.

At that he smiled, and that smile changed his solemn features, 'Do they?' he chuckled, 'Then I wish the greatest of luck to our fathers in trying to marry you pair off!'

I giggled and made a feeble jest-slap to his arm whilst Nora gasped in mock annoyance and so the strain of the moment was lost. Despite the teasing, though, as Nora launched into talk of planning her own coming out, I noticed Bastian turned quiet again, the laughter somewhat forced.

'I really should depart,' I said, after another half an hour or so of prattle. 'Papa will be cross if I am late to supper again!'

At once Bastian stood and helped both his sister and I to our feet. I brushed away the sand and then placed my hand on his arm to stroll back to the main road, the sea air in our faces as we walked. Upon arriving at the road, I almost missed the sight of my father's manservant, George. It was not like father to send anyone and so I excused myself from the company of my friends and rushed to meet him.

'Miss Maddi, at last! I've been looking everywhere! You must come home quickly!' he said. 'There's been an accident.'

My blood froze; my first thoughts for my darling father.

'What? Papa?'

George shook his head. I suppose now that he was unsure of how much information to give to me.

'Mama then?' I persisted, the knot in my stomach unravelling a little before once more coiling so that I could barely breathe. George's face showed the answer. I staggered, panic knocking me almost for six. Bastian came at once to join us, a hand on my back to steady me.

'What? What is it?' he asked.

'There's been an accident, at home, sir. Miss Chilcott is to return at once.

'Good Lord!' Bastian said, then put an arm out to me in comfort. I leaned in a little, not too much for decorum's state, although that was somewhat stretched anyhow with his clutching me in such public surroundings. Then it hit me, all in a rush!

'Oh! Oh Mama!' I gasped and before either Bastian or Nora could stop me, I set off in a run up the hill towards the house.

My home was a fine and fairly large structure right in the middle of our village known as Seaview for the views boasted from the uppermost rooms of the house. The village itself was a moderate seaside village, fairly poor really, but with a sense of community one lacks in larger towns. In the very centre was the hill which was our main street, surrounded on either side by the little schoolroom where I had taken lessons in my youth, and both a grocer and a smithy's workshop. My father's house was on the edge of a small jut, just off the hill, set at the top. Directly below us were the little shops and trader's buildings and behind us snaked out several streets of cottages, mainly small cheap dwellings where the farmer's hands and fishermen from the local agriculture lived and worked.

The village was surrounded by the sea on two sides, with woods leading out along the top of the cliffs. On the other side was yet more woodland, beside the old dirt road which led to the neighbouring villages. Between the woods and those little civilisations lay vast open moor and dotted cops of old bent trees, mostly green from moss. Other than that, the landscape was harsh, moorlands with the dangers moorlands bring: deep mires, rocky peaks, and all. Cold in the winters and hot enough in the sunshine to bake you in your skin with little in-between. Up on the hill, behind the village was a mixed tin and copper mine – indeed where in Cornwall can you go to not see one? – but the workforce was small as the vein was nearly dry so whilst we did have our share of miners, mostly it was the fishermen and farms which gave labour to our countrymen.

My father's house was halfway up the village, fairly large for its location, the grandest one in the village by some with three reception rooms, a large airy hallway and five bedrooms above. Once inside I ran up those mountainous stairs and into the chamber my parents still shared. Papa was sat beside my mother, her cold, dead hand in his and his eyes red and sore from crying. Ever my parents had been besotted. Behind me, Bastian entered the room in quick pursuit of me – we'd left Nora behind, she not so quick as us.

Papa looked up as we entered, Bastian piling into me as we skidded to a halt upon seeing the terrible scene before us.

'M… my condolences…' Bastian whispered, his eyes drinking in the prone form of my mother and his hand on my arm tightened. I suppose this must have been his first view of a dead person, just as it was mine, despite my father's profession.

Papa just stared at him.

'If there is anything I or my family can do…'

'Thank you,' Father murmured, 'that is… kind…'

Bastian paused still, then gently urged me to the chair beside Papa's, at the bed. I went without resistance. I could not take my eyes from her poor prone body. Mama was dressed in her pretty cream and tweed riding habit but the clothing was caked in mud through and through. Her hair was ragged, unbrushed and loose, and she looked as though she were wet through. I touched her hand, it was stone cold.

'What happened?' Bastian asked Papa, his hand still on my shoulder as my eyes began to widen, the shock giving way to realisation that she was already gone. Somehow, despite how she was obviously dead, my mind had taken a few moments to digest the image before me.

'I… we… we don't really know. Sh-she went to deliver medicines to the huts along the cove for me – Wi-widow Marisow needed her… her tinctures – and th-and then she seemed to go down to the shore… you know how she… how she liked to watch the waves, Maddie. B-Barnett, one of the old fishermen, saw… he saw her slip and knock her head and then the waves took her out with them. He… his boys at least, went out at once but it was too late, she… I think she has drowned... It was slippery on the rocks and… she was always so… so careless on the rocks… Oh God! Why… why was she so careless?'

Bastian sighed and then clapped a hand on my father's shoulder.

'I told her – time and again I told her to be careful!…' Papa said, hoarse, 'but she never listened! She never really believed the dangers...' he began to weep again, his hand coming up to his face and his old shoulders heaving.

Bastian paused for a moment, but then beckoned me away. 'Come, allow your Papa a moment of dignity in his grief,' he said softly.

I nodded and stood. I moved to Papa and kissed his cheek. He did not respond and so with a little reluctance, I found my feet taking me downstairs. Bastian called for Nell, and had a pot of tea ordered, then took me out into the garden. Our house, being a central one of the village, did not have an overly large garden, but it had space enough for a few fragrant shrubs and trees, and Mama's little flower garden too, half the floor-print again of the house I suppose. This was all surrounded by a red-brick wall and it was there, by that wall, that an old wrought iron bench sat. Bastian led me through the flowers to the bench and there sat me down, his hands both held tight to mine and his eyes showed a glow of soft empathy.

'Maddi,' he whispered, 'how your poor heart must be breaking I am so very sorry.'

I could not think to reply. In times of great grief, I suppose people expect a storm of weeping and tears but more than anything, I felt numb.

'Maddi, tell me what I can do,' he whispered, lifting my hand and kissing it. 'Anything! Make me useful!'

I pulled in a deep breath. 'I... my... Papa will not be able to... to sign the death certificate, as... as her husband...'

'I'll send for Dr Langton from Cattersley at once. What else?'

'I...' I looked at him helplessly. How clouded one's mind becomes when disaster strikes and in truth I was too young for such a responsibility too, not yet an adult at all.

'I... can you... can you inform the vicar and... and... anyone else who...'

'Of course,' he nodded and then paused as Nell came out with the tea-tray. Her eyes were red-rimmed too, her lips pulled down. Bastian took the tray and lay it on the little accompanying table by the bench. He poured a cup for me, adding lots of sugar, and then turned to Nell who was still loitering. 'You look as though you could use a cup too?' he said. Nell looked shocked but nodded and so another cup was poured and handed to her. Bastian did not partake, but he moved so that Nell could take his seat. She did so with a thanks and so my servant and I sat side by side whilst this young Lord served us tea.

'I'll go and run those errands, shall I?' he said once we were both with cup in hand and settled together, his tone was still so very gentle.

'Thank you,' I whispered but then suddenly all of it hit me and at last my sobbing began. Bastian moved back to kneel beside me. Nell, perhaps seeing the privacy of the moment, slipped away with her cup and a quiet thanks. Bastian allowed me my tears for a moment, but then suddenly sat himself back down beside me and, despite the impropriety of such a gesture, put his arm about me and pulled my face down onto the soft cotton of his waistcoat.

'There, I've got you safe, you cry it out,' he whispered, holding me close. 'Poor Maddi.'

And so we sat, me sobbing onto the expensive cloth of his clothing whilst he held me to him, a hand on the back of my head. At length, I pulled away and he used his handkerchief to wipe away the water at my eyes.

'There, poor dear thing,' he whispered. 'You are coping marvellously!'

I suppose, in retrospect, that is the moment it began, despite that for me that moment was filled with ought but pain. That was when first my heart began to beat for him as more than just my friend's older brother. Bastian dried my eyes and then took my hand in his again. The compassion on his face made me want to cry even more so. We were interrupted however, by the door opening again and Nell's tone informing me that my Papa felt recovered enough for me to re-join him.

Bastian nodded. 'You go,' he said to me. 'I'll set out on your errands and then send Nora up to check on you.'

'Thank you.'

'It is no trouble! Send for us if you need anything at all, I know I speak for our entire family.'

'Thank you,' I whispered again.

Bastian loitered but a moment longer, then lifted up my hand and kissed it one last time before heading out.

*****

And so it was, that the seed of love for him was born in me, albeit lost in a sea of pain for my sudden and dramatic loss. I will dwell no more on the sad months which passed, for when in mourning every day is much the same as the one before, and every light seems dim. I move then, to the following summer.

It was Nora who had suggested that we three go for a stroll on the little local beach, not so very long after my birthday had come and gone in July, making me the grand age of seventeen years. Bastian joined us with the eagerness he had to escape when Alice was visiting.

Of Alice I still knew little. As surprising as it may seem, I'd still not yet been introduced to her as Alice did not like to roam outside at all, it being bad for her complexion. She visited only rarely too, and seemed rather the homebody when she was there. Of course, I thought then, and still do think too, that Bastian took pains to keep us apart too. For never did he bring her to meet me in those early days, never did he invite me inside when she was on a visit. We lived in two completely separate spheres, and Bastian simply hopped between them, mainly remaining with his sister and I if he could.

The beach to which we went was, of course, not the one where Mama had died – that would have been too morbid indeed! – but instead was a little private cove which was situated down a flight of stone steps cut into the very cliffs by Fiveham Hall. Their own little piece of the shoreline. A darker but quieter place by far, as it lacked the hustle and bustle of the fishermen who were working out of the larger beaches in the village. The taller cliffs there at the peak made a little of shadow too, so that the beach there was always colder. I was dressed in my white cotton gown with little blue flowers embroidered and short puffed sleeves whilst Nora wore a more luxurious blue satin. Her hat was of cloth too, whilst mine was a lighter straw one. She looked glorious but was pettish and irritable, reminiscing on the days of having the glorious Caribbean Sea in which to swim.

'Even this awful grey mass of water though, seems worthy of a paddle,' she said, 'Shall we stroll down and get our ankles wet?'

'I would rather not, Nora. It's not that warm!'

'No, something of a chill in the air unusual for August,' Bastian agreed, lazing on the sand somewhat and covering his fine clothing in that damp yellow grit. In his hands was another of his little model boats, one he was just rubbing to make it smooth. He wasn't really working on it though, just fiddling with it.

'I thought for a time I should never be warm here,' Nora mused, 'Do you remember it, Bas, when first we came?'

'I do!' he chuckled, 'Oh how grey it all seemed!'

'I imagine so! Was life very different, in the Caribbean?' I asked.

A shadow crossed Bastian's face. 'It was, not always in a way I remember fondly, but often…'

'It was,' Nora interrupted, 'I was but ten when we left and still… Bas, do you remember the sugar?'

Bastian laughed with her, then turned to me, the little ship forgotten on his knee.

'Father owned a plantation – sugar – you see. Nora and I used to play out in the fields, do you know how tall sugar grows?'

I shook my head.

'And you could not imagine,' Nora took it up, 'Taller than corn or barley, and in thick clumps which were a constant source of games. Our poor governess used to despair of losing us out there one day.

'It sounds like a wonderful childhood?'

Nora nodded but again, that odd shadow showed in Bastian's eyes, 'I suppose that in the most part, yes, it was,' he finally agreed.

I looked out over the view of our grey and white sea, visible from all over the grounds of Fiveham and my mind gave me the imagined blue of the Jamaica seas set against the rows upon rows of sugar cane – what a contrast this must be, after growing up amongst the colonists.

'It is colder and greyer, in every sense,' Bastian said, as I explained the thought, 'and yet there was a darkness to life there too. Things were not always easy between the locals and the plantation owners, especially after slavery abolition, and we were somewhat tainted by that – not, I suppose, that we really understood as children. I do miss the Caribbean waters though, the soft heat and the relaxed way of life. Everything is very different here.'

'The seas are more powerful here too,' Nora added, 'not gentle waves but a teaming mass. There everything ever seemed calm and blue, other than in the stormy season.'

'Our Cornish coast must seem wild and outlandish to you then?'

'It does.'

'Come, enough of this ruminating,' Nora suddenly declared, 'Maddi, do join me? Just a little paddle at the edge of the water?' Nora wheedled, 'just your very toes!'

I laughed and finally, gave in. 'Come, then,' I managed a strained smile, 'If we must!'

Bastian laughed and put down his model. 'Come then, I think I shall join you too!' he announced, smiling.

Three

One of the things I came to know from a young age of Bastian, was that he got bored easily, and that too, should he fall to such a state, I could quite often find myself being the target of one of his pet projects. It was through this that I learned how to write in cursive using the beautiful calligraphy set he had been given the Christmas of my fourteenth year. In a similar fashion, when I was fifteen he taught me how to play chess and checkers, pushing on until I was able to beat even him. He taught me how to catch and cook a fish on the beach using his expensive wooden fishing rod, and how to light a fire using only damp driftwood and dry grass. It was Bastian who taught me how to dance, and then Nora how to play the piano – those being skills that this poor doctor's daughter had not been taught by our governess! At the turn of that year, though, my seventeenth, his latest idea was even more of a project than usual!

'I think Maddi should learn to ride, if she so wishes!' he mused to Nora about two weeks after our beach trip. 'It is as useful a skill to have for a doctor's daughter as it is for a gentleman's son here in Cornwall!'

I glanced up, surprised. 'To ride? Bastian what possible use have I for that particular competence?' I asked.

'A life skill one can never know when might come in useful!'

'I have no horse or tack…'

'You can use mine!' Nora was predictable if nothing else!

'And I have a horse in mind for you, too!' Bastian added. 'And I know nobody will mind if you borrow her!'

I glanced back down at the dry philosophy book I was still looking over despite that lessons by then were done, and then to the window – it was cold and grey without, a storm threatening. I confess, philosophy notwithstanding, staying indoors felt much more appetising.

'Well, I can't ride in this so perhaps another day,' I said indicating my gown.

'Nonsense! I have three old riding habits as well as my own! We'll just put you in one of those!' Nora said.

'I should ask Father…' I began but Nora was already getting to her feet, her eyes full of calculation and so, before I could speak again, I was dragged upstairs to once more be dressed up in Nora's cast-offs. Her full-sized, human doll. I did not mind it really, and the clothing was beautiful. Nora tore through her wardrobes awhile before finally producing a midnight blue redingote which looked to be a promising fit for me. Although Nora was of an age than me, she was larger in frame and build, being both taller and substantially wider than I was.

'You may as well keep those,' she said, 'I have a new set – and here…these match.' A further rummage and then she added boots and a hat to the ensemble and not for the first time, I worried that I might be overstepping boundaries.

'But then what will your parents think if they see me in your clothing?' I asked. 'This is an expensive outfit. Won't your Papa be angry that you give away all these fine things?'

Nora paused, discomfort flooding her features, 'We should ask, actually,' she murmured, uncharacteristically meek, then took a deep breath and rang the bell. A housemaid appeared almost at once.

'Ettie, please go and ask Papa if I may gift my old riding habit that no longer fits me to Miss Chilcott,' Nora said briskly.

I could not help but smirk, and, not for the first time, I wondered at having servants to wait upon your every whim. Had I summoned Nell in such a way I'd have received ought but a scolding for wasting her time.

Nora and I sat down to await the response, I on the chair by the window and Nora on the edge of the bed. The maid was not gone long.

'Aye Miss, you've permission' she said from the doorway. 'Yer Papa says you may do as you please with yer dresses as long as you have clothes to wear and don't be wanting new ones before time. Yer Mama said that you should give any old clothing that don't fit ya to Miss Chilcott. Saves wasting it she said!'

'There you go,' Nora said to me, matter-of-fact.

Once smartly dressed, hat and all, I stood to be critically examined by Nora a while before she nodded her approval with the words: 'It is a little small but you are quite a becoming lady!' there was something to her tone which made me look hard at her.

'A girl in a lady's clothing does not a lady make,' I quipped.

Nora's smiled a smile I could not decipher. 'No I suppose not,' she said at last. 'But none-the-less you look very fine and I am sure my brother will approve.'

When embarrassed, I find my cheeks burn bright red, no pretty, delicate flush but brightest red. Nora could not have missed it. I tried to find the words to retort that I cared not how her brother looked upon me but before I had a chance Nora laughed again.

'Oh Maddi how naïve and innocent to it all you are,' she said through her laughter. 'Go on – go! He will admire you and we need not consider how you feel on the matter.'

I laughed a little with her, still embarrassed, and then departed the room and ran downstairs.

Bastian met me at the foot of the stairs and I was gratified to see his eyes linger a moment on my frame, my dusky curls and my slightly awkward gait, before he looked away with a smile and motioned that I should follow him out of the house. Once outside, we marched in silence to the stables. He opened the door and called to a groom to 'saddle up Lily for Maddi!'

I lingered behind, my face set to passive but my heart pounding.

Bastian turned to me. 'You will be fine!' he assured, 'I taught Nora too, so I promise you will be safe!'

At first, I was very nervous of the little horse which was brought to me, but she was a timid and docile old creature and soon enough I had gained the confidence to mount. Bastian put his own hands around my boot to boost me up whilst their stable-hand held the harness tightly. My boot filled the stirrup with plenty of room to spare, my other leg across the top in the side saddle and my trembling fingers about the reins. I felt terribly unbalanced on the creature and wished I could straddle it like a man. In truth though, with Bastian leading me and calling up orders to temper my movements, before long I did not feel too terribly unsafe.

In time Nora appeared and sat herself on the fence in a most unladylike and undignified manner, as I passed she waved. 'A natural!' she called out, and for a moment I felt true happiness; I was Cinderella at the ball in my finery. I was just on my second slow solo lap of the paddock, with Bastian's bright eyes watching every move, when I saw the figure leaving the house and setting out towards us.

It was none other but Alice.

So unexpected was her appearance that panic rushed through me like a wave of anxiety. In truth, I'd not even known she was visiting! I felt my heart thud heavily in my chest, felt my stomach clench. Ever in her visits to Fiveham, I had shared a dual emotion on her; I wanted more than anything to meet her, whilst simultaneously wanting to pretend that she did not exist. I supposed, then, that I was about to be rewarded with the former. I pulled up rein and my doing so caused Bastian to look where I did.

'Oh, joy of joys...' he murmured, somewhat under his breath, but then sighed. For a moment, his eyes were so dark they were unreadable, but then, when he looked back up, I saw a tight gentleman's smile on his lips.

'Sebastian, Nora,' Alice spoke in that little tinkle of a voice I would come to hate so very much. 'Mama says you must come in before the rain.'

'Did she, indeed?' Bastian asked, still not moving. I stayed up on the horse, somewhat uncomfortable. In truth I had no idea how to dismount and Bastian seemed not to have noticed.

Alice cast her eyes over me, 'Miss Chilcott, I presume?'

'Indeed – Miss Monroe?'

'Oh, I *have* been mentioned then?' she asked but her teasing smile and her tone did not match. At once I felt less at ease. My heart sank lower still too for how lovely she actually was with her fine pale yellow hair and bright blue eyes. Up close, I could see her features were as delicate and pretty as I had imagined and her creamy skin was broken up by a sprinkle of freckles which were of the ilk to be seen as endearing. Bastian stepped closer and dropped an obligatory kiss on her hand as she reached the fence. It was a cold kiss though, no caress of the finger, no lingering of the lips, just a little kiss and then dropped fingers. I thought Alice's smile dropped a little too and I wondered if she realised how disdainful he was of her. Alice's eyes swept over me too, perhaps taking in my sharp grey eyes, my too large frame and the untidiness of my long dirty blond hair. She appraised me another moment but then turned back to Bastian

'Have you been out here all morning, Sebastian?' she asked. 'Your mama was quite perturbed that you were not at luncheon!'

The question should have been abrupt and accusing but her tone still somehow managed to stay very quiet and calm, I doubted she'd ever raised her voice in her life. I thought to my own temperament, my flash temper that reared its head every now and again, my snappish irritation, and I felt ashamed of my fire.

'Indeed? I did tell Mama that Nora, Maddi and I were having a riding lesson, I suppose she must have forgotten?'

Once more, those shining blue eyes were set upon me, anger well hidden.

'Well I suppose, yes,' she said at last. I alone seemed to see how annoyed she was at being caught in a fib. 'Would you leave me then, to spend yet another afternoon alone whilst you are at leisure with Leonora and her friend?'

My blood boiled at being so easily dismissed.

'Maddi is my friend too, Alice,' Bastian corrected her, though. 'Not just *"Nora's friend"*. My dear friend at that.'

The big blue eyes widened even more and to my absolute shock, her lips trembled.

'I am sorry,' she said, a tearful sound in her voice. 'I meant no offence!'

There were a few moments of the most awkward silence I have ever experienced, but then Bastian sighed and muttered an apology too. Alice allowed her lip to wobble a moment more, but then seemed to recover herself, swallowed nervously and smiled again.

I did not know what to think.

I could see exactly what most people found attractive about her, could see her goodness and sweetness, and yet I could see that she was the worst possible match for Bastian. He needed someone whom he could tease, someone who was playful and would bite back rather than cry if he was sharp. Before I could speak though, to ease the tensions, I was distracted by a fat raindrop falling on my head. I glanced up and sighed as the rain began to fall, and then indicated to Bastian.

'Here, help me down?'

Bastian moved at once to my side, guiding me down and placing his hands about my waist to assist my dismount. My cheeks coloured for the contact and I could not help but look to Alice again. She was paler even than before, her lips pressed tight and her eyes glaring at that intimate touch. She glared at us for a few moments but then seemed to grow faint again. It was odd to watch, the glazing of her eyes, the slump of her body. Back then, before I came to learn how contrived it all was, I too was caught in genuine worry for the girl. To my surprise she took a little vial from her belt bag and put it to her lips. Just a touch. Then she seemed to gather herself.

'I feel a little faint,' she said, 'and the rain does not help at all with my chills. Shall I tell Mama you are coming?'

'Tell her what you like, Alice,' Bastian said, not sharply but not kindly either. 'I'll be in by the by.'

'But Mama said…'

'I heard you already…'

Alice's lips puckered more so but with a coldness to her eye she turned to Nora. 'You will remain as chaperone?'

'I do not need…' Bastian began to bark but Nora cut him off.

'Yes Alice! I shall be with them the whole time! Don't give me those eyes, go on in and tell Mama we will be back presently!'

Alice lingered a moment longer, but then wrapped her shawl about herself. She got about halfway back before she turned to look back at us again. Bastian stiffened but then sighed as she turned back and continued to the house, pausing once more at the wall to rest – or so it seemed.

'My apologies,' he said.

'She's not quite what I imagined.'

'No, I imagine not. She's always been the same, since she was a child, playing on weakness and illness for her own way. Then I am scolded for being rude to her but she bloody… she puts it all on for appearances.'

'In truth?'

'Yes, I've seen it too,' Nora said, 'I think Mama does as well but she sides with Father of course…'

'You see why I dread the future now?' Bastian all-but whispered, 'Even if I am wrong and her illness is not contrived, even if she were simply this simple sweet girl, we are not well-suited!'

'It cannot be easy for either of you, to wed somebody so very different. Perhaps…' I shook my head, losing the train of thought. The rain had turned to a drizzle and already I was feeling soaked through. I gathered up my things. 'I should go!'

Bastian put a hand on my arm, gentle restraint, but when I turned he seemed not to know what to say and so with a curt nod released me again. Nora threw me her own shawl.

'To keep you dry!' she said, 'I'll have your own things sent over later!'

'Thank you', I said, and then set off home.

Four

After that, Alice seemed to find excuses to join us where first she had avoided me. Her little faintness's, swoons and coughs became as commonplace to me as Bastian's guffaw and Nora's mischievous giggles had been previously – both were sadly lacking then though. Over the next weeks, Alice's actions seemed locked into her determination to befriend me, and perhaps it was only I – perhaps Nora and Bastian too – who saw the other side of it all. How Alice only ever spoke to me in our company of three, choosing to avoid talking to me if Bastian or Nora were absent and cavort with the other instead. On the one time I had come to find her alone in the village she'd merely fixed me with a cold gaze and then turned and walked the other way. Whenever she was challenged she claimed weakness, headaches, faintness.

'It is just what she is like,' Nora said, when I confided in her, 'She's a manipulative little vixen! She makes everyone think she is a delicate flower when in fact she is whipping up little schemes of her own. Then, of course, if Bastian or I challenge her everybody is shocked at our hardness in the face of such a *lamb*!'

'I like not to think of poor Bas to be wed to her,' I said, knowing I was crossing a boundary.

Nora, forthright, fixed me with a glance, and then paused to pour tea, we were in the conservatory watching the rain on the other side of the glass, running down in rivers. It did seem to be quenching though, even as she spoke. 'You like not to think of my brother wedding any though, surely?'

'I don't have an opinion on such things...'

'You do. Come, you can't pull the wool over my eyes!'

I took the teacup and added sugar. Stirring distracted me for a moment but then I looked up at my friend. 'And what if that were to be the case? Surely it says nothing but for my foolishness?'

'Perhaps, but when has love ever been sensible?'

I smiled at that. Nora loaded up two sandwiches onto her plate as well as a good-sized chunk of cake. There was a good reason she was growing out of her clothes so quickly! I cut myself a more moderate slice.

'He feels the same about you, you know,' Nora added.

'Hush, no good can come of such talk,' I said then winced to hear the door open behind me. It was Bastian though, who entered, rather than Alice.

'Aha! I wondered if you ladies would be hiding in here,' he said, sitting down, 'another tea in that pot whilst we wait for the rain to cease?'

Bastian sat down on the wicker chair beside me and lazed back with his legs out before him and his ankles crossed. He might be a gentleman's son, but he never was so with us. Nora poured him tea and handed it to him.

'What were you ladies discussing?' Bastian asked.

'Your matrimonial state,' Nora said, then chuckled at my squeak of protest.

'Oh, not a subject I favour – but what of it, eh?'

'Maddi doesn't like Alice much,' Nora ploughed on. I wished for the wicker to open and slide me off to another place. I was well used to Nora but I hated it when she used me for her naughtiness.

'Well, then we are well matched,' Bastian said, 'and with the countdown looming!'

'It is so close now,' Nora agreed, 'three months.'

'I can scarce believe it so close,' I murmured, then stood, 'I think I should get myself home, Papa will be wondering what is keeping me!'

'Did you not want another riding lesson?' Bastian asked, 'Especially since my wife-to-be is abed with her third headache of the week…'

'At least finish your cake!' Nora added.

I shook my head. It was true Papa had been making mutterings about the time I spent up at Fiveham again, but more so, I was conflicted by shattered emotions, trying not to cry. 'No, I should go… Not to worry Papa, you see…' I said and then all but fled the room.

I got as far as the outer hall when I heard footsteps behind me. I pressed my lips, steeled myself, and then turned to my friend.

'I know why you are leaving,' he said, his tone soft.

'My papa…'

'Psh! You've never had to flee this house in a hurry before!'

I turned to face him, 'Bas… I can't do this, not now!'

'Tell me the truth at least, just once…'

'Fine! I don't want you to marry her! There, I said it!'

'I don't want to marry her either,' he said, his voice lower, 'but I genuinely have no other choice.'

I shook my head, not understanding.

'Please just… come and ride with me? The rain is easing and we'll go into the trees to be drier!' he said and suddenly his own face was sallow, his eyes tired.

I nodded, giving in and followed him down the steep garden path to the paddock at the bottom of the garden by the stables. I waited in the drizzle whilst he pulled open the gate, helped me mount and then pulled himself astride his own horse.

'We will go easy,' he said, 'and ride with care! The ground will be slippery and you are so very new to riding, but I wish to be away if you think you can manage it?'

'I am sure I can!' I moved with the horse, still a little shy of her despite the obvious gentleness of the beast.

'We'll go very slowly,' he reassured. 'I know this is your first time riding anywhere other than the paddock so I will be close!'

I nodded my head but already I knew I was better than most beginners, not for my own skill so much as for the Carfax children's gentle yet thorough teaching over the last month. We moved at a slow trot down the road and then off into the open grass-land which bordered Fiveham.

'I'm going to let Cobble stretch her legs a bit,' Bastian called over, 'see if I can shake off this mood! Don't try to keep up, I'll draw her in and wait at the other side of the field.'

I nodded and watched him canter away. His arms were strong as he controlled the animal and his back very straight. I'd never seen him ride properly before and could see that he was at least a fairly good horseman. In his shadow, I felt ashamed of my little trot and so pulled on the reins. I did not dare to travel as quickly as the gallop Bastian pushed Cobble into, but I confess I was exhilarated none-the-less as I pushed Lily into a slow canter. My fingers were white as I held the reins and I knew my gait was not so elegant as it could have been. Had anything spooked the horse I would have easily lost my grip, and yet still it was exhilarating. The edge of the field pulled in more quickly than I could have imagined and with a gasp, I pulled back. Lily slowed and I came to a halt next to Bastian who was watching me.

He shook his head but he was at least smiling again, 'Idiot!'

'What can I say? Lily wanted to stretch her legs too.'

Bastian laughed again. 'You know that if you had fallen, your father would have had my guts!'

'And so he should, leaving your pupil stranded!'

Bastian chuckled and kicked his heels once more. At last the drizzle had stopped and so whilst the moisture clung to me, I was at least drying off a little. With a laugh, I followed him down into the trees of the woods. I did not dare to canter again though.

After a few minutes more of riding, Bastian and I arrived by the old estuary which led in beside the edge of the woods. There we tied our horses to a tree near the edge and stood together watching the still water. Bastian's foul mood had gone but despite appearances, I could see a shadow still upon him.

'Are you well, Bas – I mean I know that…'

'I am well, just… pensive.' Bastian's eyes moved to my face, examining me then suddenly his façade cracked. 'I am frightened of the future,' he said all in a rush and then with a gasp he put a hand over his mouth and nose, his eyes filling up with water.

I just stared, never before had I seen his – or any man's – outer shell crack so completely.

'I am powerless and trapped in a disagreeable arrangement not of my own making!' he pushed on, 'I hate the girl Father wishes me to marry but I am not in a position to say no! I fear the loss of my freedom in it too – they say that women are somewhat subservient to us men, but by God it feels the reverse of it now!'

'Bas… it will be well…'

'No!' he insisted, still het up, 'No! No it won't Maddi! No it won't…'

'But you do have the power of your position, of your place as head of the household when your father is gone. You will be a Baron! A powerful man! And she is still but a woman who must try to love and support you always. Alice suffers too, she must for how she behaves! You are both pawns of your fathers!'

'You would have me be kind to her then?'

'I would have you be *happy*, whatever that entails. Kindness can heal better than strife, surely?'

Bastian did not reply. He stooped to pick up a flat stone and skimmed it over the water, his hand trembled though and the stone only skimmed twice before falling.

'It's easy for you to say,' he finally whispered, glaring out, 'you can go out and do as you choose without ridiculous medieval matches thrust upon you! Never underestimate your simple doctor's daughter life! If only you knew…'

'You are being foolish, Bas…' I whispered. 'Surely you cannot wish away your fine future, your position? You say you are afeared of the future but think of what it feels like not to be rich… not to have everything planned out for you – I promise you, that is equally as frightening!'

'I could be the richest man in England and still be miserable!' He murmured, 'You have no idea at all the hell I have lived.'

As I look back in my adult state, I begin to wonder if I should have reacted with more compassion then, if I should have noticed just how much he was hurting. And yet, we heard such stories of female melancholy and hysteria born of pain, but not much of men. I wish I had behaved with more care to him then, knowing how it all was to decline, but then I suppose my youth is my excuse. I really was still only so very young, and so much less experienced in such matters than I care to admit now. Instead of comforting him, of allowing him to put things together in his mind properly, I withdrew.

'Bas, I should go,' I whispered, 'Thank you for the ride but I really should get back to Papa. He'd be so cross if he knew we were out without a chaperone. He does worry so after Mama…'

Bastian turned to me and wet his lips, he seemed moved to speak but then just shook his head with a tiny motion, 'Of course, come, let me help you mount – it's harder without a block!'

*****

Bastian and I met again a few days later, another quiet retreat on our horses out into the countryside. It was a blessed relief to be alone, despite how we risked both parent's ire to be so. There we found our way back to the meadow and sat with a flask of lemonade and his old backgammon board on a blanket he draped over the still-damp grass. The board was beautiful, it was wooden and folded in the middle with leather triangles for the zones. The pieces were carved ivory and jet, or so he claimed. I won the first two games fairly easily, and then found myself laughing at his blatant attempts to cheat by distracting me and moving my pieces off the board. By the end of it, we were too much in laughter to play anymore and so he closed the board.

'I thought to bet you my board,' he confessed, 'but now I am glad I did not!'

'Never underestimate my prowess,' I bragged still laughing, 'Although perhaps let us not play chess!'

'Aha – so chess is still your Achilles Heel? Hmm! Good to know! Good indeed!'

'I did beat you once though!' I argued.

'Ah yes, and you have never let me forget it!'

I chuckled again and then lay back on the blanket. After five minutes or so, Bastian shuffled to sit beside me and then to my shock he gently stroked my hair. 'I should get you home,' he murmured, 'I asked Nora to distract Alice with a picnic but my vanishing will not be missed much longer and if word got back…'

I put up my hand to touch his, he clasped it and brought it to his lips. He stopped there though and pulled back. For a moment we both sat thus, but then he struggled to his feet, pulling me up too. 'Come on, lazybones! Help me pack up the saddlebag!'

'Such a gentleman,' I complained but pulled myself up to my feet anyhow.

Back at Fiveham, Nora was just packing up the picnic as we arrived back at the house. At once upon seeing us, Alice jumped to her feet and ran over to us.

'Husband,' she said, she'd taken to calling him that despite that they were not yet married, 'I was worried about you.'

'You need not have been.'

'Where did you go?'

Nora had struggled to her feet by then, and joined us, 'Ah, a good riding lesson?' she asked, her eye catching mine with something of a conspirator's air.

'Y-yes indeed,' I stammered.

Alice dallied for a moment, but then turned away to stalk back to the house. As she did so, however – if by accident or design, I still do not know, her feet seemed to tangle and she fell, stumbling to the ground. At her landing she gave out a little shriek and then lay still trembling.

'Oh, dear God!' Nora muttered in disgust at the girl's hysterics. Bastian's lips pressed, and in disbelief he shook his head.

'Oh! Oh my leg! I think my ankle is broken!' Alice wailed, flailing slightly. It was quite a sight and I suppose the giggle which tried to form was at least more of shock than of mirth. I quashed it, refusing to be the girl who laughed at another's pain, no matter how ridiculous the situation. Nora too looked quietly amused as she knelt beside Alice and fumbled her tonic from her belt. After an inhale and a dab – the usual dosage – Alice managed to sit back up. Her eyes flew to Bastian but he'd turned his back on her, on all of us, and had ambled away to the edge of the lawn, going back to the gate where the stables sat.

'Are you quite well?' I asked of Alice, trying to be kind.

'How he must despise me,' she whispered so faintly that I don't think we were supposed to hear it. I watched as she took that little bottle up again and took another dab.

'Nobody hates you Alice,' Nora said, in a tone which denied this, but Alice had eyes only for Bastian. Her eyes leaked, her chest heaved and I could see her pulse in her throat. This creature was so delicately fragile that I was amazed she had even made it to seventeen years of age. I suppose a better man would have felt the need to protect her, to care for her but Bastian was not a man to be easily moved by a fragile wife. Already I could see, from the way he walked, stiff and upright, that he was more annoyed than I had ever seen him, and I could not help but sympathise. Torn, I stood and ran to catch him up. To my surprise, he took my arm and placed it on his.

I did not look back at Alice, but instead left her to a rather unimpressed Nora. 'Oh Bastian,' I murmured, 'She's impossible!'

'She is!'

'Then say no! Refuse her! Say you don't find her to your tastes!'

Bastian laughed and patted my hand where it sat on his arm. 'If only life were that simple eh?' he said. 'Do you want to ride some more? I... I could do with getting away again and this morning was perfect until now!'

'No!' I cried out, pulling away and facing him head on. 'No Bastian I don't want to ride! I want you to tell me you won't marry that girl! That you won't marry somebody who is so obviously not going to make you happy!'

My temper was fired up and to my horror, I felt angry tears slip down my nose. Bastian put his hands on my arms. 'Maddi,' he murmured, his eyes probing. 'I have no choice.'

'Fine!' I said, the hot tears rolling down my face. 'Fine...' I turned and began to stalk away.

'Maddi! Where are you going?'

'Home!' I didn't even turn back to him.

'You will leave alone in my grief and anguish?'

'Why not go to Alice?' I snapped, 'She is obviously desirous of your company now.

'Maddi that's not fair!'

'None of this is fair!' I shouted the words, loud enough I suppose that Nora and Alice probably heard me too. 'Go and resolve yourself to be with her, or tell your father you won't marry her! Standing here moping about it does nobody any favours! Grow a spine, Bastian, or stop... stop sulking about it, running away and hiding with me as though I were anything more than a mere distraction to you!'

'Don't... don't say such to me when it is my affection for you which causes this pain!' he said, his voice low but his eyes bright. 'If I didn't regard you so damn highly, then perhaps it would be easier not to *sulk* at having to marry another!'

'Do not speak such words to me when your betrothed is... is...' I lowered my own voice, 'when your betrothed is but a stone's throw away! It is cruel to us both!'

He moved closer, his own voice dropping, 'how can I care when my true love turns away from me?' he whispered, 'how can I care for her pain when I love you to distraction?'

I gasped, floundered and then, with anguish I could not control, I turned and stalked away without another word.

I don't think, in the heat of the moment, I really was thinking straight. I looked not to the skies, as I stormed away, and nor did I heed the hint of rain in the air, any more than I heeded Bastian's voice behind me, calling to me. I went not to the path, to home, I could not, in that moment, bear to look upon the face of my dear Papa and have him ask why I was so filled with sorrow. Instead, I went up over the stile, and out into the trees to the clifftops. There I paused for a long moment, looking out to sea. The sea air was wet and the gulls screamed but at least it was a place for calming, for peace. The waters swirled below, a mass of teaming grey, darkest blue and white foam. I stood for the longest while, allowing my tears to fall at last, and then took myself off again, into the woods, through them, and out onto the moors proper.

I walked until my feet were sore.

The old worker's paths took me away from the coast, past the farms, past even another tiny hamlet and then back out to more open countryside. Even the rain, as it began to fall again, did not stop my pace, nor did the wind as it picked up about me, swishing my hair into a tangle of fibres and pulling at my shawl and coat. Eventually, I forced myself to calmness, and then stopped my feet. There for the first time in hours I looked about me rather than to the path at my feet.

I froze.

I was stood in the shadow of a tor, the ground before me barely even a path by then and littered with grey rocks and stones. To the west was just moorland. The coast, which should have been there, was obscured for the rise in earth as the tor formed as well as the darkening of the skies. To the east was overgrown marshy bog-land, dangerous indeed! And I had nearly walked right into it! In that moment I realised two things, firstly, that I had outwalked the day. The sky was orange fading to purple and what view I did have obscured by darkness. Already the moon sat firm in the sky above me, as the sun bowed away. Secondly, perhaps more frightening, I had no idea, at all, where I was.

Five

I stood stock still for a long moment, terror freezing me to the spot. I knew the boundaries, the edges of the moors of course, but I was well-beyond where I recognised! The skies darkened further still and I could feel the wind creeping up, making a roar that chilled me to the very bone. The moors in winter at night – perhaps one of the most dangerous places to be! I walked quickly back the way I had come, to the edge of the rise, but there I was simply met with more moorland, not even a church spire or other similar landmark to guide me! I broke into a half-walk, half-trot; my feet slipping into the wet mud which rose almost to my ankles in places. Several times, I slipped and had to stumble back to the path in the darkness, as the bogs grew deeper and more dangerous – aided in part too by the drizzle which still fell.

My best bet would be to go up the tor, I half-decided, but then shied away – the summit was littered with rocks and all-sorts. One misplaced footstep and I would be lost in the dark with a twisted or broken ankle, maybe worse!

I let out a small whimper but repressed panic as best I could. At the very worse, I told myself, I should find a small farm or something, perhaps even a little shelter to sit out the night! The moors weren't so very vast that I'd not find my way in daylight! I just needed to sit out the night!

After more slow tentative steps, I managed to find myself upon a better road than the marshy path, and there I began to walk, hoping for a light in the darkness, for any sign of home or even shelter!

None was forthcoming, truly our moors were a lonely and remote place!

'Stupid girl!' I scolded myself as I marched along, my arms holding my coat tight to save me from the rain which was now worsening again. 'Idiot girl with your foolish temper!'

I was shivering, frightened and lost. I had nothing to eat or drink, no idea of where I was, or how to get home. I had no lantern, not that the rain would have allowed for such anyhow.

Time lengthened.

For some two hours or more I walked, trying to keep myself calm, trying to remain hopeful even as the fullness of night surrounded me. Civilisation, any civilisation, that was all I needed. A friendly farmhouse, that was all. And perhaps there might have been such, somewhere, perhaps I walked in circles or further from it all – I know not, only that it was not forthcoming!

Terror can take you, in such circumstances, panic and fear with it. Suddenly every rustle of the wind was a spook behind me, every sound was a highwayman or worse, a cutthroat come to take my life. I was all but sobbing, hopelessly afraid and so very dim of spirit that I was almost tempted just to fall to my knees and allow the darkness and the marshes to take me.

I suppose had it gone on very much longer, then perhaps they would have found me the following morning a gibbering lunatic or even dead of the cold and exposure. As it happens, though, what came next started a chain of events I could never have believed. It began with a sound in the distance. It was rhythmic, sploshing, and accompanied by a clattering. For a long moment I stood, startled, and then realised what it was: the sound of hooves splashing in the mud. It was coming closer too, from the opposite direction.

My heart sang.

A flash of movement came to my eye, and then another on the dark path. Then sudden panic as I realised the danger this could pose! I was all alone, in the dark, bundled in a deep blue coat. I would likely not even be visible to a rider! In real fear that they might not see me in time to slow the horse, I stepped backwards meaning to go up onto the verge slightly. My mistake, however, was that I had not taken into account how slippery wet mud can be. And so out went my foot! I flailed but it was too late, my ankle twisted funnily on a loose piece of rock and the heel of my boot slipped. I flailed twice more, cartwheeling my arms, but it was no good and with a cry, I tumbled down the small ravine behind me into a sopping wet puddle of peaty rainwater hidden by marsh-grass. I cried out, and then again but the sound of the howling wind was enough now to drown me out. As though God laughed at me, the heavens took this moment to reopen too, sending down a flurry of rain so powerful it hurt where it hit my face.

I lay for some moments, winded and somewhat in shock, but then struggled myself to my knees. From there I tried to stand but a sharp pain shot up my leg. I gasped, still shivering and now muddy too, as well as soaked to the bone. Panic tried to set in. As long as my foot was raised, the pain abated but as soon as I tried to put any weight on it, it screamed again in agony. I panted for a moment, and then tried to gather my wits. If I could climb back up… but no, it took me only a few moments of trying, to realise that that wasn't viable. I held back a sob, choking it down inside me. Instead, using the very last of my energy, I opened my lungs and screamed out for aid. The hoofbeats came closer, seemed to go past, but then thankfully they slowed. A voice called my name.

It was Bastian!

Relief flooded me, and in a rush of emotion, I called back to him.

'Maddi, where are you?' he called.

'Down the edge!'

His face appeared over the edge of the bank.

'Oh, thank goodness! Can you climb up to me?'

'No, I am injured!'

Bastian swore, but then moved so that one foot was firmly planted in the mud at the top of the ravine then bent and all but dragged me back up to him. I just about managed it, then fell back onto the muddy verge. My dress was soaked through and covered in mud and stains from the bog, my coat in similar state. My hair hung in sodden ringlets beneath my hat which was dented and dirty too.

'Let me see,' Bastian urged, kneeling in the muck beside me. His fingers probed my ankle, pulling off my boot. 'Wiggle your toes!'

I tried to do as I was told, glad for the rain hiding my tears. It hurt too much though, pain shooting up my leg again.

'Dammit! Something is sprained – it might even be fractured!' he swore. With as gentle a push as he could, he forced the boot back onto my foot. I made a strained barking noise as he did so, not hiding the agony as well as I would have liked. I managed to stand and tried to take a step forward but it hurt too badly. I gasped and gripped Bastian again to steady myself.

'Here,' he said, leading me to the horse.

'What are you doing out here in the rain anyway?'

'Looking for you! What do you think? Your father is beside himself and I... well... I too...'

'I'm sorry Bas, I was just so angry with the world.'

'I know, I'm sorry too. Come, we are over an hour at least from home in this weather and I don't want to lose the path,' he said, wiping a sodden curl of hair out of his eyes, and holding the stirrup ready for me to mount. With a bit of a struggle, I did so, sitting astride like a man due to the shape of his saddle. Bastian took back the rein, leading the horse through the treacherous, slippery mud. As we walked on in silence, with Bastian bent over against the torrent of the rain, and me struggling to remain on his beautiful dapple-grey horse, it became gradually more and more obvious that we were not likely to make it home. As I felt the animal's feet slip for what was the second time, I took pity on the poor creature and, after calling for Bastian to halt, slithered down.

'Are you well?'

'Her feet are slipping, I don't want to risk her tumbling with my weight as well.'

'You have to ride her! We won't make it home otherwise!' he said, brushing a wave of water from his face. 'You can barely stand on that foot and we've miles to go yet!'

'I'm afraid!' I managed – hard to confess it but it was true. We were almost shouting over the rain, but then a crash of thunder rattled around us. I shrieked – everything feels so close on the moors! Beside me, Bastian took my hand in his, his lips panting in shock too as an overhanging tree bough tore free completely and crashed to the ground. At the sound of this, Cobble whinnied and reared up, her hooves splashing even more mud. I tried to hold her but the spirited creature reared again, and then bolted. I cried out in shock, but Bastian held me back as I tried to limp after the beast.

'Don't,' He whispered, 'She's gone!'

A storm of weeping took me then, perhaps allowed for my strained emotions, my sodden skin and the guilt of his losing his mount in the storm. If anything happened to the horse, I knew I would never forgive myself.

'She'll go home,' he murmured, 'Horses are intelligent beasts, they know where is safe! She'll just follow her own path back – that's all! At least you weren't on her when she reared!'

'I'm so sorry,' I sobbed, 'so sorry!'

'Hush,' he murmured, 'I'm more concerned about getting you somewhere safe and dry! Cobble will be just fine, I promise! I... I think you should sit here a moment, and I'll see if I can find somewhere more sheltered.'

'You'll be lost!'

'No, I will...' he paused, '...I will have a care and I will stay within shouting distance. Every time I shout "here", do the same! If I cannot hear you I will retrace my steps!'

I nodded, sitting and weeping into my hands. Bastian crouched before me. 'It really will be all right,' he whispered, 'I promise!'

I nodded and then he was gone.

'Here!' came the first shout.

I replied in kind.

A few minutes and then his voice again, 'Here!'

'Here!' I managed.

Thus we continued for five minutes or so until his voice became very faint. Then, for two of three terrifying moments I could not hear him at all.

'Bastian!' I screamed, trying to stand again but the pain was too much, I was frozen too, to the core.

'Bas!' I screamed again, not liking the panic in my voice. 'Bastian! Where are you?'

Nothing at first, then, 'Here! I'm here!'

'Oh thank God,' I breathed, then took up the shout of 'Here!' again until he managed to find his way back to me. All in all, it must have been twenty minutes or so.

'There's a cottage!' he said as he appeared again through the trees, 'Just a short walk! Come, I'll help you!'

The cottage was a small dwelling; no gate or grounds to announce it, just sitting squat in the middle of an old stone wall. There was gorse all around it, overgrown in places, but we managed to get through and to the building itself. An old worker's cottage maybe, a shepherd perhaps. Bastian's arm was tight about me as I limped with him over to the door. My hair was matted to my head, as was his, and even though he sought to hide it, I could see he was shivering too. The old wooden door was closed tight, the windows dark and greyed with age. Bastian left me leaning against the door which remained unopened for our knock and peered in through the window.

'It's empty,' he said, 'it doesn't look like anyone has lived here in a while!'

I tried the door, convinced it would be locked tight against us, but it swung open, revealing a single-room-dwelling beyond. The cloud of dust within seemed to fall and settle on my wet clothing as I stumbled inside. I coughed, feeling it in my lungs but moved further into the dusty and dark room. Bastian came in behind me, closing the door. Together we surveyed the strange little cottage. It looked as though the owner had left fairly abruptly, or maybe died, leaving the cottage fairly intact around them. There was still a blanket on the old pallet bed by the wall, dusty as it was, and the fireplace had a log or two, not enough for a blazing fire, but perhaps enough to create some warmth. There were two chairs and a rickety old table too, as well as a clothing chest which I opened to find empty.

'Sit yourself down,' Bastian ordered, 'I'll see if there's any tinder about to make a fire!'

I did as I was told, my addled and stressed brain beginning to relax, loosening my shoulders and the tension in my back with it. There was a cup on the sill, and I pushed open a window to collect some of the rainwater for drinking so that we did not thirst. This done, I sat back down, my wet clothing suddenly feeling cold, and my hair still running rivers around me. Bastian managed to get a little fire going, and then came to sit in the other chair. His face mirrored the worry in mine.

'They will come looking for us,' he said. 'As soon as Cobble returns without me, a search will be started.'

'You said Papa was already considering sending some men too?'

'Yes. He was worried sick... as was I!'

'I am sorry indeed to have worried you all,' I half-whispered.

'What were you thinking, going off like that in a storm?'

'I suppose I wasn't. I was quite anguished.'

Bastian's face softened, 'Because of our talk?'

'Yes...'

'I never meant for...' he sighed, 'I should not have said what I said.'

'That you loved me? No you should not have. You are to be married in less than three months' time, to another woman. It was unkind of you to... to...'

'Maddi?'

'I never hoped, you see,' I said, 'I... I have loved you for so long. I think... it began the day my mother died. The care you gave me, the overwhelming kindness in you. I...' I broke off again. 'But I always knew that we were not meant and so I told myself it was a foolish girl's fancy alone.'

Bastian sat beside me on the floor. He took my hand in his. 'And for me it was the day that you Nora and I sat in the *haunted* garden and built the model of the old river barge, do you remember?'

I sniffed again and found a smile, 'I do.' I said, although it could have been one of many such memories.

'I gave you the decking plate to hold whilst I put together the base and you dropped it in the dirt. I tried to tell you it was undamaged but you insisted that you had to clean it for me and rubbed it down with your skirts and got glue on your dress.'

I smiled again, sadly, I remembered it well, I remembered every moment we'd spent together from the childish days of play, right through to our recent companionship.

'I cannot say why or how,' he continued, 'but it was then as we laughed and Nora scolded, something about how the sun lit you up from behind, and how the beams fell across your smiling face. Then, I... I just knew. You were so bright where the rest of my life is... not so.'

Bastian broke off. He was quiet for a long moment, perhaps awaiting my reply, but I was too overwhelmed to give it. He chewed his lip, sighed, but then gently pulled away and retrieved my cup from the window ledge, bringing it before me and offering it up. I took it and drank a mouthful. It tasted dour but more for the dust in the cup than for the rainwater it contained. Bastian's face was unreadable in this, but he did not sit back down, instead removed his coat and waistcoat and put them out before the fire.

'Give me your coat, too,' he said, his voice not quite as controlled as it could have been, 'At least if we can dry some of them... I'm wondering if we should sacrifice the table for firewood too?'

'What if this is somebody's home?'

'I don't think it is, and if it is then I will replace it for them. I'd refurnish the whole damn house in gratitude for this port in a storm!'

I nodded and looked down at my trembling hands. Now I was in from the rain, I somehow felt colder. I shrugged off my coat and passed it to Bastian who then moved the chair he'd been sat on and draped the coat over it.

'How long... How long do you think it will take them to find us?'

'In this storm, probably long enough,' he said. 'Do you want to try to sleep? The bed is probably warmer than sitting there and you look cold and tired.'

'I am, both,' I said, 'but I do not want to miss the search party...'

'I'll stay awake for them.'

I nodded again and stood. It somehow felt wrong to clamber into somebody else's bed, especially in my soaking wet clothing. I hesitated but then moved to lift the blanket.

'I don't think I could sleep,' I said, 'but if we both use these blankets, perhaps we could be warmer.'

Bastian's lips pressed, and indecision slowed in his eye.

'I don't...' he paused, but then came to stand beside the bed where I had sat myself down and fussed the blanket more snuggly about me. 'I don't think it wise, that I join you there,' he said at last.

'Oh...' I flushed at the realisation of my suggestion, 'I didn't mean... I just... you are cold too...'

'I can warm myself by the fire, it is well.'

I said nothing more but held the blankets about me and tried to make myself comfortable on the bed. My stomach growled but I said nothing of my hunger. What use was there of mention, when there was no food to be had?

'What time do you think it is?' Bastian asked, 'I neglected to pick up my pocket-watch this morning…'

'Ten?' I guessed, 'Perhaps a little later?'

'Hmm, indeed, and it must have been eight when I set out, so I'd wager Cobble has likely just made her entrance now. It takes an hour or so to walk this far, and that only when the search party is formed and some idea of direction is known. I suggest we could have a good two hours here before we are found, at the least.'

'Oh, what a drama I have caused,' I whispered.

'And I behind it, with my foolish confessions.'

'Bastian…'

'No, you are correct, I should not have said what I said, all I did was upset the applecart!'

I said nothing, slipping back to silence. Bastian remained where he was, staring into the flames of the fire with his back to me. I used the moment to allow some vulnerability and let another tear or two slide from my eyes, sobbing without sound so as not to worry him further. Bastian's hand reached out for the last half-log in the scuttle and gently, he placed it into the grate.

'I think I will break down that table,' he said, turning about, but then his eyes lit on my twisted lips and wet eyes. An expression I was too young to understand came over his own features and with three steps he cleared the distance between us and sat down on the bed by my side. His hand gripped mine tightly, and then as though giving in to the breaking of some hidden dam, he slid his arm around me and pulled my blanket swathed form to him.

'Don't you shed tears over a useless fool like me,' he whispered, putting his lips to my hair. 'I am not worth this, do you hear?'

'I cannot help them. I wish…'

Bastian's lips caressed my hair again, and so I allowed myself to lay my face down onto his throat, feeling his pulse hammering there. For long moments we sat, and then he began to speak.

'I have to marry Alice,' he said, 'I have no choice in that and it goes deeper than you even imagine. Not just for my father's say so – he and I are hardly of the type to work towards each other's happiness! – but because if I do not, there could be dire consequences to my entire family.'

'I don't understand,' I murmured, still held against him.

'No, I know it. Maddi, dear Maddi, do you think that if it were just a matter of scandal, that I am the type of man to turn his back on love and marry for gain?'

'No, I don't suppose you are.'

'Then you know… you *must* know, that I cannot marry you, for reasons other than you realise?'

I lifted my head to look into his earnest brown eyes. Eyes which lingered and burned.

'Tell me?'

'I might, but if I do, now, spill these secrets then I have to have your vow that you will keep them. You cannot tell another living soul.'

'My lips are sealed.'

'I am in earnest!'

His tone forced me to more attention. I nodded, 'Go on then. You have my word.'

Bastian was silent again, for so long that I thought he changed his mind, but then he began to speak.

'Alice's father is a man named Reginald Monroe,' he said. 'He was my father's clerk, back at home in Jamaica, and helped Papa to run the plantation.'

'Just a clerk's daughter?' I whispered, she was no greater in social status than me then! Somehow, that stung more so.

Bastian nodded. 'Just so. My father is titled but the money was squandered long ago. He took into the plantation business to save face and earn back his fortune. That business was halted by the abolition of slavery, back in 1838. I was just a child at the time, and Nora still in her cloths. Papa tried twice to rekindle our fortunes, and twice he failed. He took to deeds more… nefarious… to keep a roof over our heads. He used Mama's inheritance, despite that her own mother still lived, as well as loans and pledges to fund his criminal activities, and his loyal clerk kept all the books for him, kept notes of everything…'

'So it is blackmail, then?' I asked, catching on.

Bastian nodded and then allowed his fingers to stray to my face, picking up an errant strand of wet hair and tucking it behind my ears. 'Are you warmer now?' he asked.

'I am, but come, share the blanket with me. I want you not to catch a chill either.'

Bastian seemed to hesitate again, but then nodded and slid the blanket about us both. I could feel the clamminess of his damp skin through his shirt, and the cold too. I hoped that my still wet form, where it was pressed against him, didn't in fact make him colder. Bastian slid his arm back around me, locking us together more firmly than before. His eyes skimmed my face. 'Is that better?' he whispered.

I nodded.

For a moment the heat of our closeness warmed us both, but then he resumed his tale.

'By the time I was ten years old,' he said, 'my father was almost bankrupt, despite his unsavoury businesses. There was a man in the town where we resided, Henry Augustus Lloyd, a man famed for his appearance as well as for his deeds, for he was a man one does not often see, with a white colonist as his father, and a freed slave as his mother. Mixed in blood of the two, he was still, as unlikely as it may seem to an English woman, very much esteemed and respected there on the island. He was a man of charity, a man of giving and kindness to all, even those who called at him, and berated him for the very nature of his existence. He hated the slavers though, and the plantation owners. I thought for a long time, that this was the cause of the tensions between he and my father. Of course, now I see more clearly, that there was more to it than that.'

'There was?'

'Look at me, Maddi,' he whispered, then lifted a hand up so that I could examine it in the darkness. 'I suppose, when the lights are out, it is hard to see, but you know of my look, of my skin… does this hand, when the light shines upon it, look like the hand of a white man? Does my face, my hair?'

Suddenly that which had ever been obvious, was more so indeed. I bit my lip, examining his features. So much like those of an Englishman, and yet not, too. I looked up into his brown eyes, eyes of the like I had never before seen. His hair was soft and sat in loose curls but his skin still held that dark hue, those deep bronze undertones: a colouring I had alwasy known but had barely questioned.

'This man, you think…?'

'I think he is actually my father, yes.'

I was still and quiet for a long moment.

'Does this make you think less of me?' he asked, then.

'Of course not!'

'Then you really are a unique girl.'

I fell back to silence, processing, 'and so how does this relate to your father and Monroe?' I asked, 'obviously, I presume, your father knows the truth of it?'

'How could he not? Yes, he does. As I approached my tenth birthday, tensions between those two men grew and grew. There were arguments, plots to outdo the other, it was terrible. Papa accused Lloyd of setting our outhouses – by then unused slave quarters – alight after a great fire devoured them, and tried to make the townsfolk turn against him too. They didn't though, where Lloyd had always looked after them, my father never had. Not even the colour of his skin was enough to turn the commoners against him and in response popular opinion turned against my father. Realising he was beaten, Father took us, and fled in the night with funds that I know not how he acquired, but that some level of extortion occurred, somewhere. My father was on various councils and committees – it could have come from any of them!'

'And Monroe is his witness to it all?'

'Yes. Monroe fled with us, his wife was already dead by then, and Alice still very young at seven or eight. We sailed to New York, caught a steamer there, and within a month we were here. That same month, my father made my betrothal.'

'And so through Monroe's blackmail, you came to be engaged to his daughter?'

'I believe it to be so. Papa says that it is all I am good for. He hates me, but he can have no children of his own, it seems. In selling my marriage in exchange for Monroe's silence, he has a use for me, and so I am not cast out as the half-blood bastard I am.'

The silence fell again, ringing my ears as I digested. 'At least your father was kind enough to keep you and Nora both, even despite…'

'Kind? No! No, he was not that.' Bastian's lips pinched together.

'He was a brute to you?'

Bastian shuffled away slightly from me and threw off the blanket. He paused, seeming unsure, but then pulled the shirt up from his trousers.

'Here,' he said, 'run your fingers up my back. You won't see, not in this light, but you can feel them…'

My fingers almost flinched away, the very idea of touching him so intimately almost stifling, even if not for the worry of what I would find to do so. The shirt was still sodden where it fell on my hands, but the skin beneath was soft, warming. I slid my cold hands up his flesh as ordered, but then paused at the sensation of ridges, many of them, lines in the skin of his back.

'I… What…?'

'Let us just say, Papa was not one to spare the rod... specifically the slaver canes he never relinquished from the old plantation days. This was the punishment I bear for my mother's betrayal… for my birthage, and for the legacy I carry in my brown skin. I wear these scars and, perhaps worse, his taunts and jibes… "*negro-boy, spook, darkie*". When I say my father hates me, I say it not lightly. He hates any who are associated with the slaves whose freedom destroyed his business.'

In a sudden impulse of protectiveness and anguish at his suffering, I pulled him back to me, my hands clutching his poor scarred back. I wanted to meld him into me, to take away all the horrors he had endured in his short life. Bastian shuffled closer too, his hands holding me tight.

'If I could make it so,' I whispered, 'never would any man or woman ever lay a finger to harm you again. I swear it.'

'You really are too much,' he murmured in return, 'sweet, darling Maddi. Oh God, my heart aches to have you so close and yet…' he sighed again, but then put down a hand to lift my chin, his eyes locked to mine, 'I should not even contemplate kissing you…' he said, moving his lips down to do just that. I accepted the kiss, just a fragile thing of longing and broken promises, and there returned it with the same heartfelt and overwhelming sweetness. Bastian murmured against my lips, and when I looked back into his face, his eyes were shining, a little damp.

'We should stop,' he said.

'I know, but I find I can't.. I want to… I want us to…'

'This moment is something lost, a gift to us both…'

'A memory I will long treasure. And since never again might I say it, then hear me now, I love you Sebastian Carfax.'

He pulled in a long, sweet inhale of oxygen and then nuzzled me with his face, 'and I love you, Madeleine Chilcott,' he whispered.

'We have a little time…'

Bastian's eyes ran over my face, pausing and there the temptation burned. He inhaled, slowly, and then exhaled.

'This is not how… not what I would have…'

'It is what it is,' I whispered.

He nodded, and then his lips came down again on mine. The thrill grew, more so as even in the midst of his kisses, my ears were alert for the sound of the search party, of our discovery. Bastian's kisses grew deeper still, and then he moved suddenly, laying me down against the dusty flat pillow. His hands moved to the buttons of his trousers.

'Tell me, once, more, that this truly is what you want?' he murmured.

'It is.'

He paused a longer moment still, long enough to worry me that he had had second thoughts, but then suddenly he moved, pulling himself free from his trousers and balling up my skirts about my waist. As I moved, my swollen ankle screamed, my tired limbs protested, but I ignored them all, pulling away my own under-lace so that together our skin touched skin. Bastian's lips came back to my own as my fingers slid over his ridged and scarred back. I closed my eyes, he whispered my name, and then the pressure of maidenhood being torn away encompassed me. I gasped at the pain, but then too at the pleasure of it, the oneness of being so entangled with another, with my Bastian.

I gasped and lay still a moment, and then opened my eyes to find his upon me, watching me. With a long slow moment, he moved his hips and I felt my head tilt back, my lips part to let out a gentle murmur. He moved again, his hands gripping my back and mine moving up to cup and caress his face. Another kiss, another gentle movement. I was swimming, lost in the unfamiliar sensation of being so closely one with another person. Bastian's lips went to my throat, his kissing soft on damp sticky skin. I murmured again, relishing the slowness of it all, feeling the pleasure build in a soft wave. Nobody could deny our inexperience, but still there was beauty to it in the love therein shared. His movements quickened, as he too began to lose himself. His breath was almost a moan too, his gasps of pleasure mingling with mine. Skin hit skin, wet clothes hit wet clothes, slapping together as he quickened the pace further still.

His fingers tightened so that I knew I'd be lightly bruised from them but I didn't care, allowing my own fingers to tug his hair, to grip him too. Then I felt the finish. For me the pleasure rush was small but beautiful, a gentle wave which warmed me right to my toes. For him it seemed to shatter through him, causing him to grit his teeth, to let out a barking cry as his body tensed. He gasped again, hugged me close and then allowed his sweaty head to fall down onto my collarbone as his body relaxed.

And so it was done, virginity given up for us both in that one misplaced moment. I lay still with a beating heart, holding him to me with a fervour and adoration I had never known possible. For some long moments we laid like that, but then he moved away, gently pulling my skirts back over my legs. He paused to kiss me again, but then sat up, and leaned back against the wall, hocking his trousers back up as he did so.

He was very quiet.

'Bas?' I whispered, frightened by the suddenness of his departure from me. 'Are you... are you all right?'

He put his hands up over his face at my words. For a long moment was silent, but then looked back to me and held out his hand. I moved, rearranging my clothing as I did so and laid my head down on his shoulder. He held my hand but did not speak. His body was trembling.

'I... are you... was that...' I stuttered.

'We... we shouldn't have done that... Maddi! Damnation! I'm sorry!'

'Bas...' all at once I was tearful. He moved his head to look at me and his expression was unreadable. I said nothing, but my heart was heavy too suddenly. I put up a hand to touch his cheek and he shuffled so that he was holding me properly, his face nuzzled in my hand.

More long moments passed in intimate silence but then he spoke, his voice thick and heavy, 'The rain is slowing, I should go and try to seek aid.'

'What? No! Don't go?'

'Darling, I have to… you will be safe here, and I will bring help.'

'Bas… please?'

'I'm sorry…' he whispered, and then untangled me from his body and stood. 'Don't be afraid, you're safe here.'

'I am not afraid of being alone, I am afraid of…' I bit my lip, 'afraid I have lost you.'

Bastian knelt before me and with obvious emotion, he kissed my lips again, 'Never…'

'Say again that you love me?'

'I love you, I do love you… but I do have to go now. My brain is in turmoil that I need to walk off. I'll… I'll bring help, my love… I have to… go…'

And so he did.

I lay for some time in a deep confusion but then my eyes grew heavy and I allowed them to close. My next memory is of Bastian's return, waking me from a light slumber yet another hour or more later. My tired, somewhat red and puffy eyes opened to see him once more knelt beside the bed. He took my hand and kissed it softly.

'There is a cart without,' he whispered, 'Several men of the village…'

'Oh,' I murmured, realising his meaning: discretion was required.

'You and I will talk in a day or two,' he spoke again. He seemed much recovered from his earlier anguish.

'Alright.'

He moved even closer, and then whispered, 'I love you, sweetheart.'

'I love you too,' I said into his hair, but then allowed him to help me to my feet and hobble out of the cottage. Even as the door swung closed behind me, I felt as though the incident, that magical moment, was gone.

Six

And so I come again to that awkward wedding ceremony, in our little church in the village. The dark and brooding groom – still unaware of the fruits of our one night together – and that sweetly sorrowful, pale and trembling girl at his side. I allowed my eyes to examine his back, as he moved past with Alice on his arm, to where more of the villagers gathered, throwing rice and calling out congratulations. Papa put a hand down on my arm.

'Are you well?' he asked gently.

I nodded.

His eyes bored more so into me. Papa was a doctor after all, and I think by then he already guessed my plight, but he remained wordless as he slipped his arm through mine and led me from the church. I was thankful for his support.

After the ceremony, we retired to The Cliff House to eat and drink to the health of the new couple as is tradition. I sat myself alone in a corner. My heart ached and I felt as though a million insects were invading my skin, making me hot and clammy. I wanted to sob but of course decorum rendered me emotionless. Bastian and Alice had not yet appeared in the drawing room and I wondered a little why I was still sitting there, alone. I was just standing to leave when Nora appeared at my side.

'Poor Maddi,' she said, then, topping up my wine glass. 'Here, this terribly dangerous beast can oft be used to dull the other terrible beasts within.'

I heeded her words and took a swig of the deep blood red liquid. Nora sat down beside me and held my hand. 'It'll be all right,' she comforted. 'I know it will.'

'I...' there I almost spilled it all, if Nora had not already guessed it, but I was prevented from doing so by the arrival of the groom himself. I had seen little of him, in the three months since our night at the cottage; not for his abandonment but by my own design, and never again had we had a moment alone despite how he'd tried several times to catch me. We had both been chastised by our respective parents for the gossip which rose about us after that night too, gossip which was indeed true, but none the less damaging to reputations. I know too that my shunning him hurt him, that as the days passed, he grew darker and darker whilst I silently withered too. It was for the best though, I kept telling myself, it was for the best.

'What a day eh?' he said. 'What a damned day. Mind if I sit?'

I nodded. With Nora at my side, I felt I could face him a little easier than alone, despite the absence of him in my life the previous long weeks. Bastian sat himself down on his chair and took a deep drink of his own wine, his eyes not leaving my face. In his expression I saw his tiredness, his depression – perhaps I should have heeded it more. I pushed back the feelings of protectiveness; I could not abide them under the circumstances.

'Why on earth, of all the people in the room, would you come and sit here with us now?' Nora snapped. 'Can you not see that your company the last thing Maddi needs today?'

Bastian tried to catch my eye. I looked down into my glass, avoiding him.

'If anything,' he said. 'I see the contrary, and besides, there is no one else in this room with whom I would rather sit in my misery, than my little sister and my Maddi. No matter how many other people there are in a room, you two will always be the most important people to me. When we are together like this I almost feel like we are children again, almost like the world stopped turning.'

Over his shoulder, Alice's eyes were searching the room.

'Almost,' I said in a rasp, 'but for your *wife* over there scanning the room for you.'

'Those days are gone Bastian,' Nora added, voicing my own thoughts. 'It will just sadden us all to think of them.'

'Indeed,' I said, then, not caring that Nora might hear me but in a voice low enough that nobody else would. 'Bastian, there is something... something that we need to discuss, but now – today – is not the day for it. I think I need to go.'

'Of course, your natural response is to avoid me since... since...' he did not finish the thought but I saw understanding spread over Nora's face as she watched our little exchange.

'I cannot help it, I...'

He moved closer still unmindful of all about us, of who might be watching. 'I love you so that it aches within me,' he whispered. 'Do try not to hate me at least, that I could not bear!'

I put a hand to my belly, but I could not tell him, could not explain.

'Maddi, are you well?' Nora asked as I staggered, a little faint myself suddenly. I clutched at the table a moment but then steadied myself and looked back to him, to them both. 'I think I must depart...' I said again, 'Congra... congratulations Bas, I hope you will be happy...'

'You know I can never be!'

'You must... must learn! For everybody's sake.'

He tried to grip me harder but I pulled my arm away and, as calmly as I could, walked outside onto the sloping gardens which led to the gate leaving them both behind me. There I paused though, for Papa was still within, and moved around the house some, into a darker spot where there hung a swing from an old oak. It was not long before Nora found me. The old bough groaned as she joined me on the seat, we were children no longer and our combined weight made the old tree complain loudly.

'So,' Nora said at length. 'I knew you and Bas were far too fond of each other but I had no idea that things had escalated. They have, haven't they?'

'Yes,' my voice was barely audible.

'Have you laid with him?'

I stood and paced back and forth, then decided on the truth, the night chill made the tears in my eyes burn cold, 'Yes,' I whispered.

'Oh lord! And you love each other?'

'Again, yes.'

I stopped pacing and turned to Nora, still sat placidly on the swing, watching me with her big brown eyes.

'He adores you, you know,' she said, 'I have often thought it, and *she* is nothing to him…'

'It matters not, now.'

'Surely there is comfort in finding love, even in the direst of circumstance?'

'How do you not understand?' I said, a tad too loud in my anguish. 'I am so hurt that I feel ill – sick to my stomach and so jealous I feel that I might actually tear out my own eyes if I thought it would remove the image of them standing together in that church today.'

'I know it, love…'

'You know nothing! Nora, I am with *child*!'

Nora paled so that her complexion almost matched mine. All my strength left me and I sat heavily on the damp grass. As though my heart really were giving me physical pain, I clutched my breast and cried like a child. Nora moved to sit behind me and kissed the top of my head.

'Love, is there anything I can do?'

'Just… just find Papa for me and tell him I have gone home,' I sniffed, wiping away my tears with my handkerchief.

'Hold that, for a moment,' I spun my head about to see Bastian stood at the corner by the wall. My heart thudded, but that last moment of hope that he had not heard me faded with his next words. 'You are with child?'

I nodded, still clutching Nora.

He swallowed a few times, then found a frown, 'and you didn't... didn't see fit to tell me?'

'I... of course I was going to but I... it wasn't the right... the right time...'

Bastian moved the few steps between us and helped me to my feet. His fingers caressed my face as he examined me, taking a moment to take it all in. He looked as though somebody had just slapped his handsome cheek.

'Yesterday...' he said at length, his voice so very strained, 'yesterday was the right time to tell me this. This morning even... a week ago... anytime before I...' he broke off and turned to look to his sister, eyes pleading for a solution. Nora pressed her lips but said nothing. Bastian pulled in a deep judder of a breath and then looked back at me.

'Hush, don't cry,' he murmured. 'I'll have this abomination annulled. I'll marry you. It is the only solution.'

'And then what?' that was Nora, 'Allow Monroe to destroy us all? A life of poverty for us, for your baby? You know it is only by our privilege that people tolerate us. A pauper on the streets with our skin, with our heritage. Bas, I love Maddi as much as you do but please... don't...'

Bastian's face twisted. Never had I seen another person so torn, so lost. In the face of his distress, suddenly I was the strong one. I pulled a strange calm on myself, allowing some inner strength to wash over me just as I had when Mama had died.

'Return to your wife, Bas,' I whispered, putting a hand on his arm, 'we both know you can do nothing other, now. Too much rests on your marriage which is why I did not tell you of this before. The best thing, for me, is to leave, and to stay away.'

'Please don't! I am distraught!'

'It will pass, as will our affection, I am sure. I will speak to Papa tonight about the baby, he will know... know what to do to... resolve this problem. He is a doctor after all.'

'No!' Nora gasped, 'not that...'

'I shall do what I have to, what Papa suggests... I will let him guide me.'

'Maddi...'

'You know the truth of it, my dear friend. I have to go,' I whispered, still so calm suddenly.

'Don't do anything... foolish,' Nora said, 'not without speaking to us!'

'I will do nothing without my father's say-so, I trust him.'

'You're talking abortion,' Bastian suddenly realised, his hands gripping mine. 'Maddi no! That's both dangerous and illegal!'

'I am saying I don't know what to do, but I shall ask my papa, who is a doctor...' I whispered. 'I will contact you about his verdict on the morrow and mayhap in time we shall have our friendship back... For now though, well, this time it is I who must go. It is me who does not belong in this picture.'

And then, before he could reply, I turned and walked away from them.

The edge of the grounds beckoned, as I walked, in a dark and comforting embrace. My steps sped up as I went, my heart racing but that strange calm still with me. I looked back, just once as I reached the gate, to see the silhouette of the two figures I'd left behind. Bastian had fallen to his knees, just as I had moments earlier. His sister held him, leaning over to do so and despite that I could not hear him, I could see from the shake of his shoulders that he was sobbing. I, on the other hand felt strangely calm, despite how my broken heart ached still. As I reached the edge of the lawn, Bastian wailed my name into the night, but I forced myself to carry on, away into the darkness.

How I wish I had heeded the pain and submission in that sound, how I wish that I had turned back, wrapped him in my arms and held him safe.

I didn't.

It is a decision I will always regret.

Ten minutes after I left, Bastian was seen storming up the stairs. Half an hour later, a servant caught sight of him leaving by the back door. That was the last anybody saw of him until past midnight when his new wife called her maid and complained of his absence in her bedchamber.

That maid contacted Bastian's manservant and for the first time, his disappearance was made a cause for alarm. A search party formed of the guests, panic starting to bubble when it was found he'd not even taken a coat with him. It had not taken them long to find him, however, with Nora's guidance at the places he was most likely to go.

The cove! Where else?

Bastian was already unconscious when he was found. He was laid half in and half out of the ocean where the tide had started to come in, almost claiming him. His skin, I was told by Nora, was icy cold to touch, his hair matted with sand and shingle. He had an empty bottle of Alice's "nerve tonic" clutched in his hand.

Watered down Laudanum, to be precise.

That was the night that my darling, the love of my life, gave up all hope finally. Years of abuse and melancholy suddenly took their toll, sanity snapped, and my love, my Bastian, just couldn't take any more.

Seven

Of course, Papa was called in. There were no other doctors in the vicinity anyhow, but even if there had been, my father's standing was enough that he would have been a fine initial choice. I was tucked up in bed when the knock came, a frenzied rapping which was enough to wake even the dead. I sat up, my soft blankets falling away from the white cotton of my nightgown. My heart picked up again, half expecting it to be Bastian himself, some final heroic attempt to save our broken affair. I stood and pulled on a robe, then heard the creak of the attic stairs door opening and Nell's hurried footsteps. I opened my door and found myself in the corridor with Papa, clad too in nightshirt and robe. Nell got to the door first. Her grey hair was braided and she wore an old-fashioned nightcap on her head, one of the oversized white ones. Papa went down next, and I followed just in time to see as the door was opened. The man without was a fellow I just about recognised, and already I knew him for one of the Carfax servants.

'Sir, I've been sent to ask ye to come quickly up ta the cliff house!'

'Why, what has happened?' Papa asked.

'It be young master Carfax, sir, he's done tried te to do ee-self in! Tis close to dead and not long for the world, without some intervention!'

At once the room spun.

Papa spun around at once, catching me as I fell into something of a swoon. His old eyes held a look I barely recognised. He escorted me to the hard bench and bade Nell tend to me, and then, leaving me in her hands, he swiftly departed to dress. I took to sobbing at once, hardly minding Nell's muttered "There, There" and her hand on my back. Papa seemed to reappear in no time, dressed and with his old black leather case. He paused though, and then came to kneel beside me.

'I have to go,' he said, 'I might be some time. Take this to your heart now, I *will* save your friend, if God permits!'

I nodded, still tearful to the extreme.

'Get some rest,' Papa said, 'And have George awakened too, ready to ride to Camborne, if needed.'

'I'll do that,' Nell said.

'Good… good.' Papa sighed, and then kissed the top of my head. 'Go on, back to bed, Maddi, get some sleep!'

I nodded, but already I knew such to be impossible.

If ever a person were to ask me, what was the longest night of my existence, I would say, without hesitation, that it was that night. I slept not a wink, nor did I eat a morsel or even manage more than a sip of water to drink. Nell, bless her loyalty, refused to leave my side but to go and find me a wrap when the night air took me to shivering. Her old hands were gentle on my arm and her eyes spoke the million words she did not say aloud.

Finally at the beginnings of dawn, the door opened again. I sprung to my feet and all-but ran to Papa, who was just entering. He embraced me at once, making my heart fit to burst in panic, but then stepped back and cast his old eyes over me.

'He lives.'

Oh what beautiful utterance! What warming sweetness. I fell again into sobbing, but that of the more desperate happiness, than the dreadful keen from before. Papa took my arm.

'Let me come in,' he said, 'Nell, some tea? It has been the devil of a night!'

Nell slipped away at once, leaving us alone. Papa led me back to my previous seat and there he sat me down.

'My love,' he said, 'I am dead tired and therefore cannot give you the benefit of the fullness of my attention that you deserve. I am going to drink my tea, and then go to bed.'

I nodded.

'Suffice to say, though, that your young friend is very ill… but he lives and will continue to do so. He got very, very cold whilst he lay out in the sand, so he has something of a terrible chill upon him. Worse, he imbibed rather a great dose of opium in the form of laudanum. I have had to perform an emergency procedure called a gastric lavage – a very new but effective way of removing poisons from the body – and have given him a tonic of chalk and charcoal to attempt to neutralise the drug still in his belly. His body will recover, but I fear I cannot cure the illness which led him to such a drastic act. That is beyond me.'

'Illness?'

'Of the mind. He appears to have suffered a deep melancholia, and something of mania in his frenzy as the wedding celebrations died down. He vanished, it would seem, shortly after you left, and was found having consumed a great amount of a medicine used by his new wife for her own poor nerves.'

My mind flit at once to Alice's little bottle, of how she had touched just a mere droplet to her lips. The anger towards her grew up even more so in me, my mind somehow attributing even this to her.

'What is… What is to be done, then?' I managed to ask.

'A writ of insanity will be signed by myself tomorrow, and then his parents can have him sent to an asylum to recover, or nurse him at home with my assistance, as they wish.'

'An asylum?' I gasped. 'Papa, no!'

'It is out of my hands,' he said gently, then paused as Nell brought in the tea and moved to pour it himself. 'Thank you Nelly, go to bed my dear,' he said, and then turned back to me, 'The question in the air at the moment is why. You and young Bastian are very close. Can you think of any reason why a young man so blessed, might fall to such ruin of the mind on the very day of his wedding?'

I took a cup and nursed it a little, exhaustion pulling in now that my panic was abated. 'I'm with child,' the words seemed to fall naturally from my lips, ringing out into the room.

Papa said nothing for the longest moment, but there was no surprise on his features, further enhancing the notion that he'd already known. He drank another mouthful of tea, and then put the cup down on the table.

'It is his, I suppose?'

'Yes.'

'Did he know, when he married the new Mrs Carfax?'

I shook my head, 'I blurted it out to him this evening,' I whispered, 'I meant not to but... he overheard me. He said he would have... have the marriage annulled and marry me, but I said he could not do that... I said it better that we cease any contact, and that the affection would die down. I... I suggested you might have... have some means to help us with this predicament, being that you are a doctor...'

Papa fell back to silence. He pressed his old lips together, but then put out a hand for mine, I gave it. 'I never thought to raise a child so foolish,' his voice was gentle, despite the rebuke. 'What were you thinking, Maddi, in this dalliance?'

'I...' I looked down at the floor, 'I love him as he loves me. We had but... but one encounter. The night of the storm. It was as though it were another world. We both regretted what we had done, despite the affection between us, and none other has happened since. There was no dalliance, just a mistake.'

Papa nodded, and pressed my hand. 'We will discuss this more after I have slept,' he said. 'I'm dog-tired.'

'May I go to him? Perhaps later today?'

Papa's sigh was deep and echoing. 'Do you really think it wise to go?'

'I need him to know that I do not… he…' I sighed and put the words back together in my head before uttering them aloud. 'I think the final straw for his emotions was when I left,' I said, 'I let him believe that I have forsaken him completely, that I will harm the child and maybe myself in being rid of it. If…' I shook my head again, unable to clear my thoughts. 'I need to just tell him that I remain his friend, that is all.'

'Sleep first,' Papa said, gentle, 'We'll discuss this all, later.'

In the heat of the morning air, especially on such a hot day, I found my bed sticky and uncomfortable. My heart was aflame too, guiding me more so than my head. I did try to heed Papa's words, but the truth of it is that, some hour later and with him still asleep in his own bed, my feet had found their way to the path which led up to Fiveham. The day was a warm one, with even the wind crashing over the exposed clifftops not enough to dampen the solid June sunshine – a vast contrast to that night three months earlier when the heavens had opened upon Bastian and I both. My heart thudded like a drum in my chest for every footstep. I knew Papa would be cross, when he discovered I'd gone without telling him, and already the disappointment had crossed Nelly's face, when I had left the message. I was being moved by my heart though, and nothing at all could have stopped me making that trek. At the gate, I paused. Getting up the courage to go there was one thing, but how was I to explain my appearance there? As I pondered this, however, the situation was resolved by Nora's face at a window, and then within minutes the opening of the main entrance door.

'Maddi!' she gasped, throwing her arms tightly about me, 'Oh! Thank you so much for coming!'

'How could I not? How is the patient?'

'He is so poorly Maddi! Mama says he is just sleeping and still, but they won't tell me much. He is weak indeed but your wonderful Papa has at least saved his life!'

'I'm so sorry for my part in what happened,' I whispered, breaking a little, 'this is... is all my fault. I...'

'Hush, none of that! Bastian is a grown man, you did not put the bottle to his lips!'

I bowed my head, not replying, still torn apart by guilt enough to think that I might as well have. 'Are they going to send him to the asylum?' My heart ached even to ask it.

'No, not until they see how he is once awake. Mama will not allow it!'

'Oh, now that at least is some good news,' I whispered. 'Papa said and it has haunted me to think it.'

Nora did not release my hand as we spoke, pulling me inside the house. 'We must be quiet,' she whispered, 'Alice and Papa must not know you are here.'

'My name is mud, I suppose?'

'No, not at all, but Papa has said no visitors and I am sure Alice suspects something...'

I nodded, allowing Nora to lead me quietly to the staircase and then up into the corridor to the right. I swallowed and forced my toes to tread lightly. Nora paused though at his chamber door as a woman's voice spoke softly from within.

'Alice?' I whispered.

Nora put up a finger to her lips and put her ear to the door, then shook her head and put her hand to the doorknob. 'Just Mama,' she said. 'Mama will not mind your visit.'

Bastian's chamber was bathed in darkness, and as Nora pushed open the door it almost crushed me with its utter blackness. It was quite an airy chamber, but all of the drapes were pulled to cut out the light. There was rather a stink of vomit, carefully hidden behind the flowers which I supposed had been gathered with just that purpose. Lady Carfax was sitting in a chair next to an old carved four poster bed. She sat with her back to us, talking gently to her son. Bastian was not conscious. I could not make out his features but his form lay slumped against the soft pillows. I swallowed again, my heart hammering even more so as I stepped closer, the light from the door falling on his poor dear face. I paused in shock; I had not expected him to still look so poorly.

Lady Carfax turned about and rested her eyes upon us.

'Hello Maddi,' she said quietly. 'I am glad you have come.'

The words were so very unexpected that my stomach seemed to heave as a million butterflies took it over. My mouth was suddenly very dry, but I ignored the rush of panic and managed to speak.

'I came as soon as... as soon as my Papa was asleep,' I said, owning the subterfuge.

'He has forbidden you from coming, I presume?'

'Not in so many words – yet – so I took the opportunity before he does.'

Lady Carfax nodded, and then beckoned me in. 'Come and sit by him, Maddi. Nora, perhaps you could go and ensure that Alice is occupied for an hour or so. Don't let her come here.'

'Of course, Mama,' Nora said and then released my hand and patted my arm. As I moved into the room, Lady Carfax relinquished her seat and nodded that I should take it. I did so and slipped my hand into his clammy fingers. How I held myself together to touch his cold lifeless hand, to look upon his unconscious face, I do not know. I hiccupped back the sobs and allowed just a single tear to fall.

'Hello Bas,' I whispered, and then looked to his mother who was pulling forward another chair. 'Can he hear me?'

'Your father said it unlikely. I was talking to him anyway. If perhaps our voices could lead him back, then it is better we use them... I think anyhow.'

I nodded again, and then allowed my thumb to stroke his hand. Lady Carfax was watching me carefully, but I made no pains to hide my emotions. She knew, they all knew – surely?

'I blame myself,' Lady Carfax said suddenly, mirroring my own thoughts on the matter.

'Nobody could have known!'

'I could! I should have.'

'How could you?'

Lady Carfax sighed and fidgeted the coverlet over her son's still form. Her eyes were very far away. 'Because I have seen it before,' she finally said.

'What do you mean?'

More silence and then she sighed. 'It is not well known, but my own poor dear father he… well, he took his own life too. I have seen this malady of spirit before, seen the disastrous results of it.'

'Oh!... I'm so sorry,' I whispered.

'Thank you. It was so very long ago now. Papa was a soldier, you see. He rose and rose in his regiment, he was a fine officer and an esteemed gentleman. He had it all but then war happened and he had to fight. He was stationed in the Caribbean, that is how I happened to be there when I met the children's father. It changed him, over there. It destroyed his spirit.'

'I never knew…'

'The wars are a terrible thing and life over there was hard. I… nobody ever considered that his malady hid a form of madness which could be passed down, in the family line. We really do understand so little of madness.'

'This much is true, I suppose,' I whispered. I liked not to hear Bastian described as mad, not even by the dulcet tones of his Mama.

'I know not all of it, but that after he returned home he had a funny turn again. I remained behind, having been married by then. My mother did the very best she could, to control him, but she could not. In the end, she failed to prevent his taking up his military pistol and ending his own tremulous existence just as I have failed my own boy.'

'You have not failed anybody, my lady,' I said, taking her hand in mine. Her skin was soft and smooth, much like my own. Where some people showed age in their skin, she did not so. She could not have been much above forty, yet. Too young by far to carry such burdens.

'But I have,' she whispered, 'In not heeding how similar in temperament my son has always been to my father, in not watching for the warning signs,' she said.

'You must not blame yourself, Lady Carfax,' I murmured.

The room fell silent. I dropped Lady Carfax's hand and instead lifted Bastian's again. I caressed his cold fingers in my own, wishing for something, any spark of life in that unmoving face.

'So what happened?' Finally Lady Carfax spoke of the day before, 'I knew of course that you both had an affection, and that yesterday's festivities would be wrought for you both, but he seemed well until you left. I presume that you took the opportunity to break of any tryst between you?'

'I... I did, and rather gracelessly too,' I confessed, 'I was... was upset... and I...'

I glanced over at her thin features, the darkness of her eyes a contrast to her vibrant red hair. Could I trust her? I still wasn't sure but then if Bastian's stories of his own heritage had been true, then she was likely the person in my acquaintance most likely to show empathy in my predicament.

'Go on,' she urged, gently. Perhaps she too had already seen the tautness of my gown about my belly in the past weeks.

'You see,' I said, my voice barely audible now, 'I am with child... his child. He was...was distressed that I had not told him *before* the wedding but I... I know something of the reasons why he had to marry Alice – from his own mouth - and so I chose not to...' I sighed and broke off. 'I have handled this abominably.'

'How far along are you?' she asked, not reacting to those more scandalous of words.

'It will be three months, that night that... that I got lost on the moors.'

'And there is no chance that it is... more recent?'

'No, there was just the once. I have kept myself more distant since. I am not... I am not the type of girl who...'

'We all fall prey to foolishness in our youth,' she said, 'there will be recriminations though. If you are nearly four months gone then we cannot even orchestrate a wedding to anyone else in order to pass the child off as legitimate...'

As you did! I wanted to whisper, but did not quite dare.

'I am somewhat relieved,' I said, 'I have no other in mind as intended. It has always been... always been only him, for me.'

'Well then,' she said, 'I suppose I must speak to my husband, as well as to your father, about what is to be done. If we are to get out of this without a scandal, and without offending young Alice and in turn, her father, then we will need to be discrete and careful.'

I nodded and looked down at the father of my child, unconscious still in his bed, then up to the face of his mother, who watched me with eyes burning bright as fire. At least I was to have her on my side, that was a beginning at least.

Eight

Bastian finally awoke from his unnatural slumber three days after that first morning. By the time he opened his eyes, already his brilliant mother had begun to plan the covering up of our mistake. As the day unfolded, Papa and I found ourselves at a meeting in the drawing room of Fiveham, Lady Carfax giving us her plans whilst Bastian lay in a room above us still on his sickbed. Lord Carfax had spoken again of asylums, so Nora told me, but Lady Carfax was holding her ground. *A creole would not do well in an asylum* – she'd apparently said – *even one of the good private ones*. She'd not risk her boy's life for a momentary lapse of his rationality. Somehow, she seemed to be keeping the old man at bay. I had not seen Bastian yet, in his awakening, but was determined that I would not leave the house until I had at least spoken to him too.

'Madeleine can give birth at a home for young ladies,' Lady Carfax said, glancing over our faces. I forced myself to try to attend the room, to gather my addled wits. Papa looked very tired, and Lord Carfax sat opposite with eyes as furious as the swishing sea without. Nora and Alice were out walking, a pretence to keep Alice from us whilst we discussed the matter.

'What manner of home?' Papa asked. 'I will not have her health compromised.'

'I don't want to give up the child…' I added.

Lord Carfax glared at me, but his wife interrupted.

'I suggest the child be brought here,' she said. 'It is better to be forthright, with young Alice, than to attempt to conceal and anger her. My son's marriage is as yet unconsummated. If Alice is angered, she could leave and have it annulled, in which case, there are some…' she paused and glanced to my father, '…unfortunate consequences between my husband and her father, at the broken arrangements.'

'H-here?'

'Yes. We will raise the child for you.'

'I… but then why not have… have the baby here? I want no doctor but Papa to – to tend me.'

'Because of the scandal,' Papa said softly. 'Lord and Lady Carfax want to adopt the child without publicly acknowledging from whence it has come.'

'A poor relation is easier to explain, than a bastard child,' Lady Carfax said. 'If done this way, you can still remarry. Nobody needs to know what has happened, and my grandchild will never want, never go without. You might visit – Aunt Maddi, the dear friend to the family – I am not cruel! You must never reveal though, who you are to the child.'

'And if I decline?'

'Then your reputation will be tarnished and the family will officially denounce you.' Lord Carfax spoke. 'You will never see Sebastian – or Leonore - again, nor will you ever again set foot in this house. If you attempt to spread word of the child's birthage, I will sue your father for slander.'

I gasped and felt Papa's hand on my shoulder. I was shaking all over, my guts clenching within my form. I let out a shaky breath and then looked to my father.

'We will discuss this further at home,' he said, firm, 'And deliver to you the answer on the morrow?'

'Agreeable,' Lord Carfax said.

'May I see Bas?' I whispered, 'I beg of you.'

Lord and Lady Carfax glanced to each other, and I could see the indecision there. Papa sighed, behind me.

'He is still very weak,' Lady Carfax murmured.

My heart sank.

'Ten minutes,' Lord Carfax said, gruff, 'Tell him of what we have offered. It will come better from you, I think!'

I pulled in a deep breath and then stood. My legs were still shaky. 'Thank you,' I managed and then turned to make my way out of the room and up the staircase.

The corridors above stairs seemed very dark. As I approached his chamber though, my eye alit on a person dithering at the far end of the corridor, by the window. Her figure was slight and her neatly braided and dressed hair like white fire. For the longest moment, I stared at her and she at I, taking in each-other's measure, but then she moved as though to pass me. I almost let her do so but then guilt washed over my form. Surely, she must have heard, by now, of my plight? Was it just my imagination which moved her gaze to my belly?

'Alice,' I spoke her name, the sound of it seeming to resonate but I could not bring myself to use her correct title, *Mrs Carfax*. Alice moved to continue on past me, her lips pressed and her eyes burning, but paid no heed to my greeting. Her shunning of me roused my fire, giving me more strength and as she swished past me, I put out a hand to grasp her arm.

'Alice, please!' I said. 'If you were... I mean... I could come another time, if you wanted to visit with... with your husband, now?'

Alice turned her gaze on me and truly her mask dropped. I had known she could be vile, but the expression on her normally placid face was a shocking change to behold. Her blue eyes showed steel and her lips twisted in rage.

'Why the devil would I do that?' she breathed.

'I... erm... Because he is... is your husband and he is...'

Alice's frown deepened, turning to a glower. Truly something in her had snapped. '*My* husband, is he?' she hissed, 'you noticed that then?'

'Alice!'

'What? Am I to close my eyes to your indiscretions with my husband and be a good and timid wife despite them?'

'Please... we made but one mistake and it has led to my disaster, not yours!'

'Not mine? Are you simple? Do you not know what people must be saying of me? Bad enough to my reputation to marry one with heritage thus, darkie half-blood that he is...'

Any sympathy or guilt I had been holding dissipated in a flash at the slurs she uttered. She was not finished though.

'...and now, if my marriage were not scandal enough, not embarrassment enough, I must contend with the gossip that on our very wedding night, he attempted his own life! That I am such a prospect for wife that not even a *spook* will have me! And there you go about, with your swollen belly on show whilst everyone in the entire county knows that I did not even have my wedding night with him before he chose to die rather than be my husband!'

Her hand went to her belt, to where once that tonic my darling had drunk down had hung. On finding it not there, her expression darkened more so.

'If you had any morals, you'd leave now,' she said, her voice suddenly back to frailty, 'I hope that ill luck besets you always, such as that you have cast upon me. I hope...' her face turned even darker, '...I hope you die in childbirth, your wicked base child with you.'

I staggered, more shocked I think than ever I had been in my life. 'What? What did you just say?'

Alice gave me one final scathing look, and then wrenched her arm free. She all but pushed me out of the way so that she could stalk past me and then was gone. I stayed as I was for a long moment, and then leaned momentarily against the wall, regathering my thoughts before I went to Bastian.

Inside Bastian's chamber the light was still very dim, with the drapes still drawn across the windows. The smell of illness, of near-death still lingered, as did the sombre pressure which fell upon my shoulders as I entered. At first, I paused at the silence and darkness, thinking perhaps he had slipped back to sleeping, but then his tone murmured and he shuffled to prop himself up on his pillows.

'Hello, Bas,' I whispered, closing the door behind me and leaning on it.

'Maddi?' his voice was a croak, his face peering to me in the darkness which hid his facial expression. 'Come closer? I cannot see you properly there…'

I stepped away from the door and then with something of a rush I made my way to the chair which was already pulled up beside his bed. Bastian's skin looked grey in the darkness of the room, and still I could smell a stench of sickness on him too. Sweat, vomit, lack of cleanliness. He was obviously still beset with a chill too, his forehead clammy, I was not repulsed by it though, protective and sad. Suddenly I had no words, nothing. I don't suppose the gravity of the situation had truly hit me until that moment. I took his hand in both of mine and bowed my lips to kiss his fingers, and to hide my tears.

'Oh, my love,' I finally breathed, 'My darling, what have you done?'

'I have done the last thing left to me, and see I have failed at that too,' his voice was dry, his throat obviously still enflamed.

'No! Do not speak thus. There is more to live for, I promise, there are better times coming!'

'I am sorry my love but I am done with hope. I just don't want to live anymore.'

Have any words ever been so stark? So filled with pain? So dire were those words that it took me a moment to process them, to allow them to breathe life in my gut. Finally I lifted his hand and kissed it.

'Bastian please, don't say that!'
'Why not? It is the truth!'
'It cannot be, you have… there is so much light ahead of you!'

'What light? I cannot see it!'

'You must try! For me! Think not of your sorrows but of all that is good in the world.'

His eyes moved to mine. Inside something felt close to snapping, agony to see one so beloved so very lost.

'All that is good, every memory, revolves about the one person I have lost,' he said, and then sighed, 'Every memory which ever brought me any jot of joy.'

'Oh you fool, you've not lost me,' I said, indulgence creeping in. 'Surely you know I was just wrought!'

Bastian lay back on the pillows, a bead of sweat had broken out on his brow. I shifted so that I was stood beside him, my hand still holding his tightly. He closed his eyes but his lips were pressed in anguish. I laid his hand on my stomach.

'Inside me,' I whispered, 'right here in my belly is your son or daughter.'

A tear did fall but his hand moved over the cloth of my gown, a caress. He did not speak, just lay there in silence.

'Your child,' I whispered again.

'My child that I will not know, not raise or be a father to… my child you would rather see gone!'

'Ah, but no, that is the beauty of it. You *will* raise him or her!' I said, 'I am to go away soon, just to have the baby with a little discretion, and then the baby will come here and be adopted by your mother…'

'No!' at once he was alert.

'No to what?'

'To it all. No homes, no going away, and no having the baby torn away from you, his Mama! A baby needs his Mama! More-so too I will not have any child raised here – not with *him*! Not with how he feels about people like me.'

Suddenly the realisation flooded back, of how Lord Carfax had hurt Bastian. I gasped, and then wet my lips and nodded.

'A point taken! Your mother thought it would do… do you good to have the child here but…'

'Our child is safer with you,' he said, opening his eyes again to look at me, 'Stay here, in safety and comfort with your father! Do you think I care for scandal?'

'Your parents do. Your father said that if I did not agree then…'

'What? More threats? What can he possibly do?'

'He can stop me coming here, he can stop me seeing you.'

Some of the fire reignited in Bastian's eye, 'Over my dead body,' he said, the irony lost on him somewhat, 'You leave him, and Mama, to me. You will stay in the village, and I will claim the child, when it is born. I will let everybody know I am proud to be its father, I will make sure you never go without, but I will not bring it here to be abused.'

At least he was finally thinking of the future! I nodded. There was shame attached to bearing a bastard, but our village was so small that it would not touch me, not really. 'I can agree to that, so long as Papa allows it and so long as you are sure you can manage your parents?'

'Good,' Bastian murmured, 'Good. And then the child is still close, too, so that I might see it grow.'

'You can,' I found a smile as his eyes flickered closed again. His hand still rested on my belly but he moved it to hold my fingers, I wrapped mine about his. For more long moments we sat in silence, but then he opened his eyes again and examined me. 'I am so sorry,' he whispered.

'As am I.'

'I love you.'

'I know, I love you too.'

'I wish we could be together.'

'I know.'

'Are we…' he paused, 'Are we still…'

I wet my lips and allowed a little sigh, 'You are my dearest friend, Bas, and I will always love you, but you are a husband now. Friendship is probably the most I could bear.'

'I will never lie with that girl,' he said, 'You have my word that I will not! Let her remain as my wife in name… it is enough... but I take your words and I agree, friendship only will suit us both, for now... if it were... were like it was – before?'

'Yes, like that! I miss that! I miss riding with you and the games you Nora and I would play! I miss you so much.'

'And if I were to look back on that sweetly fond memory of the cottage without regrets and with some longing...'

'Then know we are equally matched,' I whispered. I felt very grown up, suddenly, for my seventeen years.

Bastian nodded and wet his lips, 'will you kiss me, one last time?'

I did not reply with words but learned forward to touch my lips to his. His arm came up to hold me weakly as I kissed him, gripping me with as much strength as he had left in him.

Nine

After such an event, recovery was never going to come easily for Bastian. It was not a simple upward curve either. Once he was up and about, which was some week or more later, I suppose we all expected him to simply revert back but that is not the way of afflictions of the mind, and whilst some days we could have been forgiven for thinking him fully recovered, on others he was gone again to misery, hiding away in his chambers and not coming out to meet with Nora and I until afternoon, if even at all. With me he was always kind and gentle of manner – never frenzied, most of the time he just seemed sad. On a bad day, the spirit of him was gone, and he seemed almost to just go through the motions of the day. When I was present, he at least tried to maintain a cheerful demeanour, but Nora spoke of times when I was absent where he would sit for hours in silence without a smile. He would become cranky too at times, she said, irritable in a way he'd never been before.

'It is not for lack of love in him, but for lack of joy,' Nora added, as we sat in Papa's parlour with tea on the table and a tablecloth we were embroidering together somewhat abandoned between us. 'He means no harm and Mama and I know that. Father is in a royal stink about it all though and that has me on edge too. He is different since we came to England but he can be rather – startling – when he is angered.'

'Bastian told me a little of it and I... I know of his whipping scars,' I whispered.

Nora pressed her lips and nodded, 'Indeed. Poor Bas, whilst we both felt the sting of that rod, he did rather take the brunt of it all back then. Father was always at him as a boy. You know of course that we are not actually his children?'

'I do,' I said.

Nora took my hand in hers, 'It's better since we came here though,' she said again.

'I am glad of it, for your sake and for his. So tell me, how does Alice manage Bastian's moods?'

'She doesn't! More often than not, she berates him for them, but then if you had it from her, he does this purely to make her life a misery. She has not a whit of compassion for him, and yet she speaks constantly of how she loves him. I think that just angers him more.'

'Poor Bas,' I said again, 'I wish there were something I could do to help.'

Nora's eyes ran over me, 'Of anyone, you are probably the most likely to be able to help him, I'd say!'

'I don't follow...'

'You could give him hope Maddi, and let him know he is loved! Give him something to look to in the future. At the moment he is without hope, trapped in a loveless marriage, and with little to look forward to. That's a tough place to be.'

'We have the birth of the baby...'

'Yes but that too is a mixed blessing, isn't it? What of after?'

I shuffled in my chair. I was by then five months pregnant and already more than done with the discomforts of it all. Thankfully, though, I was remaining at home throughout. Despite it all, Bastian had been forceful on that point and with Papa's agreement, there was little else to be said about it.

'After is something for later contemplation,' I said.

'Later is most likely all he thinks about. Bear it in mind!'

I nodded and wriggled again in my chair. My back ached, and now my hips seemed fit to join it. At least the sickness was mostly passed, aside from that which could be triggered by very strong smells or undercooked meat. I grumbled a little, and moved the cushion again, wriggling as my movements caused the baby to kick.

'The baby is troubling you?' Nora asked, smiling.

'Aye, he's making himself known today! Here,' I took her hand and rested it on my belly. For a long moment we were still and silent, but then the baby kicked, making Nora beam.

'Oh! Just you wait until I tell Bastian of this!' she said.

'Tell him too, that I hope to see him tomorrow,' I said, 'I was thinking of walking down to visit Mrs Harper in the morning, Papa is treating her for ulcers, poor dear, and so I have promised to drop in, but I will be free after luncheon for a walk or a sit.'

'I will tell him,' Nora murmured.

Bastian came the next day as I had hoped, and came alone for Nora was helping her mama with redesigning the dining room up at Fiveham – the pair both had an eye for such things whereas it bored me completely. Where Alice was, I knew not, but she was lurking I suppose, somewhere. Bastian was not quite his smiling self, that day, but was calm and quiet as he entered the house and kissed my cheek.

'How goes it?' he asked, 'did you feel up for a walk?'

'Indeed, let me get my coat.'

And so we stepped out. As the months had rolled past, Bastian and I had become well-used to the stares and speculation of the locals – disapproving glances, pressed lips and all – and over time, they had become more accustomed to us too and so in truth those looks and tuts had lessened too.

'Where shall we go?' he asked, 'beach, cliff, moors, or woods?'

'The woods,' I said, it's cooler there and less to clamber!'

We walked for an hour that day, enough that I was well over-exerted and hot, but Bastian seemed to have a mind to walk off his cares and in that I wanted not to disturb him. At last we arrived at Cattersley and Bastian took me down to a tea-room there. Cattersley was bigger than Blossom Cove, with more amenities and such. Rather than fishermen, the dock there was filled with trade: a fish market, a bandstand, even a village green! Of course, people knew us less there too, and so rather than the hostile glances from our own villagers, we were given soft smiles and indulgent glances. I ordered a glass of water with my tea, and drank it down quickly to refresh myself, then set into a delicious feast of jams and cream with freshly baked scones. Bastian ate little, but nursed a cup of tea whilst he watched me devour the repast.

'The food is good?' he asked at length.

'Very good, yes! This damn baby seems to have his aunt's appetite! I cannot stop eating!'

Bastian half-smiled and sipped his tea, inhaling the earthy scent of it before drinking. He nodded and moved his eyes to mine, 'It's calmer here, than the bustle of our working village.'

'More civilised, I think,' I agreed.

'And nobody knows who we are,' his words echoed my previous thoughts, 'we might just be a man and his wife out on a stroll. Of course, with my colouring there will always be the odd stare, but without knowledge of who I am, they will likely just dismiss it, consider me perhaps a gentleman just come over from India, or from some other place that they can reason away with less consternation than of my being *creole*.'

'I've never understood why it is all such a difference,' I said, 'Why people cannot look at you and see the beauty I do.'

His eyes found mine, I rarely made any reference to any attraction or affection between us, not anymore. He seemed a little lost in thought a moment but then laid a gentle hand over my fingers on the table.

'I love that you think it so,' he finally managed to get out, 'I… I don't see it, but I am glad you do.'

'Always,' I whispered but then pulled back again. It did not go too well to be too open. It did neither of us any good to probe a wound.

'Come, let us have an amble around town,' I said, 'and then begin the trek home!'

'I can hire a coach or a carriage, if you are tired?'

And in the end I allowed him to do so.

Such days then, were commonplace. For the first time, I was spending more time with Bastian than with Nora, and in truth, it allowed me to come to love him more so, than less. Of course, this did mean I had to spend some time with Alice too as it was hard to lose her once she latched on. It still seemed strange to me to think of her actually being his wife – my Bastian as a husband – I suppose this was further impacted in that he seemed to treat her no differently at all, to how he had before they were wed.

'They don't sleep together,' Nora told me, when I mentioned their relationship to her, 'She has her own chamber and he his, just like before when she used to visit! On the wedding day some of her things were moved to a joint chamber they were to share, but now she's moved them all back.'

I said nothing, caught between wanting to know it and being scared to push too far into it.

'He's still yours,' Nora said softly, 'If you wanted him…'

I shook my head with a laugh, 'Now is hardly the time to think of such, is it? After the baby is born, then things will obviously rear up again but for now I am happy to be his fat pregnant friend.'

'The mother of his child,' Nora said, lest I should possibly be able to forget it.

Ten

Around Blossom Cove, there has always been a tendency for the weather to change suddenly, going from the grey whooshing coldness, to sudden and extreme burning heat in a matter of weeks. Such was the case as the summer really set in that year – one bright enough to chase some of the cares away. Then the air turned cool again for the end of September and was already beginning to threaten a return to winter. October, then, was a glory of russet and cool breezes to chase away the final memories of that awfully hot summer, without being cold enough to make us wish for its return. I suppose I was gone seven months by then, and my walks up to Fiveham were a slower, more arduous trek. I took the coastal path, mostly as it was a softer path than the roads. Still the ghost of my mother walked those paths with me, but time had loosened the trauma and after all, it was not those exact paths which had fallen, leading to her death. At the peak, before the path down to the house, I would pause often to gaze out over the water and try to balance myself for whatever mood Bastian might be in when I arrived. All was the same that day, as I stood up on the clifftop looking down onto the cove. Bastian wasn't there, it was empty, but there was such a peace to the place. Mostly the shingle was stony – not a bright sandy cove – and the waves picked it up with a softness, calmed by a dull summer breeze rather than by the frenzied lashings it could give on a winter's day. There was a breeze blowing in from the sea and it gave a seaweed and salt embrace to me and my heavy burden. I drank it in, the roar of the waves, despite their calmness, giving in to the caw of the seabirds – mainly herring gulls – and the buzz of an occasional bee as it bumbled along the pretty wild-flowers which littered the sides of the cliffs.

'He's not here,' a voice behind me startled me. I turned, my perfect moment already marring, to see Alice stood behind me.

'Ah, Alice,' I said. I never really knew what to say to her, especially with a bellyful of her husband's child. At seven months gone, it was really rather large and cumbersome too, making me feel somewhat bloated up next to her ethereal virgin's beauty. 'I was er – just admiring the view.'

She stepped closer and peered over the edge. 'No matter how sweet the day, this place makes it cold,' she said and then, on cue, she shivered.

'I suppose, but the Cornish Sea has her own beauty, her own grandness.'

'I don't see it,' Alice said, eyes of a bluer hue than the ocean itself turning upon me. 'I miss the yellow shores of my home – when I was a child.'

'Bas and.. and Nora have told me a little of it, the bright blue of the sea and the tall sugar canes…'

Alice smiled. It was the first time she'd ever smiled for me and it was somewhat jolting. 'Life was easier back then,' she said.

'I can imagine.'

Alice stepped closer again and I suddenly felt the danger. I was stood in a small space with the steps behind me and no handrail. I made a start to go forward but Alice didn't move and so I was forced to step back again.

'Alice…'

'Sebastian is in the house,' she said, 'he was dull this morning and lay in bed still and sallow.'

My heart ached. My poor love! Alice said nothing though, her face showed no compassion at all.

'It is difficult for him,' I said, cringing.

'It is difficult for us all. Did you want to stroll down to the cove?'

I stared in surprise. Alice wanted to stroll – with me?

'I erm – you want to stroll?'

'I thought you did? Is that not why you came? For a *stroll?* I am sure it was more my husband's company than mine you crave, of course, I am no fool – but no, I offer you this pale consolation as he is unwell.'

My discomfort was growing, an itch just under the skin. I glanced down at the slippery steps, and then the rocks below. Our little cove did not make for an easy stroll, but a slippery causeway of potential dangers. There was a little of sand, here and there, but the jutting rocks, covered in seaweed, mossy clumps, and the muddiness of silt from where these particular cliffs were formed in soil as well as rock and stone made for a difficult walk. On the other hand, I was wearing my good boots and if Alice wanted to stroll, well, perhaps it was an olive branch!

'I... here?' I asked

'I don't see why not, if you can manage it in your state?'

Oh, there it was, a challenge issued. I should not have risen to it of course, but how could I resist when it was she who issued it? I turned back to the steps. There were about thirty or so of them, all hewn in roughly to the cliff-face in blocks of six or seven. They were not straight down but zigzagged a little. In places there were handrails but not for the top three sets and then sporadic going onwards. The cliffs were not the highest there, further on they gave drops of more than the height of Fiveham, but here the cliff dropped so that it was lower. I stepped out onto the first step.

The stone was slippery from the spray and the autumn shower we'd had earlier, but not too much so. I tested it and found it safe enough. With more confidence, I began my descent. Alice followed me, close enough that I could feel her body behind mine. I paused for a rest after the first six steps and then began the next, still with my shadow in tow. The next batch were trickier, a storm had pulled away a chunk of one of the steps in a deep gouge, so it was uneven and difficult. I put down one foot, telling myself that I would speak to Bastian about getting a handrail fixed here at least, around this tricky step, but as I moved to place the other I felt a hard and definite shove in my back. I gave out a cry, my fingers moving for purchase on the silty cliff-edge, but even as I grappled, the stone and bud of moss I grabbed for came loose. I screamed again, maybe her name, and then felt a hand skim my shoulder as though she'd repented and tried to grab me at the last moment. It was too late though; I was already falling. My free hand spiralled wildly as I went down on the hard steps, out in the air of the sheer drop. Thankfully, I managed to control the fall so that I did not go over the edge, but instead went sprawling face-first onto the cold slabs. One final cry escaped me as I landed but, unable to make purchase, continued to tumble, going down another two sets of steps and then landing in a heap where they twisted, jarring my back on the rocks.

At first there was no pain, shock dulled me to it. Then the rawness started up, spreading to encompass both my head where it had crunched against the cliff face, and my belly.

Oh God! Not my belly!

I wrapped my arms around myself, gagging on the sensation as pain rolled through me. Out in the distance, dulled somewhat, I could hear Alice screaming. She called my name twice and then came the sound of her running down. She seemed all of a frenzy, panic and tears all over her face. Had I imagined the hand in my back? It was difficult to believe that her attack could be so malicious as I looked up upon that face.

'Oh my goodness, Maddi, I'll get help!' She said, 'I'll… don't move! I'll get help!' and then she was gone again, those pattering feet moving away from me.

I groaned and curled up, still dazed and starting to feel pain in those lesser of important places, my wrist where I had fallen on it, my knee and ankle. I groaned and forced myself to sit up. The landscape spun and suddenly the sound of the waves crashing was oppressive and overwhelming. I moaned again and put my hand on the step. If my intention had been to rise, it was sorely misplaced. My wrist was broken, I know that now, but then it was simply agony, unable to hold my weight. Panic started to set in. I groaned and then, to my horror, my body expelled my breakfast, thick ropy vomit leaving my lips in a torrent. I have heard it said this happens in a trauma – the body choosing to concentrate on mending rather than the digestion of food. Twice my stomach heaved, causing more pain across my whole form. I tried again to stand but even if my hands would have allowed it, my body could not do it, weakened and jarred as it was. I put a protective arm about my belly. My baby. I glanced up. I was about halfway down the steps so I could not see the top from where I sat waiting for help.

Then the sudden thought struck me that if Alice had intended maliciousness, she might not actually send for help. This notion suddenly set me in a panic. If Bastian was in one of his low moods, and Nora was tending him, how long would it be before somebody even walked this way? The thought had me struggling to move again. I pushed my body forwards, towards the last step down which I had tumbled. I forced myself up using my one good hand and my knees. I wobbled dangerously and my vision blurred. It was too dangerous, if I fell there was still at least fifteen feet of sheer drop on my righthand side down onto jagged rocks. I began to pant; I was already shivering with cold and now my energy reserves were failing me. I let out a murmur and felt hot tears on my face. In defeat, I slumped down onto the steps. Just a short rest! Just a moment to regroup, I told myself, and then I would try again.

I was spared this though, by the sound of my name being called.

I felt my breath grow ragged again, but this time with relief. 'Bas!' I called back, 'Bas I am here! On the steps!'

For a moment, my mind brought me that other time he'd found me injured, seven and a half months past when I had fallen off the road in a storm. The night we'd gone to the cottage. My heart hurt, suddenly, for the memory, and my eyes welled up. This was more serious though, already I knew that.

Bastian's footsteps came to me then, and I glance up to see him skidding down the steps so quickly I was scared he too might fall. He was not alone, either, my eyes brought me the sight of Nora's worried face, above, and then that of one I had not expected – Baron Carfax himself!

Bastian got to me first. He navigated the crumbling steps and then sat himself down beside me. His eyes were frenzied but his movements had authority as he examined me, then pulled off his coat and wrapped it about me.

'Nora, Father, can one of you go for Maddi's Papa?' he called up. 'She's ice cold!'

'I'll go,' Nora's voice drifted down, 'Father can help you bring her up better than I!'

'Send for some servants too, girl,' Baron Carfax said, 'We might need help here, and blankets!'

Bastian murmured an agreement, and then, finally he spoke to me, 'Sweetheart, can you hear me?'

'Yes,' I managed.

'Are you in any pain?'

My eyes welled up again, 'Yes.'

Bastian's whole jaw clenched, but he let out a long breath and then was calmed. 'W-where, where does it hurt?' he asked.

'Head, arm, belly, foot.' I couldn't quite form full sentences.

From above I could hear more footsteps and moved my eyes to see Baron Carfax coming down too, making his way with less familiarity than his son had.

'What can I do?' he asked, not the monster he was made out to be in my mind, but a concerned helper in my distress.

Bastian shook his head, 'We have to move her,' he said, 'Can you help me, she's in pain and she's…' he wet his lips, 'bleeding…'

Was I? I stared in shock but had not the words to ask.

Baron Carfax loomed above me, but at least his form blocked out the horrible bright sunshine. He shuffled so that he was knelt above me, and then slid his hands under my shoulders. This allowed Bastian to slide his hands in around my waist, lifting me so that my weight was against his shoulders. He lost his own balance momentarily, but Lord Carfax put out a hand to steady him and Bastian grasped it. Perhaps, had I been more aware of what was going on, I might have marvelled at how these men who liked each other not at all, worked together to rescue me. Disaster can move even the firmest of enemies to camaraderie, or so it seemed. At last, Bastian had me. He was panting with exertion already, I was hardly light to pick up in my heavily pregnant state, and he was no labourer with brawn built in work, but a lord's son only. Somehow he did it though, shuffling so that I was slumped against him, my arm over one shoulder with his hands about my waist, the other holding my legs. From above, I heard the call of other voices – servants and Lady Carfax. As Bastian carried me up, his father moved before him, holding out a hand to aid in case he too fell. He didn't though, and in a momentous effort, he managed to carry me up the steps, dumping me down on the grass at the top of the cliff face.

From thereon in, things become a little more blurred. I know now, of course, what happened but in the moment all I felt was shock, panic and pain. What had happened, was that my fall had caused a slight tear inside, pulling the placenta a little away from the uterine wall. In truth, I was lucky indeed that it was not more so, for that could have led to a haemorrhage and then to my death.

What it did do, however, was trigger a premature labour.

After his near on heroic carrying of me up the steps, Bastian allowed his father and the servants to strap me to a board to carry me in. He walked at my side though, my hand in his and tears all over his face. Lady Carfax too seemed wrought, walking at my other side and promising me all would be well. I was somehow serene. The pain had moved to every part of me but somehow it was dulled, background noise. I did not know then, how pale I looked, how still and white, how cold I was to touch. There was blood about my head from where I had hit it, a wound which would cause a slight indent to my skull forever more, even once healed. There was blood on my legs too, I could feel the wetness, but it was not so much as I feared then, as it was mingled somewhat with the amniotic fluids of my waters breaking whilst I was below on the steps.

And I remember very little of birthing my son.

Papa was there, as were the midwives and a maid. Bastian, tearful but strong, was allowed to stay with me for the first leg of it, about two hours, but then Papa had ordered him out. At only seven and a half months gone, I knew as well as they all did, that I was likely going to lose the baby. Children born that early just did not survive. Labour lasted for eight hours, in total. It was exhausting – isn't it always! – but more so for doing it under such circumstances. Papa, despite being a doctor, was not involved in the actual birthing process and allowed the midwives to work, only interfering where he had to, and so spent most of the time holding my hand. His job was to begin once the baby was out, to stop the bleeding and to save my life. I cannot even imagine what he must have gone through then, in those long hours. Once the baby was born, though, he jumped straight into action. Whilst I strained and craned my body to look upon the weakly silent thing in the arms of the midwives, Papa injected me with something, and then packed me up to stop the bleeding. With this done, he finally laid the boy in my arms.

Oh, but he was tiny.

I had never before seen a new-born at all, let alone one born too soon! Papa covered me up with the coverlet on the bed, laid as I was in a nest of mattress protecting towels and a newly acquired clean sheet which was not soaked in blood. I had eyes for nothing but that tiny face, though, those little closed eyes and lips which moved but did not manage more than that strange mewing sound.

'Call for Master Carfax,' even Papa sounded overwhelmed as he came to sit on the bed beside me. His fingers reached out for the baby, and then gently caressed the little hand. He'd cut the cord himself, and brought the infant to independence from me himself. He said nothing, but a tired hollow fell onto his old features.

'My dear,' he said, and yes, there was emotion in his tone, 'you must steel yourself…'

He was interrupted though, by the door and Bastian's entering. At once Papa stood to give Bastian his place at my side.

'You have a son.' Papa managed, but then his old lips pressed again and he let out a long breath, 'And... and I council you now to seize these precious moments, both of you.'

My chest heaved, but I knew it already. Bastian nodded, too full to speak.

'H-how long?' I managed.

'Just tonight, I should think,' he said, 'He'll grow weaker, he'll pale and go floppy, and then his gurgles will cease, most likely.'

'He'll feel no pain?' Bastian asked, his voice was strained indeed.

'He'll feel no pain,' Papa agreed. 'I'll leave you both alone now, and I will make sure nobody distracts you or tries to come.'

'T-thank you,' I whispered.

'It is the least I can do.'

Once he was gone, Bastian wasted no time in joining me on the bed. He shuffled in close and then slipped his left arm around me, using his right to touch the cheek of our son. He cooed a little and murmured a few words to the baby and then looked to me.

'He's beautiful,' he whispered.

'He is.'

'We should name him, before…'

'Yes!' I interrupted before he could say it, 'What… what name?'

'If you would allow, I would like to name him Lloyd…'

'Lloyd,' I murmured, 'Like…'

'Like Henri Lloyd, my real father.'

It would cause a stir, I knew that already, but I was too tired to worry overly on that, 'Lloyd,' I murmured, 'It suits you well, little one, do you like that? To be Lloyd? Your Papa has given you a precious name my darling!'

Bastian seemed to deflate then, an inhale which rounded his shoulders and dimpled his chest. He was trying not to cry again, I realised. I touched his hand and brought it back to our son. We were both so raw, so close to tears. I clutched my precious bundle to me, leaning back on Bastian as I did so. He held me tightly, holding us all together. Both of us took it in turns to murmur to the boy, sweet nonsense but we could not help ourselves for it.

Thus an hour passed.

'Should I try to feed him?' I murmured at last, sad to think his little guts would be empty.

'Perhaps it is kinder not to, it might cause him pain if his tummy is not fully developed.'

I nodded, I wanted desperately to, but I could see the sense in that.

'What of you, do you need any water? Food?' Bastian asked,

'No. Just this.'

He nodded, and then pulled me closer still and kissed my forehead, 'And I,' he murmured. 'This is my family, here, in my arms. My Maddi and my newly born baby son, this moment is as things should be, and in a matter of hours it will be gone.'

'So let us savour it,' I murmured, 'Don't dwell on the sadness until it is time. Let us be present for Lloyd!'

'Indeed,' he sounded braver, good!

'I'm so tired.'

'Rest awhile then, if you need to. Here, lean on me.'

'I don't want to miss…'

'It's all right, he is stable for now and I can hold him so that he is close. He is well for now, if his condition changes, I will wake you up.'

I nodded and then passed the baby over to his father, minding my bandaged and throbbing wrist. Bastian slid him onto his arm and then laid back a little so that I could lie down and close my eyes. My hand moved back to the baby, resting on his little tummy, and then, despite how I wished for every second with Lloyd, I allowed myself to begin to doze.

I was asleep for but an hour I suppose, for the sky was just turning to red, making it close on seven or eight of the evening when I awoke. Bastian was still holding me, and the covers about me were grasped in his free hand. He was still awake, his eyes still on our boy but I was instantly aware that it was his gentle tone which had awakened me.

'Maddi, darling.'

'Hmm?'

'He's growing quieter, my love, and his little gurgles are becoming less rhythmic.'

For a moment, just a fraction, I wasn't sure what he meant but then it all came rushing back and I sat up a little more so with an "oh!". Bastian passed our little boy back to me, tenderness in his hands as he supported that little head onto my arm above the broken wrist. He was right, Lloyd was beginning to fail.

'Oh my little darling,' I whispered, 'Don't go so soon…'

Bastian dropped a tear, and I followed it with one of my own. Neither of us sobbed though, just the quiet agony within as the pulse in the baby's neck began to weaken, his arms stopped moving, and then his legs.

My chest heaved, and my breath caught. Bastian laid a kiss down on Lloyd's head, pausing there for a long moment and then looked up at me with eyes which were raw with pain.

'It is over,' he whispered, choked, 'he's dead.'

Much of the rest of that night was lost to crying, to a pain which would not abate. I cried until my already sore head was pounding, until my eyes were bright and raw. Bastian stayed with me after the initial movement to fetch Papa, who gently but firmly removed our sweet precious bundle from us. Downstairs, preparations were being made. Various knocks came to the door – mainly Nora to beg our guidance, did we want the vicar to bless him? Would we object to him being buried in Bastian's christening gown? Did we need anything?

In those moments, I moved through every emotion. I cursed Alice for making me fall, Bastian's family for keeping us apart, myself for being so pliant and foolish, even him for being wed to her. Bastian took it all, knowing it for what it was, mere grief. He held me through the fury, through the unbearable sobbing, through the quiet times too, when all I had the strength to do was to lie back on him and weep. It was in one of those moments, that he picked up on what I had said earlier,

'Alice pushed you?' the words were softly spoken, but with fire beneath. I had not intended to tell him that. In the end, he had still to live with her, he had still to be her husband and his knowledge of such was more a pain to him, than a solution to anything else.

'I don't know,' I replied, 'I... I am certain I felt a hand in my back though, between the shoulder blades, and then I was falling.'

'Then she and I are done.' Bastian whispered, fire burning in his words, but then pulled me back to him, 'I'll make this right, I swear! This farce has gone on long enough!'

Lady Carfax came to us, next, close on midnight. She looked stern but her manner was so very gentle and sweet that I gave in and offered her entry. She sat herself down in the chair beside the bed, her hand taking mine. Bastian sat up beside me, his arm about me to give me strength.

'My darlings, Nora and I have dressed out a fine wicker basket for baby until the coffin is made. He is comfortable and peaceful, wrapped up in cotton and lace. Would you have me bring him to show you?'

I shook my head.

'Are you sure?'

'I am, I have said my goodbye,' I murmured.

'And I the same,' Bastian whispered, 'Although I shall see him again, before…'

'Of course. Now, and this is important, do you want the vicar to baptise him before he is put into the coffin?'

'I think that we do? Yes,' Bastian said.

I nodded.

Lady Carfax smiled a thin, sympathetic smile, 'And… and did you have a name in mind? For the moment he is just being referred to as Baby Chilcott but…'

'It's Carfax,' Bastian interrupted, 'and his name is Lloyd. Lloyd Sebastian Carfax.'

Lady Carfax let out a rush of air from her lungs. For a moment she looked very pale but she brought herself under control quickly. She bit her lip and glanced between the two of us. 'Are you both certain that you want to…'

'Yes,' Bastian said, firm, indeed, I'd never before known him to have such a strong tone, 'I am certain. And Mama, ready yourself as things might become a little… difficult from here on in.'

Lady Carfax looked as bemused as I felt, 'Difficult?'

'Yes, because as of tomorrow morning, I intend to make the beginning enquiries to seek an annulment of my marriage to Alice,' he said, 'Mama, I won't live this way anymore, I'm going to annul my false marriage and marry Maddi, just as I should have in the first place!'

Eleven

Those first few weeks were the worst to bear. Even as my body recovered, my milk was dried up and my stomach fell flat, I was met everywhere with reminders that I should have a baby, and I didn't. Bastian felt it too, I know he did, but whilst I sat in mourning, back in my own home once I was able to get up and walk about once more, once my pulled ankle and broken wrist were mending. Bastian threw himself into his crusade for an annulment of his marriage to Alice. I suppose it was his final hope, the last thing he had to cling to!

'I have written to Monroe,' he said to me, when I finally got up courage to ask of it, 'And I have outlined it all. I hope that I'll not have to go against him.'

'Father is furious,' Nora added, 'He is a bear at the best of times, but he is…'

I glanced up quickly enough to see Bastian shake his head minutely at her. Even still they protected me from what a brute he was, still I was not to know it fully. I could guess though.

'He is, yes, a bear,' Bastian said.

'Has he… has he hurt you, again?' I dared to ask.

'No, and never more shall he, but he frightens Nora still when he rages.'

At once, I hated the old man again, despite how he'd helped Bastian to rescue me.

And so it fell that we played a waiting game. Letters went back and forth between Bastian and Mr Monroe, and to his father too, from how I heard it. Constantly, Bastian assured me that things progressed but still Alice remained where she was, and still the marriage remained sound.

'I'm so on edge, all the time,' I confessed to Nora. We were taking a stroll on the beach together whilst Bastian was out assisting his father on estate matters. 'I know he is doing all he can, but I am impatient.'

'I would be too! Rabidly so!' Nora agreed, stooping to pick up a shell, brush it off and put it into her pocket. She designed little mirrors and boxes made of them to give as gifts at Christmas. 'Are you and he…'

'Oh,' I flushed, 'No, we agreed after Lloyd, that we would remain platonic until the day we can be married.'

'Indeed, good grief, no wonder you both look forlorn, then,' Nora chuckled.

'It is sweet, I think, that we…'

'Sweet? It's daft, if you ask me,' she said, 'Once all this business is done with you will be married, and it's not as though you've not already been lovers! Or even that anybody hereabouts would believe you weren't!'

'I suppose,' I said. There were two little shells sat together on the edge of a rockpool so I dipped to collect those for Nora, pausing to look for little crabs or fish in the pool as I did so. Beyond, I heard Nora squeal and laugh as she raced the waves to avoid having to clamber over the rocks. The sound was one to bring a smile to my lips, as so was the dissolving of my own determination to keep Bastian and myself apart – as Nora said, who would we really be harming, anyway?

I chose my moment well, the notion of becoming once more his lover becoming an idea that once conceived, could not be put away. The perfect opportunity came to pass on the night of his birthday, some three months after we'd lost Lloyd and so a year since that adventure out at the cottage. Nora was my co-conspirator, helping to arrange so that there was a bed made up for me in the room next to hers, on the correct side of the house for least detection. There was to be a celebration of Bastian's birthday so I would attend that, sneak away early with a headache and with Nora to care for me – in truth to help me prepare. Then to go to his chambers and be there when he arrived back upstairs. It was foolish and childish, but it was what it was!

The day went much as planned. Despite all that was in motion, I had to dine in the large dining room with Alice sat dour opposite me. Alice had point blank refused Bastian's suggestion to go home whilst the formalities of the annulment were negotiated. She was still fighting it, in her own way. The situation was absurd, with Bastian openly inviting me to spend time with him, with our engagement all but ready to go as soon as the annulment was finalised. Still, Alice wasn't done yet, and Monroe had not yet given his take on it either. Lady Carfax treated me already like a daughter, whilst the old Baron tried time and again to overrule the invitations the family sent.

However, despite all of this, I was still in good spirits as the day died. Nora glanced at me close on nine and winked, and there I was struck down with a "headache" which rendered me unable to remain below stairs. We were almost scuppered by Bastian's trying to follow us, worried for me, but Nora put him off and then we were above in the chamber that had been assigned to me. Nora was giggling like a schoolgirl herself as I went inside and closed the door behind us both. She could not hold it in, and I wondered at her behaviour a little: I suppose I had lived ordeals she had not and so where she was still a little childish at times, I had to fight to retain that girlish mirth. Nora kissed my cheek and then with a word that she would return shortly, she vanished. When she did come back, about five minutes later, she had in her arms some clothing and to my surprise, some makeup.

'Well,' she said, 'do you really think my complexion so fair, in comparison to Bas?'

'You pale yourself with powder?' Somehow that felt sad to me, Nora was so beautiful and I hated to think she felt the sting of her heritage too.

'Hush that,' she said, 'Come, now we have to get you ready for Bastian! Here, a gift!'

The "gift" was a delicate nightgown in a subtle cream chiffon and silk. It had no shape to it, of course as such items do not, but the cloth was very soft and billowy. I resisted the urge to hold it up to my cheek, but instead took a long moment in examining the folds of material, the little pink silk rosebuds on the sleeves. Upon examination, I realised too that the rosebuds were set with tiny pearls at their hearts.

'This is…'

'Is something I had made on a whim and have never had any cause to wear,' she said, 'put it on… if you like it, that is!'

'It is very beautiful but it must have c…'

'If the next word from your lips is "cost", I shall strip you down and dress you myself!' Nora scolded.

I laughed and, I confess, such gifts were commonplace enough from her now. I lifted the beautiful gown and slipped behind the dressing screen to wriggle free of my corsets and gown to don the robe. It was like wearing spider's silk and I was lost in a cloud of it.

'Here, you look very fine!' Nora said as I came back out. 'Perfection! If Bastian can take his eyes from you then he is blind. You look beautiful! Like a medieval maiden!'

'Oh, no, it is just the gown which is pretty.'

'Hush, nonsense! Here let me sort your skin for you!'

I fell to silence as Nora took up her powders. In silent contemplation, I allowed her to apply the stuff to my face, a layer of powder, tiny amount of black to the corners of my eyes. Her final act was to remove the pins from my hair so that it fell loosely down over my shoulders in a sleek wave which she brushed briskly and braided over one shoulder. At last, she was satisfied and led me to the mirror.

A tiny seed of nerves began to eat away at me once more as I looked upon Nora's handiwork. I truly looked more like a bride adorned in her wedding garb than anything else. I wondered how Bastian would react when he saw me, would he appreciate his sister's gesture or would he turn from me in disgust?

'Oh Nora, you have done a great job with me,' I said. 'But this is inappropriate – distasteful, even – I am not Bastian's bride!'

'Not yet! But it is a little push for him towards that! Let him see what he is missing! Let's get you to his chamber before he goes to bed, I want the surprise to be perfect!'

'You act as though I am a gift to be given...'

'Your love is a gift to you both. After what you have suffered you both deserve a little happiness. Now, let us get you to his chamber before he comes upstairs!'

Nora took one of the candles from her dresser, I took the other, and quickly the pair of us slipped out of the room. I was terrified that someone would catch us but as we passed the top of the grand staircase, I could hear only the piano from below. We walked quickly across the corridor and down into the back of the house where Bastian had his rooms. I felt dizzy with nerves, dizzy and a little ill. As Nora turned the handle of Bastian's door, she saw my face and smiled.

'No need to look so frightened Maddi,' she soothed, suddenly seeming so much more grown up than I. 'It is Bastian remember, this is what you both want and there will be nothing to fear! You've done this before, and with him too!'

'Not... not this! A childish fumble in the extremes of emotion, not a calculated encounter.'

'Indeed, so this will be better!'

I nodded, nervous beyond belief and almost to the point where I wanted to give up the charade and leave before I was discovered. Nora was watching me silently and when my eyes rested on her, I saw that her own were shining with mischief. Everything was a game to Nora!

'I'll go and lure him up, shall I?'

For a moment, I felt such a strange tension in my stomach that I thought I might actually begin to cry. I was so nervous, so afraid that something would go wrong, Bastian was pursuing the annulment in order to marry me, I knew that, and so he might think it better we wait! He might put me aside, gently chastise me! After Lloyd I worried too that he might not want to take such a risk again. The thought of the baby was enough to stall me too! If nothing else, until Bastian and I were wed we really needed to have a care! I worried too that a servant might come in before he did to stoke the fire or turn down the bed. How could I ever explain my presence? What if the hypothetical servant called for Baron Carfax? So many what-ifs, so much to worry about that I felt a mass of knots forming in my belly. I took a few deep breaths to calm myself. I could still leave, I told myself, there was still time to just go – but that thought was not appetising either; I was so riled up with expectation that to just sneak away would be nothing but an anti-climax.

Then I heard a noise outside of the room. The time for changing my mind was done.

Nora's voice came flittering through the wall, first, but I could not make out what she said, then the door opened and Bastian was in the room. With a wink at me, Nora closed the door behind him. As Bastian entered the room, his eye flittered to the candle on the side, surprised to see it lit, and then to me, sat delicately on his bed in all my splendour. He just stood for a moment, staring, and then pulled off his coat and waistcoat and laid them on the back of a chair. His eyes burned me but he was silent. I began to feel uncomfortable in his stare, in the fact that he did not speak to me.

'You might want to lock the door,' I said, more to break the silence than anything else.

'What is this? I thought you had gone to bed?'

'I… and so I have…'

'You seem to be in the wrong chamber though, and dressed so... Nora's doing, I presume?'

I flushed, unsure of what to do. Bastian didn't seem overly cross at my presence though, more confused. He undid his cravat and then found his way to my side and sat down on the bed. I could smell a gentle scent of gin upon his breath.

'I understand if I have made an error in judgement in coming here,' I finally said, 'I am sorry, I'll leave?'

'The devil you will!' at once his hand came out to grasp my form, pulling me in to his arms. His lips tasted my throat, my shoulders, oh heavenly forbidden touch! His hands worried the cloth of my nightgown but even still, he paused and then pulled away again, conflicted.

'Are you very sure?' he asked, 'You want this? Before I have achieved my annulment? I am still a married man, as it is, that is a worse sin even than what was before.'

'Yes,' I said. 'I know, but I have trust in you and in God to straighten out this mess. I want to... I want to taste you properly, without a fear of people walking in at any time. Not a childish fumble in the dark like what was before I – I want to...' I flushed, '... I want to make love to you, Bastian, properly.'

He sat in silence for a long moment staring at the room beyond, my hand still prisoner in his but his mind obviously whirring. Hardly the seduction I had intended, but then how had I really expected him to react?

'We will be married soon enough,' he said at last, looking up at me, 'I will be yours then.'

'You *would* prefer I leave then?'

'I didn't say that!'

'Then what?'

'I just want to ensure that if we are going to... that we both understand what we face, the rules we are breaking.'

'Well *I* do... Bas, don't think my coming here is rash and not thought out – I've thought of nothing else for some weeks now.'

Bastian pulled in a long breath that swelled his chest up, and then looked back to me, 'And you are healed? I won't hurt you?'

'I am healed, and... and we can have a care, not to...' I paused but no, it had to be said, '... we can have a care to ensure we do not make another baby – yet!'

Bastian's eyes searched my face, still unsure, but then suddenly he lifted a hand to touch my cheek, 'Come here, then,' he murmured.

A tingle started up in my very toes and spread through me, running up my form, through my fingers. I bit my lip with my top teeth, feeling that plump flesh pull free of them as I gave out a little rush of air. Bastian slid a hand into my hair, cupping my face with his soft hands. He leaned in until his lips were almost upon mine but paused for a tantalising moment, breathing his breath onto my lips. The moment pulled, but then he closed the distance, kissing me again, softly. My eyes fluttered closed, my heart speeding up and my belly turning itself into knots. I kissed him back, then shuffled closer as his hand slipped from my face down onto my shoulder and then into the small of my back. His kiss grew deeper and I melted into it, a surrender of everything I had held in for so very long. Bastian's other hand caressed my collarbone, and then ran down over the soft chiffon of the nightgown.

Our movements became fluid as our bodies touched, the silk of my gown encompassing us both in an almost dreamlike softness. Bastian stripped off his shirt so that I could feel his flesh against me, something I'd not been allowed that first time, and I found myself moving with his rhythm, melding with him. He was hot to touch, soft, malleable where my fingers gently pressed and explored his flesh. I started to become lost in the sensations, my own conscious being slipping away to the intensity of the moment. Then the nightgown was gone and where we had been encased in the layers and layers of soft chiffon, instead it was bare flesh to flesh. His body moved with mine, his hands caressing me and his lips straying to parts of my skin he'd not had the ability to kiss before: my breasts, my belly. No rush this time, no cause to break free of that unharried exploration of each other. My hands gained confidence too, unbuttoning his trousers and sliding them away, his short-trousers too and then running my hands over his flesh. The touch made him pause briefly, and pull in a deep intake of breath. I found a smile and as he opened his eyes he smiled too. His lips possessed mine again and then with a gentle hand he pushed me back down onto the pillows. The chiffon nightgown was under my back and head where we'd not thrown it aside, it embraced me in a cocoon of softest silk as Bastian slowly slid a hand up each leg, parting my thighs. I lay still, enjoying the anticipation.

As he joined us, there was some fumbling still, we were both still so very new to the experience, but then there was unity as he brought us together. I fell to his rhythm, my legs about him, my hands tangled in his hair. He moved slowly, encompassing me entirely in him, then quicker, building up a pleasure in us both. My hands gripped chiffon, my head pushed back to soft pillows and my body was at his mercy entirely. My lips moved to his collarbone, biting my lip and repressing any sound as might be heard beyond our room. In unison, I felt his hands grip me tighter, his breath tickle my shoulder as it left him in a long exhale which ended in something of a quiet moan. He stiffened, two final deep heavy pushes, and then with a gasp he pulled away, leaving my body abruptly. At first I frowned confused at the sudden loss of him, but then I realised it, felt the wet heat on my belly where he spilled. The best way to not make a baby that we had open to us, was not to allow it inside.

And then we lay still for a long moment, Bastian buried his face in my shoulder, his hands tangled in my hair. He kissed my neck, my throat, my shoulders, and then moved away. I shuffled to sitting, watching as wordlessly he fetched a washrag from the bowl of water on the dresser and came back to clean away where he had stained my skin with sharp cold water.

'There,' he murmured, still lost a little in his emotions. I spoke not, just curled myself up into his arms and closed my eyes. It was bliss and I dared not allow myself to think, lest it spoil the moment with the reality of our situation. For the first night since Lloyd had died in my arms, I felt myself slipping away to a natural sleep, completely at peace.

The following morning, I awoke abruptly to the sound of knocking on the door. In my dazed state, I knew not where I was for a moment and glanced about me frowning. It was still very dark. The drapes were pulled but from a split within them, I could see it was still darkness without, not yet morning. Then remembrance took me of the night before, and my whole body froze. Beside me, Bastian stirred and rubbed his eyes, then looked up at me and a smile took his lips until the knocking came again, seeming loud in the quietness of the house.

'Who's there,' Bastian called, but his eyes left me not.

'Only Nora,' came her call. 'I was afraid to just walk in.'

'We are sleeping! It's early!'

'It's five – the maids will be up soon!'

'Give us twenty minutes!' Bastian called back, and Nora left with a chuckle. Leisurely, Bastian stood and I felt myself blush as I averted my eyes from his naked form. He chuckled at my shyness but wrapped himself in his robe which was draped over the foot of the bed. First, he crossed the room and turned his key in the lock, then turned back to me. Shakily he smiled.

'So what now Maddi?' he asked.

'I… I suppose I should get up and find my way to the chamber I was supposed to sleep in.'

'Don't go yet?'

'I will be but a few rooms down!'

Bastian came back to me and sat on the edge of the bed. he kissed me twice, then pulled way with a soft smile. 'And was last night a… a one-off, or can I expect such a surprise again?'

'Until we are wed, it should be infrequent, at least,' I murmured. 'I wanted to give in, I couldn't fight it any more, but we need to be so very careful now.'

'I agree,' he said, but then caught me again as I moved to stand, spilling me into his lap, 'I'm not letting you escape that easily this morning though!'

'Nora will be back!' I laughed, but already I was acquiescing to his kisses.

Twelve

I suppose, then, that we come now to the hardest part of my tale to write, the moment when my life tumbled back down around me and crashed into flames which once fanned, destroyed it all for so very long. This, the moment where my dalliance turned to pain, to destruction and then was lost, along with our hopes. I was so certain, in those early days that the annulment was soon to be finalised and then we would be wed. So certain was I that I threw caution to the wind. Bastian and I began to play at games, then, dangerous games – sneaking him into my chamber at Papa's house, or escaping off together to hidden coves and secret places, hiding, being as one, living as though we were already married.

Of course, life is never so kind for very long.

Monroe finally broke his silence just a few weeks after Bastian and I had rekindled our affair and refused, via a sharply worded letter, to withhold his evidence if Bastian were to annul. In response, Bastian took up council with a legal man named Jones. The two of them went together into the parlour and there were gone for some three hours. When Bastian came out, he gathered Nora and I to him and we slipped out of the house, up to the garden at the back where we had played as children. There, he spoke quickly against the howling winds.

'If Alice does not agree to testify that the marriage is unconsummated, then I cannot seek annulment on those grounds,' he said. 'I can apply for a document from parliament to issue a divorce only if she – not I – has been unfaithful.'

'Oh!' I whispered, shocked and feeling the ground sinking below me, 'so what is our next move?'

Nora took my hand. Despite her fine gown, she was sat on the floor with me. Bastian was up on the wall but it was only a half-meter tall. He glanced between us, his eyes dim.

'There is another route,' he said, 'In cases of insanity upon marriage, a person might seek an annulment. This is actually supposed to protect a man against marrying a woman who is not in full control of her faculties…'

'Lovely…' Nora muttered,

'…but! Jones thinks in my case, I might use it as a defence in having married whilst insane.'

'Because of your suicide attempt?' I asked, all the colour leaving the scenery around me in my shock and disgust.

'Yes. Your father signed a writ of insanity upon me, on the day after my wedding! It was to last a year, and meant that I could have been committed to an asylum had I worsened, and that I am not capable of managing my own affairs in this time. He is set to review it soon, actually. If we are careful in our wording and of how this is presented, this might be what we need to release me from this farcical marriage!'

I shuffled back, my back against the wall behind me, and put my head down on his thigh where he sat above. He slid his fingers into my hair, gently caressing it. We were in view of the house but in that moment I did not care.

'And this is our only route?' Nora asked.

'Yes.'

'So what of Monroe and his blackmail?'

Bastian drew in a deep breath, 'That is something I will need to discuss with Father,' he said.

'He won't help! He hates us both!' Nora said, grim.

'And so he might, but he loves his money, and his freedom! What we have here – this house – it is untouched by whatever the old fool did in Jamaica! If the worse comes to the worse...'

'Then we shall be poor as church mice, rattling around in a drafty old house we cannot afford,' Nora said.

'We have enough to get by, I am sure, from estate rents and the like. Father has the most to lose, because he risks arrest for God-knows what! If I can get him on our side...'

'I think that a better plan,' I agreed, 'If he will tell us the stakes, then we better understand the gamble!'

'Exactly. And then we can challenge Monroe again,' Bastian said, 'And call his bluff, as it were. I'd still rather work with him than against him.'

'So then,' Nora said, 'we are agreed?'

Some four days later, Bastian received yet another letter from Monroe, and then vanished again into his chambers, not coming out for the whole day. It was the first time he'd done that in some weeks, and at once Nora and I were on alert for bad news. I snuck up the stairs after tea and cake with Nora and her Mama, somewhat on pretence of having already left. At my knock, he came to the door but did not open it, not even for me.

Bas,' I whispered, putting up a hand to his cheek, 'what is the matter my love? Is there bad news?'

He pressed his lips to my forehead. He was bedraggled indeed, with tear-tracts all down his face.

'Yes,' he murmured.

'Oh God, would you not tell me?'

'Not yet I – I am still digesting. Go home Maddi, please? I'll see you tomorrow, my darling, but I hate for you to... to see me like this.'

'All right then,' I'd learned better than to push with him, I knew his moods well and was still waiting for the day he'd let me in rather than shut me out. Still my heart ached, and yet more new worries stirred. 'I- if you are sure you are well?'

'I will be… I promise.'

'And you won't do anything foolish?'

'I have already promised you that never again will I allow myself to fall that low.'

I nodded my head, deflating.

Bastian seemed to see it for his lips again touched my brow. 'I'm sorry my love, give me one night to digest this latest rock in our path. Kiss me, know I love you, but come back tomorrow and we shall discuss it then.'

I stood to receive the offered kiss, my fingers holding tight to his arm for a moment, but then he gently but firmly, stepped back and closed the door.

With my heart aching, I removed myself, walking slowly towards the main stairs. Normally I was careful not to be seen as I departed the house once I'd already said my goodbyes, but my mind was filled with Bastian's sorrow and to my horror, I nearly bowled into Baron Carfax.

'Madeleine?' he asked. 'I thought you'd gone home?'

'No sir,' I said trying to sound casual. 'Bastian and I were to play chess in his rooms but he is feeling unwell.'

'Chess? I see. That will explain why that rascal is locked away upstairs again, I suppose?'

'No sir, he is unwell,' I whispered, frightened of the look in his eyes. Baron Carfax continued to glare upon me and I felt my stomach churning, I could well see how this was a terrifying man even besides the things I knew he'd done. I hoped that I was leaving Bastian safe and that his father would not go up to his chamber.

'Well I don't suppose there will be much time for playing chess in the future…'

A chill went down my spine. 'Yes sir,' I whispered again. 'I should go, sir.'

'You should.'

The skies were becoming darker outside and I felt the chill of the air on my skin as Lord Carfax himself opened the door for me. 'Goodbye Madeleine,' he said, and again I felt the sliver of fear on my spine. I nodded in return and fled the house almost as though the devil himself were chasing me.

The following day, however, Bastian was back to his usual good humour and shrugged it off once more.

'And what of the bad news you had to tell us?' Nora demanded.

'Nothing that can't be gotten past,' he said, despite how his eyes darkened and his features shifted just a little.

And so it went on. At the turn of another month – that making it three since I had begun our affair again with my visit to Bastian's chamber, and nearly seven since he'd first started seeking his annulment – I snapped.

'How much longer?' I barked, as he came down the stairs to meet me one morning. The question was abrupt and was uttered without even a greeting but I'd been laid awake all night in a state of anguish – not for the first time – and enough was enough! Bastian sighed and pulled me by the hand from the hallway where we stood, into the parlour which overlooked the sea. It was one of my favourite rooms in the whole house, bright and airy, tall ceilings and a wide window to let in the white light of the ocean skies. There he sat me down and rang for tea. Nora joined us presently, her eyes worried as she caught the tension between us.

'We will get the annulment,' Bastian finally said, 'Monroe is bending. We all agreed it was better to work with him than against and now I have a communication going. He is slow to reply though, which is what lengthens the process.'

'But you have his agreement?' Nora asked.

'Yes, with some provisos I am working through.'

'What provisos?' I asked.

'Nothing you need worry yourself with. I promise, we are nearly there!'

'How long is nearly?'

'A month, maybe two.'

'Another month! You said such last month!' I sulked.

'We are both in the same boat darling! I think we are closer though, come here,' he murmured, trying to pull me in. Angrily I resisted though, tearful.

'Leave her be Bas,' Nora murmured, 'she's upset!'

'We are all upset!'

'Are we? Because it seems to me that you are rather having your cake *and* eating it!'

Nora gasped at my words, her lips falling open, but poor Bastian looked as though I had slapped him. He stuttered but I gave him no respite and with a barked farewell to Nora, I turned to stalk away. Outside, though, between me and the gate, was the worst of obstacles! Alice was out on the lawn. She was dressed in her finest, with her long hair braided away. She was flying some strange brightly coloured kite. I paused, I hated by then to even be near her, but then I made to stalk past. She saw me though and there, despite it all, she saw my tears and she smirked. My temper, always a little on the side of flash in a pan, snapped.

'Oh! Smile and smirk at my tears, will you?' I snapped, shouting the words like a common fishwife.

Alice stared in shock at my outburst, her eyes widening. She seemed indecisive, and then wrapped the kite wire about the sill and came over to stand face to face with me. She'd grown a little fatter lately, and her skin was a little blemished and greasy. I refused to notice these signals of stress though, not wanting to see weakness in my foe that might bend me, and so I merely held my glare.

'And what reason would I have not to smile?' she finally said, 'When my husband scolds his mistress and kisses his wife with tenderness.'

'My Bastian would rather gargle soap than kiss you, you horrible liar!' I snapped.

'Think what you like. See, I was worried at first, when he asked for an annulment but now I see it was in my favour, for as he comes more and more to realise that he'll never be free of me, the more he will have to learn to live with me.'

'You manipulative little bitch,' I growled, trying out the unfamiliar word, 'You didn't even want him!'

'No, but I do rather enjoy looking forward to being a baroness one day!'

'You never will be! How dare you! The annulment *will* go ahead.'

'Oh,' she laughed, 'I'm sure…'

'It will!'

Alice just smiled again, I bit my lip and pressed my thumbs into my palms in an effort to restrain myself from slapping her silly. I, in my fury, turned from her but instead of doing the sensible thing, I turned instead back to the door of the house. Alice dipped off back the other way to collect her kite. I barely noticed her. I stalked back into the parlour where Bastian was now alone, Nora having gone elsewhere. Bastian looked up as I entered, his eyes were wet but rather than pity, this fuelled my anger more so.

'Oh! Don't you sit and weep,' I snarled.

'Maddi!' his face was a picture of shock,

'How dare you weep? If you are in pain then be stronger and do something about it! You have the motive, means and legality to annul this marriage. If you loved me, if you did seek a future with me, then you would use them.'

'Damn it all, if you think it is that easy!'

'It is,' I knew I was shouting, I could control it not, 'It is that easy! Just put in your papers and all is done!'

'And what of Monroe? What of my father?'

'Damn your father to hell!' I shouted, 'He is as much a monster as the other! Even to you! Why the devil do you deny us our happiness in the place of the man who beat you?'

'I don't! I hold back to protect us! If I were to give in to this, now, we'd be paupers! We'd have nothing but these stone walls! What's more, if Carfax denies me then I am not just a penniless creole, I am a penniless bastard creole! It would be the workhouse for us, and how do you think we would fare there?'

'This is ridiculous,' I said back, 'It would never get so far as all that and you know it!'

Bastian shook his head, 'I'm doing everything I can,' he said, 'the wheels are in motion! You have no idea what I do, the sacrifices I have made and will continue to make to secure our future!'

'Why, you make no sacrifices at all,' I snapped, 'none whatsoever. You sit up here on this hill and you enjoy all the luxury of your position and you don't give a monkeys about the rest of us, about me!'

'You are an idiot if you think that!' he said, no longer shouting but hoarse and hollow.

'And you are a fool if you cannot see why I think it,' I said, the same tone settling on me. 'I'm tired Bastian, tired of all this!'

'I just ask for patience, Maddi we are so close now.'

I shook my head, 'I can't do this anymore,' I whispered, 'File that paperwork tomorrow, or lose me for good. I can't… I can't keep doing this.'

'An ultimatum? Really Maddi?'

'Call it what you will,' I said, still dull, and then in a panic I suddenly turned and ran away.

I spent the rest of my day locked away in floods of tears. Papa was out attending the final rites of one of the old labourers over at Home Farm and so I was alone. Every moment I expected to see him, to hear a knock on the door, but Bastian did not come. I think that irked me more so, and then became agony as the clock drew us away into darkness. Nell tried to bring me hot stew but I could not bring myself to eat it, so very low of spirits.

As the clock struck ten, I heard the sound below of my father coming in from his house call. I thought for a moment to ignore even him, but then tiredly let myself out of my chamber. At once upon seeing my face, he opened his arms despite that he too looked exhausted. I fell into the embrace just as I had as a child, and there I simply sobbed, my Papa holding me tight.

'Here,' he said at last, 'My poor little girl – it's him again, isn't it?'

I said nothing, still sniffing. 'Let us brew some cocoa,' he said, his old arm about my shoulders leading me through to the kitchen, 'just like Mama used to, yes?'

And so Papa and I sat, that miserable night, and together we drank cocoa, never once suspecting what was happening up at the Carfax house, the panic and frenzy which was going on as Alice's maid came to Lady Carfax and told her that the girl was gone away somewhere. The beginnings of the search, the horror as the hours ticked on and she was not found. Whilst Bastian and his mother and father went out to shout her name across the clifftops, I sat and sipped on warm liquid chocolate, oblivious to it all.

Alice's body was found in the early hours of the following morning. She was brought in by a local fisherman who'd caught sight of something on the rocks in the water, about a mile between the house and the village, a scarily close re-enactment of my own mother's death. Alice had been in the water longer though, she had been beaten against the rocks all throughout the night and her body was much battered, broken, almost unrecognisable but for her unusual, almost white hair.

The gossip reached us quickly, before even the summons for Papa to come and examine the body. As soon as I heard it, I ran the distance to Fiveham. The family were talking to the authorities though, and I was forbidden access to them or the house and so, dejectedly, I walked home. My heart felt as though somebody was squeezing it in their hand. Terrible suspicions began to form about the man I loved, despite how I pushed them away. It seemed too much a coincidence! We'd quarrelled and then just a day later, this! I tried to tell myself that he was not capable, that he was too gentle to ever hurt a soul but then I would remember how much he was hurting, remember how once before he'd turned an act just as violent in onto himself and I would wonder.

It must have been hours later that I was shocked out of my terrified musings by Nora's knock. Her face was ashen and flooded with tears, her hair uncurled and her face unpowdered.

'Alice is dead!' she gasped.

The cup slipped from my fingers and smashed as it hit the coffee table. I trembled, unable to make sense of my befuddled thoughts. Suddenly Papa was at my side, holding me up as all my strength left my body.

'What?' My voice was low, shuddering.

Nora threw herself into my arms, sobbing. 'There are two officers and a coroner at the house,' she wept onto my shoulder, 'they are calling an inquest, but he said it looks on first glance like Alice was murdered – and Bastian is the main suspect!'

Thirteen

Often, an inquest was held at a local alehouse, or sometimes even a spare room in the courthouse but, as was also often the case, with the deceased being of The Cliff House, the coroner took his men there. A coroner's jury was made up of men of the village, and sometimes a little further afield too. These men were our townsmen of note, and in a normal case, Papa and Baron Carfax might have been amongst them. Unlike a trial though, these men mingled in with the rest of us, not separated by different locales in the room. In fact, the whole event seemed much less formal than I had expected, and the coroner at least seemed kind enough as he led Papa and I inside.

Bastian, Lady Carfax, Nora and I all sat quietly in the small parlour whilst the men examined the body under the guidance of my father. Also in the room was Alice's other doctor – the man who had prescribed her medications – Dr Lent. He was a Londoner, and had made his prescriptions from there only seeing her once or twice in the time since she'd married. Finally a handsome gent with fair hair and blue eyes like Alice had had. The notorious Mr Monroe, the blackmailer. He was something of a surprise though, I had expected him to be old! My own Papa and Lord Carfax were my only real guides to how a Papa should look, and so this fairly handsome creature who seemed so young was nothing as I had been picturing him. Late thirties, I supposed, close to forty – he must have been young indeed when Alice was born! His glittering and earnest eyes remained firmly on the floor and his smooth hands twisted something between them. At a closer glance, I saw it to be a cloth and peg doll and with a pang, I wondered if it had been hers. I wondered if he felt guilty. Whatever had happened to Alice, he'd driven her to it by this forced marriage, by his blackmail.

'Tea?' Lady Carfax finally whispered to Alice's father. He shook his head but the other doctor, Dr Lent, nodded for a cup. Bastian was silent, he had been for the whole time we had been sitting, and Nora sat at his side with his hand in hers. I felt strangely outcast, especially for my usual closeness to both. Lady Carfax poured tepid tea with too much sugar and handed out the cups. I took one but Bastian did not. His eyes came up to meet mine though, and they looked much as they had on the day of his suicide attempt. The very thought chilled me. How very broken all of our lives, for that one ceremony, for a marriage of so-called convenience.

By the by, the party returned. Papa was at the head of it, followed by the coroner himself, and then misters Michaels, Squire, Carmack, and Hanley all men of the village who were to stand as jurors. Lady Carfax bade the men sit, and so they did so, taking chairs about the room and pulling them all up to a big square table in the middle of the room. We all moved to take our seats too, about the table, and it turned out that I was sat close to the coroner, and opposite the family Carfax. So informal a gathering, one could almost forget its dark purpose and possibly dire consequences.

'Good morning all,' the coroner spoke.

I nodded, and the others said hello quietly as Lady Carfax rang for more tea.

Mr Holden cast eyes from one to the other of us. He smiled though, and was gentle just as he'd seemed before. I decided I liked him.

'Now, first and foremost, you have my commiserations, Mr Carfax, Mr Monroe, and the rest too of course. Before I begin, we do appear to be missing a person called herein?'

'My husband has…' Lady Carfax wet her lips, 'Baron Carfax went out last night and has not returned.'

'Indeed? Curious?'

'Not so, really. He… he does from time to time take the alehouses and so I… I am sure he will be here in due course.'

Sympathy showed in Mr Holden's eye, but he kept the rest of himself straight, 'Never mind, he is not key in this matter and so his absence will not detain us. Ladies and gentlemen, you have all been invited here today to help us to ascertain the cause of death of Mrs Alice Carfax of this very house. An inquest has been called due to the suspicious circumstances in which this life was extinguished.'

I pulled in a deep breath and locked eyes with Bastian. He was unreadable, although his eyes did linger on me.

'It is often the case when a person dies that they are surrounded by loved ones as they slip away, and their passing is one of peace, sadly this I cannot say of Mrs Carfax whose exact cause of death is still under debate,' Holden continued. 'I am Mr Holden, as you know, and I am the coroner who certified the death of this young woman. It was also I that called you all together for this inquest. To bear witness, we have Dr Chilcott and also Dr Lent, who both have attended the poor dead girl. Mr Sebastian Carfax, the husband of the deceased. Miss Chilcott, friend of the deceased, and Miss Nora Carfax, the late Mrs Carfax's sister-in-law. The poor lady's father has also asked to be present. All of these witnesses give evidence without duress and of their own free will. I would like to also reiterate that this is by no means a trial; no accusations will be made during or as a result of this inquest and no sentences will be passed. If it is found that Mrs Carfax's death was not as it should be, we have only the power to request a trial of murder, not to deliver a verdict of such. In a moment, a series of witnesses will give evidence, and then might be questioned by any person present who wishes to do so.'

I was shaking with fear, my hand trembling and my brow hot. I hoped the ordeal over quickly, I could not stand for this to drag on.

'The circumstances so far appear to be thus,' the coroner went on. 'That on the day of the seventh of April, in this the year of our lord 1849, the body of Mrs Alice Helene Carfax, previously Monroe, was discovered by local fishermen lying on the rocks below the coastal path between Blossom Cove and Fiveham. This was approximately halfway along the two mile stretch. It was high tide and so it likely that her body could have been picked up by the tide and deposited there. Doctor Chilcott assures us that bruising on her back and shoulders, face and abdomen, were post-mortem and not from a struggle. Mrs Carfax was missing her shawl but we cannot rule out that it was taken by the sea. An empty bottle of her nerve tonic was found near the downed gate just north of where her body was found, alongside a broken fence. We surmise this was most likely where she fell and if so, it would seem that she fell approximately between twenty-two and thirty feet onto rocks below.'

All this I listened to carefully, but my first impression was of relief; an accidental overdose of her tonic perhaps? A fall under the influence of such? Or perhaps Alice had committed suicide? My surprise at this revelation brought it home, though, how much I actually had suspected Bastian's involvement. It was not my most comfortable thought.

'To start these proceedings, I call to bear witness Dr Chilcott.' Papa stood and stated the same as Holden. That Alice had most likely died from her fall, but that either way, there had been no struggle.

'And what of her mental state?' Mr Holden asked.

'The girl was delicate, always, but was attended more so by her own physician for such…'

'Alice was not *delicate*!' Monroe interjected, standing, 'not until she came here, at least!'

'Sir, you will have your own chance to speak,' Holden said.

Monroe muttered something incomprehensible but was still, sitting back down. Dr Lent stood, it seemed the formality when speaking. He was a tall man with blond hair and small spectacles. His clothing looked more expensively made than my father's and I suspected his services were not cheap.

'Alice Monroe – that is Mrs Carfax as she became – was…' Dr Lent paused, '…she was a sweet girl with a disposition for quietness. She was only nineteen years old at the time of her death and I do think this should be taken into account.'

'And she was taking medication you prescribed to her?'

'I prescribed her tonics to help her to remain level-headed for she would become flustered and dizzy easily.'

'And would you say that this was more so after her wedding, as her father ascertains?'

'She had declined a little, but she was always delicate. I had been prescribing the tonics since her return to England, in 1842, sir.'

'1842? By God man, she must have been a child still!' Papa interjected.

'She was eleven. A delicate child, sir, as you said.'

'And these tonics contained opium?' the question fell heavily, from the lips of Mr Carmack – one of the jurors.

'Laudanum, in it's diluted form, rather than pure opium.'

'The distinction is noted, but your tonics did in fact contain the tincture of opium, commonly called laudanum?'

'Not to begin with, but I added the ingredient upon a worsening of her condition in…' Dr Lent rifled his papers, '1847, sir. It was not a great dose, but it was present.'

I glanced at Bastian, wondering his thoughts. He of all people, was lucky that the dose had not been large – otherwise it might have killed him when he'd tried to end his own life. Then another thought nagged at me. If Alice had killed herself, surely this was almost a mockery of Bastian's attempt? A horrific parody. I bit my lip, storing the detail.

'And have you recovered her tonic now, to be disposed of?' Holden asked.

Dr Lent picked up a familiar bottle from the table. 'This is the bottle recovered from the site of her apparent fall,' he said, 'It's empty, but I sent her last prescription just two weeks ago. Either the solution was poured away, or she took a hefty dose before she died.'

It was all sounding like suicide. My mind took me back to her that day though, to her triumph and her goading of me – it didn't seem possible!

'Are there any further questions for either of our medical witnesses?' Mr Holden asked of his make-shift jury.

'No, sir,' they spoke as one. I wondered to what extent these local men were happy to remain uncontroversial; all the locals took much trade from the Carfax family, even my father. The room turned to quiet for a moment, as Holden looked from one to the other of us, and then he spoke again. 'And so it would seem that Mrs Carfax's body showed no sign of foul play, and a potential for suicide. Now we must try to recreate her last day, and examine any motivations for anything unseemly having occurred. Who, if any, can begin this pattern?'

I stood, shaking, and suddenly all eyes were upon me. I glanced to Bastian and he nodded, very discreetly.

'Miss Chilcott, did you see or speak to Mrs Carfax, on the day of her death?'

'I... I did sir.'

'In what manner?'

'I... Alice and I quarrelled, sir,' I whispered.

'You quarrelled, about what?'

I could feel every person in the room squirming on my behalf, but I could not stop now. I had to tell the truth. 'Sebastian and Alice were negotiating for an annulment,' I said, 'she blamed me and my... my close friendship with her husband.'

I looked over at Mr Monroe, her father, his eyes glowed with grief, though, not dislike or anger, just grief.

Mr Holden's eyes burned into me. 'And the manner of your "closeness" with Mr Carfax, was it carnal? Were you lovers?'

'Sir, must we really…' Papa said, standing too.

'I am afraid we must, yes.'

My face burned hot but I found the strength to nod. 'Yes, sir.' I glanced to Papa but he did not react.

'You have had a child too, I have it told? A stillborn which was born early and did not survive. The child was his?'

My cheeks burned, 'Yes, sir. Alice pushed me… she pushed me down the steps to the cove beyond the house, sir, and I lost the baby.'

A murmur went through the people gathered, but again, my eyes flit over to the stranger, to Monroe. He surveyed me with an expression which seemed to mingle sorrow and sympathy equally. I wondered if he believed me, if this sort of behaviour on the part of his daughter was no shock.

'I see,' Mr Holden, 'and had this any bearing on your quarrel with Mrs Carfax?'

'Yes, sir,' I whispered, 'I was upset after having had sharp words with Sebastian on how long the annulment was taking and when I came outside, Alice laughed. I… I spoke harshly to her to chastise her in her enjoyment of my misery.'

'Master Carfax had made promises to you, for after the annulment was achieved, then?'

'He had,' I knew it sounded damning but caught on the spot I could not stop the admission.

'I see. And what time did you leave her?'

'I… this was about four in the afternoon, I suppose… Alice stormed away to… to collect her plaything with which she'd been dallying, a kite, and I found my way to Sebastian in the… in the parlour and there we too quarrelled.'

'And do you have you any more to add to the timeline of *Mrs* Carfax?' Holden asked me.

'No, that is all. I left Fiveham House and went home where I cried it out until my Papa came home.'

'And you did not see Mrs Carfax again?'

'I did not, no sir.'

'That is all, you may be seated. Mr Carfax, I have some questions now for you if you will allow?'

Bastian stood. He looked terrified and who could blame him? He caught my eye, but then glanced away. A bead of worry took me for his unhappiness, the memory of what he had done before, under extreme pressure, but I pushed it back – he'd grown beyond such foolishness now – or at least I had to hope he had!

'Mr Carfax, Miss Chilcott ascertains that you were seeking an annulment on your marriage to the deceased?'

'I was.'

'On what grounds?'

'On… on the grounds of nonconsummation, at first, but such is hard to prove and so we moved to insanity.'

'Her insanity?'

'No,' Bastian whispered, 'my own. On the night of my wedding, I attempted suicide. I had a writ of insanity placed upon me for one year by Dr Chilcott. I was to move that this insanity had existed earlier than identified and impaired my decisions in marrying when I did.'

'Despite that you had had a long engagement?' Mr Monroe spoke without standing.

'Indeed, as you know when I wrote to you of it. My reason had been compromised for some time. This is why… why it was more complicated, though. It wasn't a straightforward annulment.'

'But you are recovered now?' Holden asked.

The room was deathly silent for a long drawn out moment. I willed Bastian to speak but he seemed to be thinking it through, unsure of how to reply. He did not want to lie, I realised. My heart thudded.

'Perhaps,' Papa stood, 'as his doctor, I am more qualified to comment thus?'

'Go ahead.'

'Master Carfax suffers a melancholia which can lead him to dark days where he struggles to function properly. He is sane, but he is troubled by melancholy moods. He is still under my care and I have recently renewed my writ upon him, but with decreased symptoms …but his malady is not frenzy or madness, as you are thinking.'

Not enough to kill his wife, my father's words seemed to ooze as an undertone. I realised it was calculated. Papa was working with us after all. The thought warmed my heart.

'I see. Thank you Dr Chilcott. Master Carfax, Miss Chilcott ascertains that you quarrelled on the day your wife died?'

'Yes, sir.'

'Is this so?'

'Yes sir.'

'On the basis of the annulment?'

'Yes, as she said.'

'And afterwards, you and your wife were both present for supper?'

Bastian shook his head. 'After I quarrelled with Maddi… with Miss Chilcott… I took myself to my own chamber but Alice was there awaiting me.'

'Your wife and you shared a chamber?'

'No, not… not ever.'

'I see. But she was there then?'

'Yes, she was… she was quite wrought.'

'From her quarrel with Miss Chilcott?'

'No, from…' Bastian looked to me, and sighed, 'she said she had been with child,' he finally whispered.

I tensed, biting my lip. I knew not why he would say such a thing – surely she could not have been, if he was telling me the truth about the nature of their relationship? A dread settled upon me.

'Mrs Carfax was with child?'

'So she said, although the timing makes this admission close after the quarrel between both her and I, and Miss Chilcott and I, and so perhaps it was…' he paused, 'Alice liked to feel sympathised with and she'd pick things that... that resonated.'

'Such as the baby you and Miss Chilcott lost?'

'Yes.'

'But either way, she maintained that she'd lost a child, and that the child was yours?'

'Yes and I did believe her. Alice was, for all her sins, not the type to stray.'

The ground was swallowing me up. My mouth was dry, my heart thudded and my pulse was too loud. I gripped my hands together under the table to hold myself together. I willed Bastian to look to me, for some indication that he was lying. He did not, keeping eye-contact with Mr Holden.

'And so your original request of annulment on grounds of non-consummation was...'

'False sir, this was why I had to seek a new grounds f-for it. Alice refused to say our union was unconsummated.'

'She refused to lie?'

'Y-yes.'

'And so back to that night.'

'Yes, I... So Alice said that... that she had lost the baby. She wanted to... to try again, because... because she thought that it would strengthen our marriage...she said that she'd seen Maddi off. She said I had to try again, to get her with child again.'

'And so she wished to...'

'Yes. She was all over me like a damned...' Bastian paused and checked his words, 'she was... was seeking intimacy,' he corrected himself, 'I told her that I... that I would rather – well, something impolite. I was stung from... from just having quarrelled with Miss Chilcott and so I was harsh with her.'

'So you and Alice too, quarrelled?'

Bastian nodded. 'Alice could be very devious,' his voice lowered, 'she had an edge that few people saw. She said that she would have her father expose... there is some issue betwixt her father and mine, some scandal – I know not even what it is, but she... she threatened and cajoled and... she pushed me and pushed me and would not leave me be. I tried to leave but she stood between me and the door, not allowing me to leave her... and so I... and so I did as she wanted, despite it not being my wish or desire.'

His eyes met mine. Mine pleaded, his apologised. I was imploding, everything shattering completely.

'Mr Carfax...' Mr Holden interrupted our silent exchange. 'go on?'

'I... I made love to my wife as she wished me to, in a fit of passion and... and then I went down to the cove, this must have been about suppertime, and I... I walked into the sea to try to... to clear my mind of... of.. well, of it all. I swim, sir, to clear my head – at times when the clouding comes again, as it did when I was ill, before.'

'And so we come then, almost to the moment of Mrs Carfax's disappearance. 'Mr Carfax, did you see or hear anything of your wife again that night?'

'No sir,' Bastian said, then glanced to me again. He parted his lips, sighed, and then he did the worst thing he could possibly have done at that moment, the one thing to convince me entirely of his guilt.

He lied.

'I left the cove and went straight to the village where I... where I met with Maddi, that is, Miss Chilcott.'

Another murmur started up, a few hostile glances in my direction. I merely sat in stunned silence though. Why would he say that? What reason did Bastian have to lie?

'You went to see Miss Chilcott?'

Bastian's eyes did not leave my face, and now I understood the expression, 'I did,' he said. 'She snuck me in by the back door as she had done many a time before, and we went into her chamber. Her father was out on a house call, if I recall correctly, and so it was easily done. Maddi was still upset, wrought and so instead I comforted her.'

'You made love?'

'We did.'

'So you lay with your wife, took a walk and then went to your mistress, with whom you also lay? Within a couple of hours?'

Bastian squirmed, his cheeks reddening – I wondered if he'd considered that fact, in his lies! 'Yes, sir!' he whispered.

'And what time did you leave Dr Chilcott's residence?'

'Not until her father was abed, so about midnight if not a little later.'

The room was very hush for a long moment. The glances to me were more hostile, Papa just looked shocked. Was he remembering, as I was, how I had greeted him when he returned home? How we had made cocoa together? I hoped not.

'Miss Chilcott, please stand.'

I did so, trembling, knowing that what I was about to do, to say, was perjury even if this were not a true court. The alternative was to show Bastian up in a lie. No matter what he had done, I still loved him enough not to condemn him to trial – murder was a hanging crime! I'd not see him hang.

'Miss Chilcott, is what Mr Carfax is saying the truth?'

'Y-yes sir,' I whispered.

'You may sit down, please rise Mr Chilcott,' Oh God! He was calling my father! Papa stood, looking somewhat confused.

'Mr Chilcott, you were on a house call the night that Mrs Carfax died?'

'I was.'

'Did you witness any evidence, upon your return, which collaborates this story unfolding here?'

There was a long pause. Papa looked to Bastian, and then to me. He wet his lips, then cast his eyes across the table. 'My daughter thinks an old man is a blind one,' Papa spoke, his old voice soft and calm like when he was giving a diagnosis, 'Often she'd sneak the boy in and think I knew not.'

'But this specific time?'

Papa glanced to me again, he was no fool, 'This time too, yes,' he lied, 'There were boot marks by the back door and two tea-cups upon the table. My daughter remained above when I came in, which was unusual if she was alone. I heard voices, muted when I passed the chamber, but loud enough when I was on the stairs. Yes, the boy was with my daughter, that night.'

And so there it was, Bastian had lied to give false alibi, and both my Papa and I had backed it up. My eyes filled with tears, my lips trembled. I glanced at Bastian but he was looking at his hands, Nora's hand on his back in support. His mother looked to me, speculation in her eyes. In the far corner, the jurors were all talking quietly amongst themselves, I closed my eyes to block them out. At length, the muttering between the jurors was quieted and then Mr Holden spoke again.

'It would seem then, that we have a timeline leading up to the evening,' he said, 'but still nothing afterwards. Mrs Carfax first quarrelled with Miss Chilcott and then went to her husband's chamber, there she waited until he arrived, and the pair first quarrelled and then engaged in intimacies. After this, at about supper time, Mr Carfax left the house without supper. Was Mrs Carfax present at supper?'

Lady Carfax stood, 'no, sir,' she said, clear.

'And did any see her, after these intimacies were supposed to have occurred?'

'Might I call in her maid?' Lady Carfax asked. 'She would have seen her afterwards, I would presume.'

Mr Holden nodded. I sat, numb and refusing to allow Bastian to take my eye as the maid was called in. The girl was about twenty five years old and blond like Alice. Miss Hargreaves, she was named. Her eyes were red and her lips pressed. She looked like a person in distress indeed. Other than Mr Monroe, she was the only one who looked as though she were truly in mourning at all.

'Hello young lady,' Holden gave her his kind look, the one which no longer rested on me. 'Do you understand what an inquest is?'

She nodded, her hanky clutched tight in her hand.

'Might I ask your relationship to Mrs Carfax?'

'I was her personal maid, sir.'

'You were fond of her?'

'Yes.'

'You came from London with her?'

'No, sir, I'm local, from Cattersley.'

'Thank you. We are looking for some information on the whereabouts Mrs Carfax on the night of her death, after approximately six of the evening.'

Miss Hargreaves nodded again.

'Can you offer us any light on this?' Holden pushed.

'I was with her, sir, after Mr Carfax left her.'

'So about six?'

'More like seven, sir.'

'Seven in the evening, then?'

'Yes. After Mr Carfax left her, Alice rang for water to clean herself... she was in good spirits then, and said he'd come to her. She said he was drunk his passions for her, and asked me if that denoted he was coming to love her more so. I claimed ignorance on the subject, sir, I am not yet married.'

'And this was your final conversation with Mrs Carfax?'

'No, sir,' she shuffled her feet a little where she stood – nobody had offered her a seat. 'She called for me about eight, sir. I went in expecting more of her questions but her mood had changed dramatically. She said her husband had gone out – to see Miss Chilcott at her guess – and then went on to call Miss Chilcott some names. I tried to calm her down by brushing her hair as she liked when she was wrought but I snagged her hair and she shouted at me to leave her too. She was... she was very upset.'

'Upset enough to commit suicide?'

'Oh, sir, I couldn't say!'

'That is fine. Do you have anything further to add?'

'No sir, only that it was I who discovered she was not in her chamber at ten o clock. I went in to put her to bed and she was gone.'

'Was anything amiss in her chamber?'

'Not that I noticed, no.'

'Thank you my dear.'

Dr Lent stood, 'Miss Hargreaves,' he said, 'can you attest to Alice's claim of pregnancy? She spoke not to me of it…'

'Nor I,' Papa added in a tired voice, not standing.

Miss Hargreaves sighed, 'I don't know, but it wasn't likely. Her husband only visited her two of three times in the year they were married and there was no instance that I knew of where she lost her monthlies. She'd say she was with child from time to time, but I never gave it much credence.'

'Thank you, dear,' Dr Lent said, and then sat down. Mr Holden wrote out a note or two on his paper.

Mr Monroe stood then. His eyes moved over us all. 'My daughter was not suicidal,' he said. 'You use words like delicate and fragile, and mayhap these words are correct, but suicidal, she was not. I fear foul play here, I fear it in my very bones.'

'And what evidence?'

Monroe locked eyes with Lady Carfax, she with him.

'I know only that there was some bad blood between Baron Carfax and myself,' he said. Oh he was being careful not to show up his blackmail. 'I knew of some misdeeds from… from time spent as his clerk and…'

Lady Carfax sprung to her feet. 'Not these malicious lies, again,' she hissed.

'Malicious lies, you say? And yet enough for your husband to marry his son – or at least your bastard son – to my daughter in order to keep me quiet! I suggest sir, knowing that I had given Alice knowledge of these deeds, that perhaps this does give motive for murder, after all, had she used it! Not of the young man but of his supposed father… who by chance is not here tonight!'

Monroe bent to rummage in his case and brought out a handful of documents which he gave to Holden. Mr Holden took the papers and skimmed them, but then sighed.

'This is wildly off track, and purely circumstantial,' he said, 'I am afraid I cannot take these rumours into account, in relation to your daughter's death.'

Monroe's lips twisted and I could see he'd hoped his evidence would create a stir. He looked to Lady Carfax again and she glared back. Something unsaid passed between them. 'I suppose I shall have to present my other evidence to a court of law, then...' he said.

'Do your worst...' Lady Carfax herself looked set to kill!

'Now, now! let us have order,' Mr Holden said, 'gentlemen, ladies, unless there is anything else I need to hear, I am ready to allow the jurymen here to deliberate on cause of death of Mrs Alice Carfax, nee Monroe.'

Nobody spoke for a long moment, but then Bastian stood. He looked so tired.

'I have nothing to add but personal testimony,' he said, 'The night my wife died, she discovered more so than ever before, the level of my disdain for her. Whilst that says nothing good of me, it does give her motive for suicide. The way she died is pertinent too. She left behind her an empty bottle of nerve tincture; the same I used when I myself tried to commit suicide, and she is said to have jumped not too far from where Maddi fell and lost our child. I cannot think these things coincidence. Alice loved children and despite everything that she was, I do know that she felt guilt at her part in the loss of my son. If she *had* just lost a baby of her own then perhaps that too played into this.'

The room was silent, all eyes upon Bastian.

'I claim no sainthood, and I make no excuses for my own appalling behaviour, but I do believe, above all, that Alice committed suicide.'

Holden nodded, an odd appreciation in his eye for Bastian's frank words. 'Very good then, thank you Mr Carfax.

We will deliver our conclusions when we are ready, Lady Carfax, do you have another room we could use?'

'Yes, certainly, and more tea…'

As the party broke up, I took the opportunity to slip away. Both Bastian and Nora spoke my name as I went but I shook them off and all but fled from the room. Outside, I made my way up to my little sanctuary, that overgrown garden behind the house that as children we'd called the haunted garden. There I sat in a numb sort of silence. The flowers were dying off now, the bluebells and campions, although the tiny pink herb Robert flowers still poked through the cracks in the tumbled down wall that surrounded the garden. The air was hot and scented with lilac and buddleia. There in that silence, maybe an hour or so passed, enough that even the cool September sun burned my skin to bright pink and for two days following I was a little dizzied and ill from more than just the events of the day. At last, Nora appeared, though.

'I thought I would find you here,' she said, sitting putting her arm about me. I laid down my head on her shoulder. I had shed no tears but my gut felt hollow and empty. 'Your Papa is worried,' she added.

'He will understand.'

'I am sure. There has been a verdict…'

'Already?'

'Yes, it did not take them very long. I am afraid though, that you must resign yourself from here on in for being blamed for Alice's suicide…'

'Suicide?'

'Yes. Bastian is clear of suspicion. Monroe is swearing and throwing about accusations but he sounds like a mad-man deranged, rather than anything to really worry on. I suppose Papa will feel some repercussions when he returns home…'

'I am glad for Bastian's sake,' I said, 'At least I can let go of this panic bead within me.'

'And I…' Nora said. 'Will you come back and speak with him?'

I shook my head.

'What, why not?'

'Because…' I paused and glanced about, and then back to her. I spoke in a whisper, 'Because his alibi is a lie,' I said, 'Because I've just committed perjury to cover for him.'

Nora blanched, 'What?'

'He wasn't with me,' I said. 'I quarrelled with Alice, and then I quarrelled with Bastian, and then I went home and wept all night – alone but for Papa.'

'But… but your Papa said so too.'

'He lied to cover for me,' I said, 'I too am without alibi, perhaps Papa thought Bastian and I had planned this, or perhaps he really did think Bastian was there, I don't know, but I know it wasn't true!'

'So where the devil was he?' Nora asked, 'He wasn't at home!'

My heart sank even further, 'You are sure?'

'Of course I am! After Bastian's own suicide attempt do you think I would not be looking, we all heard you quarrel! Bastian cannot be trusted not to do stupid things when he is wrought! I saw him set off out to the cove and he never came back – I turned the house upside down looking for him!'

I shook my head, flummoxed. 'Come,' Nora said standing, 'Come, we'll ask him ourselves!'

'I can't.'

'What? don't be a fool, come!'

I shook my head but then I began to weep again. 'Nora – he lay with her,' I whispered, feeling a little broken within. 'He never told me – he said that the annulment would be easy because he'd never laid with her and then he… he… and she was with child! Oh, God! God!'

Nora crouched back down and grabbed my hand. She seemed a bundle of emotion too, almost fit to burst.

'And so I cannot trust him,' I added, 'He has told lies of such magnitude to me, and then he has used me – and Papa! –

to give false alibi. I have no idea what to believe now, but Nora, I'm so very afraid at what this all means.'

'You think he...'

'I don't know,' I wept, 'God, Nora! How can it be that I don't know?'

'Maddi, you are my most treasured friend and so I will overlook that you just accused my brother of murder. I excuse it too knowing how well you love him, and so how much the conflict within you must be. I have to go home, I suggest you do the same. Get back into the warm with your Papa and cry it out. I will send Bas to you in a day or two once you have rested, we are all very tired.'

I nodded, pulling myself to my feet.

'Be safe,' she whispered.

'And you and Nora – make sure Bas doesn't... doesn't do anything foolish!'

'It is upmost on my mind,' she reassured me, 'Go, I'll look after my brother.'

It was but one night before he came, just one long night of no sleep and many tears. His knock on the door was loud, resoundingly so, and then I heard his voice call my name. I shook my head at Nell as she went to answer and pulled it open myself. I knew I was somewhat bedraggled. I had barely slept, a million nightmares threatening and even in wakefulness I was haunted by the awful truth that if he had killed her, he'd done it for us. My long hair was an unbrushed snaggled mess, pulled back with combs to try to tame it. I wore yesterday's crinkled dress and my eyes stung badly enough to realise that they were likely red and sore looking.

He looked worse. By far.

'Maddi, can I come in?'

'No.'

'Maddi please, my darling please!' his eyes were almost frenzied and his shirt was misbuttoned, his hair in disarray. If he had slept, I would be very surprised. He reached out a hand for me but I stepped back, out of reach.

'I said no, I have nothing to say to you.'

'But I have a great deal to say to you Maddi! Hear me out at least?'

'I don't want to hear it. How could I even believe a word? Please Bastian, just go away. Just… go away.'

I made a motion to close the door but the look of sheer misery on his face made me pause a moment, he used this time to slip his fingers into the door, gazing at me passionately, he shook his head and whispered the words, 'not like this…'.

'Oh, for God's sake Bastian! Fine, come in then if you must…' I stepped back and let the door swing open. Bastian was inside in an instant, trying to embrace me and for one pure moment of self-indulgence, I allowed it, but then pushed him away.

'Don't touch me, I can hardly stand to look at you, let alone be touched by you.'

Bastian stepped back and surveyed me. His eyes crinkled, emotions spilling again. 'Oh Maddi,' he whispered but I pushed off his anguish with harshness.

'Don't! Just say what you need to say and then go.'

'G-give me five minutes? Have you, is there somewhere we can go?'

I paused again, but then led him from the hallways of our house, into one of the corridors which led to the front and there opened the door to Papa's study. Somehow, I couldn't bear to have him in the rooms I frequented and used.

'Sit,' I whispered, indicating the chair by the desk. He did so and I sat by his side, in a more comfortable lounging chair by the window.

'What have you to say to me?'

'I'm sorry Maddi I…'

'Stop! I don't want your apologies.'

He sucked in a sharp inhale, 'I apologise, none-the-less for… for putting you on the spot like that. I didn't know what else to do.'

'Because you killed Alice?' the words should not have slipped out with such ease.

'What? No! Of course I didn't! Maddi!'

'So where were you?'

'I was home, alone in my chamber.'

I reeled, tears springing into my eyes for another blatant lie. I panted a few times, trying not to cry, but then let a tear spill anyway. 'You're still lying to me,' I whispered.

'No, Maddi! No, I swear!'

'Don't! your sister already told me you were not there! She was worried about you and so she searched the whole house! She already told me that! …and you weren't here either! So where the devil were you?'

Bastian muttered a curse under his breath and then ran his hands through his hair, 'I am telling you the truth,' he said. 'I went back in and Mama saw me because she was just returning from town where she was visiting Mary Callow up at the parsonage. I avoided her and I avoided Nora. I *was* in my chamber, Nora just didn't see me go there and when she knocked I slid down beside the bed so she'd not see me if she opened the door. I knew my family would just fuss, and that if Alice knew I had returned she might…'

'Might what? Expect her husband to lie with her again? Now that he had shown willing?'

'Oh Maddi, it wasn't like that!'

'No? Then how was it?'

'It was – it was something I never wanted to do, believe me, and it was not… I did not make love to her Maddi – I expelled my frustrations on her after she had goaded me and tormented me and pulled at me for bloody hours! It was not love, it was hate, it was fury and passion and everything was just – it was a blur of madness.'

Still I said nothing, I could imagine it well and it made me sick to my stomach and that wasn't even the worst of it. 'But it wasn't the first time?' I whispered. 'Even if she wasn't with child, she sought to make you believe she was which means there must have been at least a chance…'

'She said she'd work with us, if I just gave her a child. It seemed an easier path.'

I shook my head, 'You fool,' I whispered, 'If you'd given her a child, you'd never have been rid of her.'

'I never would have been anyway, I don't think. Legally I could get the annulment, but the cost was disaster for us all. I couldn't risk it.'

'And so you killed her?' I whispered, expecting that confession to follow. My words seemed to jolt him though.

'No! Maddi for christsakes no! I did as she wanted me to, then I left the room and made my way away, out, past where you fell, down across the slippery rocks to the sea! There I stood contemplating how easy it would be to…to… but I didn't because I knew that would break you apart and so instead I just went home and hid myself away.'

I looked at him, at the state of him. He was in pieces and I knew well what such a mood could put upon a person. I loved him so powerfully, I wanted with all my heart to believe him, but I just didn't.

That realisation hurt.

I didn't believe him.

'Bastian, I want you to leave,' I whispered.

'Please, don't do this! Believe me!'

'I…' I began to cry, my hands going over my face. At once he was at my side, holding me, kissing me, and I could not bear it.

'Get away from me,' I whispered, 'Stop this!'

'Maddi, please! Don't cast me off for a crime I did not commit! Goddammit! I love you so very much… All I want is us!'

'Enough to kill for?'

'No! Maddi! You should know this! I thought you knew me!'

'So did I!' I shouted, shoving him, 'I thought I knew you too but you've been lying and lying!'

'If you think that I could ever harm a person – even Alice – then after all these years, you don't know a damn thing about me!' he hissed, furious too now, despite the tears he was spilling. 'You don't know me at all, let alone love me!'

'How dare you say such things?' suddenly all my fury was released, 'how dare you question my love for you? It was you who lay with *her*!'

'Maddi – I have explained…'

'Yes, you have! Rather well!'

'You take this moral high-ground, Maddi, but in truth look at you! You are more angry that I lay with her, than that I might have killed her!'

I paled, my heart thudding so hard it hurt. 'I want you to leave!' I whispered, 'get out!'

'I'm sorry, I didn't mean that!'

'You did and I want you to leave!'

'Please… don't do this, not now! You will throw away everything if you do, even the potential for our futures.'

A strange noise escaped my lips and I felt the tears not just well up and drip from my lashes, but explode from my eyes. At my whimper, he tried to approach me again but a violent fit of rage ate me up and, in a frenzy of temper, I picked up the paperweight from the table and threw it at him. The heavy glass object, thrown in such a passion missed him entirely and smashed against the wall behind, showering him in broken glass.

'Get out! Get out!' I screamed, grabbing at anything else that came to hand, the ink bottle exploded next and then a heavy book which happened to be on the table.

'Maddi, for God's sake!' he made towards me again but I was too angry, livid in my fury.

'No! Get out of my house!' Another book I happened upon, and then a wooden box filled with clips flew towards him.

The noise of the study door opening shocked us both and I stopped in mid-throw to spin to the door. There, in the doorway, stood Papa. Slowly his eyes took in the scene before him.

'What on earth is going on here?'

I looked at Bastian with pleading eyes, willing him not to make any more fuss. Papa was frail enough without Bastian upsetting him.

'Bastian was just leaving, Papa,' I mumbled, my fire gone in an instant.

Papa looked less than convinced and walked further into the room, putting a hand on my arm.

'I see. Well goodbye then, Mr Carfax.'

Bastian viewed us both with tear-filled eyes.

'Dr Chilcott! If I could just…'

'Have you not done enough, young man?' Papa asked. 'Have you not brought enough shame upon yourself and upon my daughter?'

'Sir, I…'

'I think it best you leave,' Papa interrupted, 'Perhaps you should think on how other people suffer at your actions, and ponder upon that before you grace my hearth again, sir…'

Bastian staggered, physically, he looked to me, 'and you wish me to really go, forever?'

I nodded. I did not trust words.

Bastian inclined his head, then nodded. He opened his lips once more, but then pursed them again and walked out of the room. As he left, I turned to Papa's breast and began to sob, the dam finally breaking. The old man said nothing, simply held me tight.

Fourteen

I will not examine the next year in detail, it is not worth the heartache and in truth, very little of note happened therein. Still our day-to-day life continued on, still Papa treated the sick of our little village and I began to assist him in that too, becoming something of a nurse in some cases, or a charitable companion to the sick and dying in others. Papa seemed old suddenly, I suppose the inquest and its consequences had done him in as much as they had I! Still he was diligent in his work though, and, when he was done for the day, still he would come out with me to walk on the beaches, or to sit with me in our little parlour.

Nora still visited, too, but I saw nothing at all of Bastian but a few odd glimpses in the village – always ensuring he did not lay eyes on me. Nora was devout to her brother of course, but after a quarrel or two, we agreed to make him a taboo subject: *"For now of course"* as she would state! We'd gossip a little, sometimes read together or do some darning, and then she'd leave again. Never did we go out walking though, that remaining somewhat a solo pursuit for me, a place to be alone and take off the mask of indifference I showed to the world.

As I grew away from it, a strange serenity took over my mind. I no longer felt impassioned and I found that I no longer lashed out as I once had, the fire within me dimming a little. I did not so much feel lonely, I had Papa and Nora and that was enough for me, but my whole life seemed to shimmer into a strange meaninglessness. Finally, in the June of 1851, some year and a half after the inquest, I finally acquiesced to Papa's request for my visiting London – his home before he'd retired down to the country with me as a child – to spend the season. To finally "come out". I was, by then nineteen years old and so it was high time.

'London is not such a terrible place,' Papa said, 'And I am homesick! This is where I made my fortune, as a young penniless doctor – it is a placemark in our history as a family. You should come at least once and meet your cousin Simon, and your Mama's cousins the Bellinghams... they were instrumental in Mama and I meeting, you know!'

'I know the stories well,' I smiled, 'Mrs Bellingham threw a ball and there you met Mama, but her own doctor said she must leave the city and so you moved all the way from the grey and the smog down to our own little paradise to follow her.'

'Indeed, and we will not be gone long, but half a year! And just think, you can attend some of the officer's balls and perhaps even something a little grander!'

'That does sound appealing,' I agreed. In truth I knew as well as Papa did that I needed some change in my stale life. And so with trembling hands I began to pack up my things. I would not be far from home, only in London, but even before I went I wanted to come home again.

'My brother is in agony,' Nora told me, sitting on my bed and watching me pack.

'I guessed he would be.'

'Will you go out and meet some fine London gentleman, fall in love and get married, do you think?' There was sorrow in Nora's tone, but also curiosity. 'That is what a young lady seeks in her coming out, is it not?'

'I don't know. I don't think so, but I crave adventure, stimulation. Perhaps if I were to find the right man.'

'How could you when *the right man* is waiting here for you? Don't you see it still? He never gives up dreaming that one day you will come back to him.'

'I won't and so he should cease that dream,' I said softly. 'Now come, let us speak of other things!' I picked up a little velvet jacket and brushed away the dust before folding it and placing it in my travel-chest.

Nora patted it. 'I'll give you some clothes,' she promised. 'You will look like a tired little mouse in these. You might be a mere doctor's daughter, but nobody needs to know how dowdy you are!'

'Surely Bastian would not approve of you dressing me up for other men?' I could not help but spill it.

Nora laughed. 'Very true,' she grinned. 'I'd best not then! Will you see him, before you go?'

'I don't think so. If he and I are really destined to be, then nothing will happen, and I won't meet anyone and get married. However, if another man can steal my heart – surely that is a sign?'

'Mayhap, but it has been over a year Maddi, how can you make such a gamble without even seeing him first?'

'It is for the best,' I said, patting down the jacket. 'Now stop, I hear Bastian's voice in your words. You have done your duty to him and said what he willed, now shush and help me to pack!'

'I wish a man would love me as loyally my brother loves you, and I wish you could see it, if you could then you would understand. There aren't many men who just... wait like this.'

'If he is unhappy then he can remarry too,' I said, and even after so long, I felt my heart pound to even say the words.

Nora saw my sudden pallor and laughed. 'You don't fool me, Maddi!' she said. 'I fully expect to see you home in six months' time, still unmarried.'

I said nothing, she was probably right.

Papa still had old friends and connections in the big city, men and women I had heard him mention over the years but never before met. Even if he had not, though, I was to find to my shock that Papa had something of a status of celebrity in London – and for what, but that he had managed to successfully administer the gastric lavage technique when he had saved Bastian. This technique, I was to find, was something relatively new and to have used it on such a highly ranked member of society had spread up into all of the London society papers.

And so Papa had become "The Famed Dr Chilcott", yes, *the* Dr Chilcott, who had *saved the life of Baron Carfax's son with the gastric lavage*! This might have faded, but for another heroic performed by my timid old Papa some two weeks into our stay. It happened whilst we were taking supper at Sears restaurant, on the strand. The man at a table adjacent, unknown but well-dressed and quaffed, suddenly began a dreadful coughing. He clutched at himself and spluttered over and over. At first, this caused a stir for the unmannerliness of the coughing but then, as the man's face began to turn a shade of purple, suddenly Papa was on his feet, running to assist.

One moment of his quick thinking and yet another life saved. The culprit, a cherry pip from his pie, flew from the chap's lips, leading the man to once more be able to suck in oxygen. I sat, basking in the applause for him, as Papa tended the man and then returned quietly to his own supper as if nothing had occurred, despite a little flush to his cheeks.

'Oh my,' Mrs Bellingham – the aforementioned cousin to Mama – said, 'what a hero to have at our very table!'

'It was nothing my dear,' Papa murmured, wiping his hands with his napkin.

'Nothing! Do you not know who that was? That gentleman yonder is the Duke of Bournemouth! Second cousin to his majesty!'

'Was it then,' Papa murmured but already I could see he was more interested in his own pie.

Suddenly, then, Papa was overwhelmed with wealthy Londoners who wanted to become his patrons. Patients willing to pay the big city prices for his care and cures. Poor Papa seemed more overwhelmed by it all than anything else! Dutifully he continued on though, as tenderly as before he'd treated the sick of our little village, now he turned his talents to the big city, and the "important" persons therein.

And so it went on.

Some few days after the cherry-pit incident, I was invited to a ball at the very house of the old chap Papa had saved. A grand affair indeed, and whilst the Duke of Bournemouth himself never approached us with thanks, Papa seemed to think the ball invitation adequate indeed as recompense. In truth it was a very grand affair, enough to warrant a new gown and a firm chat from Papa on my manners. It turns out, I was to meet both of the people who would shape my time in London there: Angela Grippon, and Mr Harrington.

The whole house was decorated in lanterns, hazy blue decorations and chiffon, that night, a large house on the edges of the city with enough gardens to allow for milling outside too. A band played in the corner of the main ballroom, and there were chairs here and there. A detour to the back of the house led to two rooms set for cards, a huge buffet hall and then the kitchens, if you were to stray too far as I did whilst exploring. Papa led me through with ease, he a man with his own type of elegance. He sat me down and muttered he would find us some refreshment. I sat and fanned myself peevishly, not enjoying the hustle and bustle, nor the heat, when a voice behind me spoke: 'quite dreadful isn't it all?'

I turned to face the girl. Her skin was pale, her locks red and her lips thin. She was dressed as was I, in a silk gown although her peach was a little more discrete than the deep green Papa had procured for me.

'It is! Is it always thus?' I asked.

'Normally!' she smiled, and then offered me her hand, 'Miss Grippon – Angela.'

'How do you do?' I remembered my manners, 'And I am Madeleine Chilcott'

'Chilcott? Hmm… I don't know you.'

'No, it is my first time at a ball like this.'

'Your first night and having not been a debutante! Hmm, that makes you unusual enough to be interesting! Which Chilcotts are you of? Old Bernard Chilcott's Northumberland line, perhaps? Or of the Surrey Chilcotts?'

'No indeed,' I corrected, 'I am of no line – I am simply here with Papa who is here at invitation given in thanks for helping his lordship when he was in distress – Papa is a doctor, you see..'

'Oh!' Angela giggled, 'You don't want to be saying that too loudly, no one will want to befriend you without connections!' Her eyes twinkled with mischief though, and her smile was wide. 'Well, Miss Nobody of Nowhere, I am of the Essex Grippon, daughter of the most esteemed Frederick and his good wife Margaret and I assure you that if I were of finer temperament, I should already be thrice married.'

I smiled, this girl was outlandish but I decided I liked her. 'Does my lady have a temper?' I teased.

'Atrociously so!' she broke into a grin. 'Why, only last week my latest betrothal was dissolved after I struck my young man about the chops!'

'You did what?' even I was shocked.

'The great oaf kept standing on my toes at dance,' she explained, 'and I thought, well, better to break the troth than to spend the life dancing with a man who has no caring for his wife's dainty feet – wouldn't you say?'

'Indeed!' I laughed and was about to add more when suddenly Angela's face straightened.

'Old Mr Harrington!' she hissed, pointing her fan discretely, 'Now there is a fine specimen indeed despite being old enough to have fathered us both.'

I glanced at the man stalking towards us. 'Handsome,' I said, feeling very much unlike myself to be talking so easily to a stranger. Back at home I rarely saw a face which was not known to me. But Harrington, the man she pointed at, was fairly handsome, if aged. He looked to be perhaps forty-five or so. The height of fashion in his plain black and white attire, he sported the staple mutton-chops and moustache, but with hair a little longer about his ears than some of the other gentlemen in the room. He walked with confidence and a straight back, and as he moved in closer, I could see the touch of grey at his temples. Distinguished, rather than aging his features.

'Isn't he just! I bet he'd be... Ah! Hello Mr Harrington!'

'Miss Grippon,' the man spoke lightly and took up Angela's hand in his to kiss her very dainty fingers, 'And Miss... I don't think we have had the honour...'

'Chilcott,' I said, and then glanced sideways at Angela, 'Of the Cornish breed.'

Angela sniggered but Mr Harrington seemed oblivious to our jesting, 'Charmed, my dear,' he said, 'might I offer my hand for a dance?'

I floundered but my new friend all but pushed me out of my seat. I danced two dances with Mr Harrington and when I returned to my seat, Angela had gone. I felt sorry for it, but I spied her off dancing with a younger sweet looking gent. 'Let's just hope the sop minds her toes!' I muttered.

'What was that, my dear?' Papa asked, having returned to my side with refreshments. Quickly I told him all about my new friend.

'Well, I am not sure I approve,' Papa chuckled, but he was smiling and I realised he was enjoying socialising more than I'd imagined possible. Seeing him tap his cane to the music, smiling to the new faces, I could not help but be pleased I had come, for his sake. 'There are to be fireworks, I am told,' he added, 'would you like to come and watch with me?'

Outside, the air was chill around us, as chill as London gets, anyhow. The stars were very bright, visible even through the smog of the city. There us and at least a hundred other people all stared up at the sky in expectation. We were not disappointed. With a sudden loud squeal and then a boom which seemed to shake the whole house, suddenly the sky was lit up in orange and blue fire. I gasped and ooohed with the rest. I'd never seen such a spectacle before and it truly was awe inspiring! Another whistle, and then another firework shot sparks into a star above us. I confess I was somewhat mesmerised.

'Magical, are they not!' I murmured to Papa.

'That they are! But that your mother were here to see this!'

Another tug in my guts as suddenly everything seemed to merge back together with the memory of her. My first trauma, my first loss. The weight began to settle more so. I tried again to shake it off. I was obviously just in a funny mood, I told myself!

'S-she probably would have been afraid,' I managed, trying to sound light-hearted despite how I ached within suddenly.

'Perhaps, but whilst your mother could be timid, she was brave too. She faced things as they were, always. You are a lot like her.'

I bit my lip. I knew as well as Papa did what lengths I was going to, to run from my own problems. I knew not how to voice it then though, nor whether I was quite ready to yet.

'It's... it's quite a life we have made for ourselves since she died,' I managed instead. 'What do you think she would say to it all?'

Papa glanced at me and smiled a sad smile, 'she'd scold me for spending all this money on your dress, that's for certain,' he teased.

'Indeed! And the food bills we put in would have had her talking to Nell too, I should imagine!'

'Just so!' he managed a small smile in return.

'Mama never was one for waste, was she?' I found once I had begun talking of her, it was difficult to cease.

'Indeed. Your mother and I were not wealthy when we began out,' he said, 'It took a lot of sacrifice to lead us to where we are now.'

Sacrifice. For some reason, the word brought me them again – Nora who should have come out at a ball much like this one, but who never had! As it always did, thinking of her led me to him and, oddly a flash of that terrible night that I had lost my son, with Bastian holding me, telling me that here was his family. I bit back on that hard. I had never expected my trip away to somehow bring my lost love back so vibrantly. This could all be his life though, I realised, if he ever chose it and left the village. For him – the Baron's son – it would not be an invitation as a favour, but a certainty. He'd hate it though, and the gossip would swallow him whole.

'You are very quiet,' Papa said, under another glow of cracking red and orange.

'Can I be frank?'

'Always.'

'I was thinking of Bastian, and how this is his birth-right and yet how he would hate it all.'

'Do you still think of him often?'

'I.. no, but that is more through repressing it, than through lack of his presence in my heart.'

'You two were very close. I am surprised that you did not reconcile.'

'How could I?' I whispered, 'you know as well as I that he lied at the inquest…'

'Hush,' Papa said, not urgent but firm, 'let us not discuss that here. Come, the fireworks are almost done, shall we get an early night in? These soirees do run late and I am an old man!'

At the following ball, a smaller one which was held three days later at the home of one of my father's old city friends, I was accosted by Mr Harrington before I even had a chance to find Angela. He took me out at once to dance, and then, afterwards, steered me into an alcove and there served me a glass of white wine. Thus intimately removed from the event I, for the first time, began to feel uncomfortable. Bastian's face tried to swim before my eyes but in truth, it was that which pushed me on to sit a further ten minutes with this older man. He spoke softly of a great many things and I smiled and nodded, finding myself reluctantly impressed with his knowledge of so many topics.

'Ah, see, age is not always undesirable!' he smiled when I told him of this, 'it does have the potential to make us wiser.'

'Indeed, so long as we heed its teachings,' I tried, not sounding as wise as I aimed for. Mr Harrington cracked a wide white smile though and found I smiled back as he touched my cheek gently with his thumb, an affectionate gesture. I allowed it, but was steeled to pull back if he tried any more intimate forms of contact. He was truly in his element though and drew back again as the gentleman he was. I drank another sip of wine as he continued to talk on, his words becoming somewhat droning as he became more relaxed.

After the glass was finished I used Papa as an excuse for escape and left the alcove, but there was accosted by Angela too, who had spied me taking my leave.

'He's much taken with you,' she remarked, nodding towards where Mr Harrington stood on the other end of the room, furtively sending little looks my way.

'He is a sweet man.'

'Rich too, you could do worse... much worse, Miss Nobody of Nowhere! I'm rather impressed that you've bagged him if I am honest!'

My heart dipped low, 'He is a sweet man, and yet, I am not lost in love nor lust.'

Angela laughed, calling me a romantic fool, but then she paused, her eyes at the door, 'Oh – speaking of – now there is an interesting creature...' she said.

I followed her gaze but then my stomach lurched.

Reginald Monroe stood in the doorway.

Fifteen

Monroe looked much as he had at the inquest. Youthful, fashionable, handsome! He was dressed in the finest of clothing, a top hat being handed to a valet and his walking stick holding at least one stone that sparkled in the bright lamps. For the first time, I found myself wondering at how a man described as a simple clerk could afford such finery. His coat was cut very fine indeed, his cravat of silk and all of the most fashionable styles. His eyes skimmed the room, suspicious and wary – I suppose that when ones only child is torn away as Alice was from him, a wariness is more usual than not.

'His daughter was murdered,' Angela whispered to me, making me jump slightly as I had been lost in contemplation of that man who once I had deemed my biggest enemy.

'M-murdered? Surely the verdict was suicide?'

'Oh, you have heard the story then?'

'Only whispers – tell me of it?'

Angela beamed, she did so love to gossip! 'Well, it's a shocking one indeed,' she said, settling back with her back against the table and helping herself to some grapes, 'So you see, the story begins not with him but with another man – man named Carfax. Over in the Caribbean, back when the slavers were being abolished, this man Carfax had made a name for himself, with Monroe there as his trusty clerk. Carfax was the son of a baron, but a younger son and so set not to inherit a thing. Rumour states that he was a slaver and a plantation owner right up until the end, all his livelihood depended on it. Then suddenly, when all hope seemed lost to him, his brother back here died, making him the heir. There was little of financial compensation left to go with it though, compared to the fortune he'd amassed over there and so illegally, he continued on with those poor captives, using them work his big plantations until his father died and gave him the title.'

I said nothing. I'd not heard some of these details and so the gossip was rich.

'Well, so it came to be that this man met and married a lady over there – a girl named Sylvia who was living alone with her father; Naval Surgeon, Gerald Paxton…'

Bastian's mother! I had not known her father to be medically minded, perhaps this was why she took so much to me! Another little titbit of information to store!

'Well they met and they were quickly wed, or so it seems – likely an agreement! But then, when a baby was born shortly thereafter, it had the dark skin and facial features of one of the slaves – a creole child, half-blood!'

Well, I knew that much! My heart gave a little pang though, for my Bastian, suddenly being washed in memories of caramel skin, gentle brown eyes and fine curly hair as soft as feathers.

'Now suspicion of fatherhood fell,' Angela was still talking, 'on some fellow who was the son of a freed slave. A dark and beastly chap it is told. The baby was much the same and when the good lady, four years later, produced a second child, she was much the same too!'

I bit my lip not to correct her.

'Well, nobody quite knows what happened,' she concluded, 'but that there was trouble between the local man and Carfax, serious trouble which caused the family to flee – that man Monroe with them!'

She nodded to Monroe who had found himself a drink and then had locked eyes on to me. He looked shocked enough to see me there, almost as shocked as I had to see him.

'Monroe was still merely a clerk at the time, although he has made himself in factories since. His young wife died in childbirth and so he was a lone father to his baby daughter from birth. Who knows why or how, but he managed to secure a match for his little motherless daughter to the Baron's supposed son – the boy who had the creole blood! They were betrothed, apparently, when the girl was still less than ten years of age!'

'This I had heard,' I said, no longer sure I wanted to hear our tale told from the lips of an almost stranger.

'Indeed, and I am sure you read of the death of that girl in all the societal papers too? How the boy grew to a man, but how he was a lunatic – wild and violent as such a breeding would dictate! He had other lovers – one in particular, a doctor's daughter! Some people even say that he got her with child but it seems uncertain! What is certain, was the beastly man's wild temper and one night – after first raping her – he dragged his wife, Monroe's daughter, up onto the cliffs and there he threw her off to her death!'

'Surely not,' I whispered. Lord, was this really how the story had played out in the London tabloids?

'Well, who knows?' Angela said, 'The gossips do like to embellish.'

Yes, I thought grimly, so I can hear! Already I knew I would fight tooth and nail to prevent Nora from coming to London if she ever suggested it.

'In truth, the inquest did find a verdict of suicide,' Angela confessed, 'and who could blame the poor dear either if that was the case, being married to such a creature?'

'Indeed,' I managed to demure, but then froze to see Monroe was approaching us. His stride was still not the suave walk of a gentleman, but the pace of a man who had much to be about in business. There, he reached us fairly quickly across the crowded room. At once, Angela was set to charming, standing up and fluttering her eyelashes demurely. Suddenly I hated it all. I met the man's gaze, but he did not look angry or sharp, more wary and curious.

'Miss Grippon,' he said, lifting Angela's offered hand, 'and, if I am not mistaken, Miss Madeleine Chilcott?'

'Sir,' I nodded as he grasped and kissed my fingers. His moustache tickled.

'I thought it was, sometimes, it is difficult to place a person out of context. And how are you these days, my dear?'

'You are acquainted?' for the first time I saw Angela flustered. I enjoyed the moment, more so as Monroe gave a thin smile and nodded.

'Miss Chilcott was acquainted with my late daughter, Miss Grippon.'

Angela flushed even more so, going quite pink and I wondered how much of what she'd said in gleeful gossip she was now regretting.

'And her husband's family,' I added, then I suppose just in spite for her colourful version of events, I added, 'my father was physician to the Carfax family.'

Angela's eyes were like saucers as suddenly the penny dropped. Her lips parted and then suddenly bowed to a smile as her embarrassment faded, and amusement took its place. 'Oh, indeed?' she grinned.

Monroe examined my face in detail, perhaps comparing me to his lost child, trying to figure it out, how Bastian had loved me and not her. He continued this stare for about a minute, and then produced a calling card.

'I should like to borrow you for a few moments if I may – tomorrow perhaps, you could come for tea?'

All the amusement of the situation crashed back down around me. I swallowed and took the card, 'Regarding?'

'Regarding a gentleman we both know as a mutual acquaintance…'

Was it a threat? I knew not but inside I was all suddenly aflutter with butterflies. I glanced to my friend who was watching this exchange with gleeful eyes. For a moment I wished her gone and Nora in her place. Clever and sensible Nora who would have known exactly what to say, how to fend him off!

'I... er... certainly,' I managed. 'Tomorrow then, to this address?'

Monroe nodded and then smiled that sad smile again. He wished us a merry rest of the evening before leaving us alone. As soon as he was gone, Angela turned to me with a pressed smile and enthusiastic eyes...

'At *any* point,' she said, 'at *any point at all* in my story, you could have stopped me in my embarrassment! At any point! But instead you let me witter on and, well... I...'

'Sebastian Carfax is not wild and nor is he a lunatic,' I said first, wanting that said and understood, 'Nor is he dark and beastly as you describe. He is a fine and handsome young man with skin like caramel and... and he is a kind and gentle soul who feels too much and whilst yes, he was given a writ of madness by my father, he faced it not for his *violent temper* – for he does not have one – but for his trying to end his own life. He is a troubled soul, not a monster.'

Angela was gobsmacked – probably unused to such straight-talking from her wispy and chivalrous peers of society in London.

'I once loved him very much, it was no mere fling. We were close friends from childhood you see and he... he loved me completely too,' I went on, it was hard even still to say those words, 'And his sister, Nora, is my very dearest friend and always has been. Alice Monroe was not murdered. She committed suicide, there was much evidence for it! I was there when they deliberated! I gave evidence at the inquest myself!'

Angela said nothing for a long time, but then put a hand on my shoulder. Her face had lost the amusement in it though, her eyes sharp. 'Stop!' she said, 'People will hear you and… and imagine the scandal!'

'Oh, I care not for scandal! I have felt it's bite enough already not to care for it!'

Angela smiled again, 'Oh I knew I liked you,' she said, 'you have pluck! Something one does not see often about here. I promise from now on, I shall ensure that I correct the stories when I hear them!'

'Thank you!'

'Good, now, here, take my handkerchief and pat your face, you are awfully red and Harrington is moving this way again!'

After a breakfast of kippers and eggs, the following day, I kissed Papa and left him to the three patients he had booked in that morning. I had fast given up on reminding him that we were supposed to be at leisure and left him to it! He did so like to be busy and was making good money too, I suspected, with all these finely attired ladies and gentlemen – much more so than in tending the persons of our little village!

'Where are you off to this morning?' he murmured as I kissed his wrinkled old cheek.

'Just to the park with Miss Grippon.'

'All right, be home before two, we have a late luncheon booked with the Bellinghams.'

'Yes Father,' I whispered.

Monroe's rooms were much more modest than the man himself. A simple suite of rooms just a hansom-trip away from Papa and my apartments. They were set across the second floor of an old townhouse which overlooked the smelly Thames and, when admitted, I found them sparsely decorated and dull, with windows which let in beams of light which did nothing but to show up the dust.

Monroe came in shortly after the landlady admitted me, he was dressed in a coat and gloves which he removed before asking "Maybelle" for tea. We made stilted small talk the tea was prepped and delivered, and then he turned to me with eyes I could not read.

'It was fortune indeed which led me to you, this past day,' he said. 'I have a hope you might be able to assist me in a few details on…'

'I came to London to get away from all that, and I did already answer all questions posed to me before the coroner,' I said, firm.

'Indeed, but there are some actions since that I wish to probe. I am certain that Alice was murdered – no, don't look thus – I do not suspect young Bastian of it!'

'Then who? Me? I never…'

'No, not you either, although God knows you had motive too! No, it is another I suspect – the old man himself. Baron Carfax and I have had a difficult relationship…'

'Yes! Blackmail can cause turbulence in a friendship!'

'Blackmail? You mean how he paid me off to cover up his secrets? That was not my blackmail. He threatened me with disaster should I speak of it, and he took my girl from me as assurance.'

'You claim, then, that the marriage between Bas and Alice was Carfax's orchestration, not yours?'

'I do! And I confess it true that I did not fight it too much, because my girl was dappy for young Sebastian, always…'

'Not so,' I said, shaking my head.

'And what do you claim to know of it?'

'I know that she called him a darkie and a half-breed…' I said, 'she said these things to me, she said she was disgusted to have had to marry him.'

'Then that is a testament to how much you both broke her! As a child she adored him. She was his shadow, always, joining him and his sister at their games, playing amongst the sugar crops and swimming in the beautiful blue oceans.'

I paused, the memory flashing of Bastian and Nora telling me of such games. They'd never mentioned Alice as being present but I supposed it followed that she must have been.

Had they invited her in? I wondered, or had she followed as they'd played, wanting more than anything to be invited to their games? Suddenly I felt sad for her. 'In truth?' I whispered.

'In truth. When I was Carfax's clerk, I saw many unsavoury things, many things to turn a man's stomach – especially in his treatment of his slaves. Carfax is an awful and dangerous man. I never would have placed Alice with him if I had had a choice and the only comfort I had was that she loved Sebastian so very much that she saw little else in it.'

I sat, reeling. I could believe it all, what doubt was there? I'd seen the scars on Bastian's back with my own eyes, had run my fingers down those broken ridges there his father had gone for him. I could not deny that Carfax was a brute. Did that mean, then, that I had misjudged this man? And his daughter?

'Saying I believe you,' I managed, 'What… for what reason have you brought me here?'

'Firstly, are you still in contact with Sebastian?'

I shook my head.

'No,' he mused, 'I was told as much by my investigators. A shame, really, as you might have been able to assist me more so if you were. I am interested in why you left, but also more urgently in another matter – that of the whereabouts of Baron Carfax?'

'I… I don't understand?'

'So you are not aware? Hmm. Perhaps your father might be more in the know, as his doctor?'

'I'm very confused,' I whispered.

'Then allow me to fill you in. Since the inquest, I have had investigators looking into the matter. It has become known to us that not only did Baron Carfax skip out on the inquest, but it would appear that he never came home at all?'

At once I set to wracking my brains. Had I seen him, at all, in the past year or so? Suddenly I didn't think so! The family had stopped attending church in the aftermath of the scandal and so I had not seen him there but surely I'd have seen him about? More so, and strikingly so, surely Nora would have at least casually mentioned it, if her father was missing? Surely?

'I... I remain good friends with Nora,' I managed, 'She's said nothing at all but it is true, I've not... not seen him...'

'No, and nor have any. I begin to fear – to grow suspicious.'

'But what motive?' I asked, 'More so if she was his assurance of your staying quiet! Surely he would want her to remain alive and well, if holding her for assurances?'

Monroe sat in silence, buttering a scone with long languid motions, his eyes were far away.

'Because of the annulment,' he said at last. 'Sebastian was losing patience with it all and was about to go ahead with the annulment anyway. I had stepped back from it all by then – I just wanted my little girl home and safe away from it all. I had made my fortune in a few sensible purchases and so I was willing just to let it all go. Alice was less inclined to leave though You said she was devious, and I suppose she was, my clever girl. She'd already tied young Sebastian up in her own scheme and she was determined to remain where she was. I told her time and again to just leave it – he obviously didn't love her, but Alice was headstrong!'

'She was blackmailing Bastian?' I whispered, taking that nugget from his sudden rush of words.

'She was. She wanted a baby. She said she'd give him his annulment if he gave her a child, but in truth she hoped that the act itself would bring them closer. She told him that if he gave her the baby, she'd give him the annulment but if he did not then she'd tell you lies to make you believe that he betrayed you.'

'This makes my poor darling sound even more guilty, although of course I know he is not!'

'It is damning but for the fact of Alice's final letter to me,' he lifted a piece of paper from the table, 'It reads, in part, "*I grow weary. If Sebastian still continues with the annulment, then I shall go to his father with what we know. Edward will make him drop this foolish notion. I am his wife, he cannot just put me aside!*', here,' he handed it to me. I skimmed it. It was filled with anger and a young girl's frustrations.

'Why did you not bring this up at the inquest?' I asked.

'It was in the pile of papers your coroner looked over,' his voice was soft, tired.

'He read this and still pushed you aside?'

'Carfax is a powerful man and I supposed at once that the coroner was in his employ when he did not push for him to be present!'

'Good Lord,' I murmured. 'But now Carfax too is missing?'

'It would appear that way. I have made enquiries and he is not at the ruins of the plantation, nor is he with mutual friends either in the Caribbean or in New Orleans. He must be in hiding, and I suspect he's doing so in this country.'

'This is all…. So much…'

'I know it must be difficult to trust me. I have been played as a villain in your story, I know, but…'

My mind took me suddenly, strangely, to the day of the inquest, to Monroe twisting the little cloth dolly in his hands. It was a gesture too tender to have been contrived. 'I trust you,' I said, and it was true, I did. 'But what do you want of me?'

'I have a boon to ask of you,' Monroe said, 'A small thing indeed, under the circumstances.'

'What boon?'

'When you return home, ask your friend Nora of her father's disappearance. Ask her, and push her a little if you will. Discover his whereabouts now, or his whereabouts that night! Do what the coroner would not do, and investigate Baron Carfax too… and if you manage to uncover anything at all, write to me?'

'I could not betray Nora like that!'

'It need not be betrayal – you could tell her everything I have told you, take her into your confidence! Tell her why you need to know, to absolve her brother from the lurk of suspicion which still lies upon him.'

I pressed my lips tightly but I nodded. If I could prove that it had been the baron, and not Bastian, who had killed Alice, then it would ease my own troubled mind too.

Sixteen

I left quickly after that, with little more to be said, and there I went home and pondered it all in silence. It made sense, especially with the Baron going into hiding, and Alice's final letter, that there was perhaps more going on that we'd not considered. I thought of Bastian too, as the possibility of his innocence after all washed over me. I suddenly found myself lingering on the other side of it too. Alice had blackmailed Bastian, so her father had said, but I did not believe suddenly, that that was wholly the motivations for him having betrayed me to lay with her. Bastian and Alice had known each other their whole lives, and in the end, she'd asked one boon of him – a child before he left her. In Bastian's shoes, would I have done any differently? I wondered. In some ways, the love Bastian and I had shared had still been somewhat childish, despite what we'd suffered together, was his and Alice's relationship really any different?

But then it struck me too, was I really now feeling sympathy for the girl? For Alice who had ever been my nemesis, who had most likely pushed me and killed my baby. My mind brought me the panic in her voice as I'd fallen, the way she had screamed. She was devious but was she really so good an actress? Suddenly I didn't know any more. Last I had seen him, Bastian had accused me of caring more that he'd lain with Alice, than the suspicion of him as a murderer but it was not until that moment that I actually considered that accusation. Was my jealousy really the issue at hand?

In which case – what of the false alibi, of Bastian's lies to the coroner? Could they really have just been his fear. He knew as well as I, what motive he had.

I picked up a pen to write to Nora, but I could not find the right words and so put it down again. How could I begin it? How could I ask her, outright, if she thought the man who had raised her was capable of murder? But then hadn't I all-but accused her brother of the same? In frustration I put down my pen again, but then lifted it back up and began to write down each scenario and the evidence for and against it, or who may or may not have killed Alice. When it was done, Baron Carfax and Bastian still stood neck and neck at the top of my list of suspects, but at least now, Bastian had company there. At least I was no longer painfully certain he'd done it.

I did not see Monroe again whilst we were in London, I know not if he purposely avoided me, or if he was merely away again after our meeting. I found myself, however, much distracted by the obvious intentions of another. Mr Harrington took to calling at the house where we rented rooms almost daily. He took me on adventures, as he called them: out on a boat on the Thames, out on a picnic to Hampton Court and one evening, a starlit stroll down the narrow London streets.

'I do believe he will propose to you soon,' Angela observed in a whisper to me. This was late upon a Sunday afternoon and we were at picnic. I, Angela, Papa, a Mr Gregory and his wife Patricia, and of course, Mr Harrington.'

'I hope not,' I lamented, 'surely he realises he is too far my senior? He must be double my age!'

'One would think it but that is not the way of society…'

She was interrupted by Papa arriving beside us and remarking upon the fine summer's evening.

'Indeed, very warm,' Angela purred, taking my father's arm, and then I was left to walk alone. As always, Mr Harrington made a beeline for me.

'Rather lovely days we are enjoying at the moment,' he said quietly.

'Just as Papa said to Miss Grippon, very.'

'Are you well? You look a little pale.'

'I am well,' I smiled.

Mr Harrington took my arm gently in his hand to hold me back from the rest of the party but with Angela's words ringing in my ears, I all but tugged myself from his grasp and ran to Papa's side.

The proposal could not be put off forever though, and after only five months of being in London, I was asked that soul shattering question: 'I would be pleased, nay overjoyed, if you would consent to become Mrs Harrington...' were his words.

I put a hand onto the wall as though to steady myself and looked upon his open and honest face. His eyes gleamed in earnestness but even the utterance of his words showed their impossibility. To never return home to Cornwall? Never to see Nora, and indeed, Bastian again? To forsake it all and live in the city with my rich old husband. Suddenly all the glimmer of London was gone and I felt desperate to get away.

'Sir, I am flattered,' I began.

'Do not say no!'

'I am sorry, Mr Harrington, I must!'

'Why must you? We get along, we are friends, are we not?'

'I don't love you sir.'

'Love grows, Maddi, you must first find somebody with whom you can share a life, the love comes afterwards. I will make you happy, I will elevate you... come, do not close yourself off to this idea.'

He looked sorrow stricken and for a moment, the briefest moment, I entertained the prospect of saying yes but I knew, had known all along, that Mr Harrington was not for me. An idea struck upon me. 'I cannot marry you, sir, for I have not my father's permission.'

'I have it,' he interjected.

'You... do?'

'Indeed yes, he has already granted me his blessing.'

'I see.'

'Will you reconsider? Knowing this?'

'No sir. You are so very kind and I wish with all that I am, that I returned your affections but I do not. I am sorry, my answer is no.'

'Then I too am sorry.' He said and took my hand, lifting it to his lips, 'Sorry indeed,' and then he took his leave.

Vexed, I ran straight to Papa who was taking tea and a little fruit bread in the parlour of our rented rooms. 'Are you so very tired of my company that you will hand me over to any old man who asks for me?' I demanded.

'Hello lass, it seems that I have offended you?' my father's expression was mild and helped to quench my anger.

'You have! Papa! Mr Harrington? Did you really suppose that I would have him?'

'You seemed fond of him?'

I stumbled there, 'I am but...'

'And is he not rich enough to give you a good life? Handsome despite his age?'

'Yes but... he's... he's...'

'Not to your tastes?'

Sometimes I resented my father's ability to stay calm in a crisis and as he sat looking blandly at my furious face I began to wonder of Mama's temperament. Had she been fiery like me?

'No Papa, he is *not to my taste*...'

'And nor is he of curling hair and brown eyes and a childhood sweetheart to boot.'

I reeled and physically stepped back, 'Papa?'

'Deny it!'

'There is nothing anymore between Bastian and I!' I said, 'It has been nearly two years since I even saw him!'

'Then write to Leo Harrington and tell him you have changed your mind.'

A tear rolled down my face. 'No, Papa, I do not want him.'

'And the next? And the next?'

'Papa please!' I was close to actual sobbing now.

Papa looked me with a long glance over his spectacles and then spoke quietly, 'Maddi, you are twenty years old now, a girl no more. Tell me, what do you plan to do with your life?'

'I don't know,' I whispered.

'But your life is not here? Do you want to go home? We are booked until Christmas but if there is no point then we might as well go home…'

'If I say yes?'

'If you say yes,' he said mildly, 'then we will go home but if we do so it is on the understanding that I shall not again offer you a chance of a season in London. You will have to resign yourself to only what Cornwall has to offer… do you understand?'

'You mean Bastian?' I asked, confusion rocking me.

'I mean that you should go wherever your happiness lies. If this time in London has given you clarity, then follow it.'

I stood frowning, had Papa orchestrated this whole thing? In truth? I could not tell, Papa was unreadable.

'This was a test?'

He smiled then though and shook his head. 'Sometimes, the heart wants what it wants,' he said, 'and sometimes it does not. I hoped that yours could be swayed, that is all. It seems I was wrong, so let us go back to where we belong. I am weary of London anyhow.'

And so it was. Our things were quickly packed away and our trunks loaded. The stagecoach picked us up promptly at ten of the morning, on the third of November, and then we were off towards home. The stage let us off at the closest town, and then we had an hour to wait for the little closed carriage from the Sailor's Rest to scoop us up again and begin to take us towards home. Papa and I had a little tea in the tea-room, and then headed out to be met. Already I could smell the countryside, the sea, and my heart sang to once more be coming home. As the roads turned bouncier, the air started to smell fresher and that good old ocean breeze whipped through the carriage, making me pull my shawl a little tighter. I smiled though, that just meant I was nearly home. The carriage rolled on, bouncing us enough to jar our bones but whilst Papa sat with his eyes closed, adrenaline began to pound through me. We reached the fork in the road where the path split, one for Fiveham and one for Blossom Cove, and I looked out at The Cliff House, drinking in the sight of it. To my surprise though, it was Papa who sat up and called out. 'One moment please, can you halt the vehicle?'

The carriage came to a rocky, juddering stop.

'Papa... what?'

'Go,' he said.

'I don't understand...'

'Go, sweetheart, forgive your young man and accept any proposal he makes you, with my blessing.'

All of the blood rushed to my face. I could not breathe, could do nothing but sit shocked, looking at my Papa.

'But Papa... there is still so much...'

'So much of what? Maddi?'

'So much... distrust. He lied to me, he lay with Alice!'

'My dear, I know this is not what you wish to hear, but let me make this plain. You were the mistress! You were the one who chose to share him! His wife was his right, and he hers. Surely inside you know that?'

'But he lied about it.'

'Would you not have done the same? To save his feelings?'

'I... I suppose I don't know. Aside from the fact that he lied to me, there is the false statement too! You gave false testimony, just as I did. Why would he have lied at the inquest if he was not guilty?'

Papa leaned back, 'It's true – but I do not think he lied because he was guilty. I have my own theories on that and I suspect they are much like the reason I lied.'

'What, I don't understand?'

'Because both our lies gave him an alibi, true, but they also gave you one…' Papa said.

I sat back, my heart thudding, considering it for the very first time.

'Me?'

'Young Sebastian's lies stopped anybody from ever eying *you* with suspicion.'

'But I didn't do anything to be suspected for! Oh… oh God! You do not think people suspected *me*?'

'I doubt it, but you *were* alone in the house, you had no other alibi. It made you safer too, sweetheart. Think about it.'

'Oh…God… and I threw a paperweight at him,' I breathed.

Papa smiled. 'So you did,' he chuckled. 'But look into your heart of hearts, look to that young man you claim to love so dearly and ask yourself – is he a murderer?'

I shook my head, almost tearful, I couldn't imagine it, not really.

'Go on then,' he smiled suddenly, his weathered old lips matching the genuine emotion in his eyes, 'Go – go and claim your happiness! We both know why we are coming home so let us not be coy!'

'I will…' I had to stop to breathe, 'I will be back within the hour…' I said, '… to help with unpacking and…'

'Be as long as it needs, my dear. Nelly can help me unpack. Send a boy if you will miss your supper!'

I nodded again and then leaned in to kiss Papa. 'And you are sure?' I whispered.

'I yearn to see you happy just as you yearn for that young man. Go – go on – go and offer your forgiveness now if you wish to do so. This has gone on long enough, I think!'

I nodded and then unlatched the door. Old Mr Briggs, the coachman, looked at me with surprise but then knowing showed in his eye too. Who in our little village did not know of the saga of Bastian and I, in truth?

I nodded, found a smile and then pulled my shawl tighter still as I started up on the road to Fiveham. My usually robust constitution had climatised from this harsh seaside weather to favour London's blandness so whilst it was indeed only early autumn still I felt it all, every gust of wind, every splatter of the drizzle rain which was coming over. I walked in determination though, half-running at times in my eagerness but then pulling back as I remembered the bridges I would need to rebuild too. I had accused him of murder – there was nothing at all to prevent him simply turning me out and I knew it. I didn't think he would though! Not if all Nora spoke of him and how he held on for me was correct and not just her trying to coax me back.

At the old gate, the last of the gentle slope, I paused again and forced a few long breaths whilst I tried to unknot my belly. A person could change a lot in a year, nearly two! – how was I to know he was even the same man? And yet, had I not known him enough years to know he was never changed? I glanced to the paddock and stables where once he'd begun to teach me to ride, where Nora and I had giggled long at his antics. And then of course, where he and I had quarrelled over Alice, where I had called him weak for marrying her. I pushed the memory firmly away and then realised I was being watched with interest by a young stable-hand. I swallowed my stress and waved to him, then climbed the stile by the big black iron gates. Bastian had built the stile himself, to save us having to faff with the gate every time we went in or out – not that we as children had used the main gate overly – preferring the cliff-walk.

And then I was inside.

The house up on the hill squared off with me, suddenly seeming so far up the sloped, layered gardens. Slope, then steps, then more slope, a bend and then more steps, right up to the house itself. Back in the day, when Dame Evelyn had entertained, this had ever been a point of contention – or so Papa had once told me – coaches had had to drop their owners at the foot of the slope and leave them to climb up to the house against the fey ocean winds in all of their finery. The slope was too steep, and the wind too wild to risk driving up past where I now stood. I could almost imagine it now, the sighs and the swearing as shawls were pulled away and old tricorn hats threatened to be taken by the thieving fingers of the wind. With such daydreams in mind, I began the ascent. My belly felt hollow and I was still not sure I'd actually be able to knock.

It was not until I was about halfway up that I saw Nora. I paused again, my eyes filling with tears that were more than just the effects of the sharp wind. She was about halfway up, cutting a bunch of long-stem roses from one of the pretty rosebushes which littered the tier before the tall steps. As she glanced up, she saw me too.

For a moment we both stared at each other but then I was running and so was she, flowers dropped to the ground, and so we met to embrace in the middle, me puffing to have run up the slope.

'Maddi!' she beamed, kissing my cheeks and squeezing me. Never have I ever known a moment of doubt in Nora's affections of me but if I had, it was quelled then! 'Oh! You are home then! Oh and look at these fine London fashions! I approve! You are better dressed than I am! You look so well – how the devil are you? Shall we go and have tea? …at your Papa's house, I know, as you won't come in here you stubborn creature but…'

'Actually,' I broke her off, 'I wish to… I have come to see Bastian…'

My words silenced her enough that it might have been the first time ever I'd seen her speechless. She looked confused, then happy, then wary, all in one split instant.

'What.. why…?'

'Because… because…' I paused, still breathless and crazed, 'because in London another man asked me to marry him and in that very moment I knew that I could never, not ever do that… I can't marry anybody else!'

Nora smiled but it was still somewhat wary, 'You wish to…'

'Reconcile.' I whispered the word, 'I wish to reconcile!'

At once Nora's smile beamed again, her eyes brightening and her pearly white teeth coming on show, 'You do? Oh! Oh well in that case come, here grab this basket of roses for me and I shall take the gardening tools… here,' she looped the basket onto my arm, and then her own arm through the other and led me up to the house. I found a smile, a small one in truth as I was more nervous than eager, as at the door Nora paused and turned to me.

'I'll get these tools away,' she said, taking the basket from my arm too, then pushed open the door and shouted her brother's name into the echoing hallway. I flushed so warm my cheeks felt they were aflame but I could do nothing but stand like a lemon as she scurried away.

And then there he was.

Bastian appeared from a corridor to my right, and strode into the hallway. The slight annoyance on his features to be yelled for in such a manner vanished when he saw me in the doorway.

'Maddi?'

And then I was weeping, hot tears running over my cheeks which were both flushed with emotion but battered cold from the wind and rain without.

'Maddi?' he whispered again and I realised how strange all this must be to him. Two years of nothing and then me stood wordless and weeping in his hallway, unable to speak. I could not yet work my lips to explain and so I let my body do it. I strode the ten steps between us, closing the gap and, a slight pause to gather my nerves, then threw my arms around his neck, burying my face in him, holding him pressed tightly to me. My gesture worked better, I suppose now, than any words could have done. He caught me up and held me tight, pressing his face into my hair. Thus we stood, unspeaking for some long moments, but then he spoke.

'With such an embrace, either you are coming here because you love me still and want me still, or because you have come to break the news to me yourself that you have chosen a husband in London and are saying goodbye,' he murmured in a thick husky tone 'and for the life of me I cannot tell which it is.'

I looked up, pulling away enough to hold his eye, to examine every inch of that handsome profile.

'If it were the former?'

'I pray to God that it is the former!'

'You fool, of course it is the former!' I nuzzled his shoulder with my face and pulled him closer, drinking in a scent I had once found so familiar. 'I am so sorry I left,' I finally whispered. 'So sorry I left you.'

'I am sorry too, oh sweetheart you cannot understand even for a moment how much I have regretted it all – my subterfuge, my lies...'

'Stop, say no more! I saw Monroe in London and he confessed it all. I know... I know everything.'

Bastian put his head down against my cheek again and there I felt his body shudder suddenly, a release of emotion. He murmured something but it was just a whisper I could not hear, praising God I suppose. I drew our faces together, guiding his with my hand, and kissed him, first on a wet cheek, and then on the lips.

'If you had... had anything to ask me,' I murmured, 'then now might be the time.'

For half a moment, bless him, he looked confused but then realisation dawned in his face. He did not release me, did not pull away, but with his lips against my cheek, near my right ear, he finally murmured out those so perfect of words:

'Will you marry me, Maddi?'

'Yes.'

'In truth?'

'Yes!'

And then we were both crying, both holding each other and moving to kisses despite how we were both so wrought. His hands gripped me so tightly, the urgency in him was so raw in that moment. I wondered how I could ever have left him at all. A woman's clearing her throat stilled us and with reluctance we parted to see Lady Carfax on the stairs. She was smiling though, not disapproving.

'Mama!' Bastian said and then turned again as the door opened to reveal Nora too.

'Here,' Lady Carfax said, seeming to float down the stairs. She came to us and placed something into Bastian's hand.

'Nora came to find me and tell me what was about to occur,' she said, 'I thought this might be appropriate. It was grandmother's.'

I glanced down to see the ring in Bastian's palm. My mind flit back to that delicate old lady, that one time I had met her as a girl.

"It will be worth the wait", she'd said. Those words jolted me then, echoed through my head. Bastian's hands shook as he lifted the ring up and forced himself to move away from me. At a short arm's length, he stood, inhaled a few times, and then finally smiled. 'A bit more officially,' he said so that just I could hear him, then, louder, 'Madeleine Chilcott, my darling Maddi, will you allow me to present you with this ring and in doing so consent to become Mrs Carfax just as soon as we can be wed?'

In the doorway Nora gave a little clap of excitement, rendered childish again in her joy.

'Nothing would give me more pleasure,' I said, beaming. 'I want nothing more than to be your wife, Bastian!'

Bastian's smile widened again and his eyes shone. He took up my hand and slid the ring onto my finger, 'then it shall be,' he whispered and then we were both taken up in hugs from his mother and sister, along with Nora's squeals of happiness. Truly, it was a fine moment indeed.

Afterwards, Bastian and I escaped by heading outside to watch the sunset over the water. The day was still fairly bright, despite the lateness of the hour but already over the water the sky was turning to a deep pink. The sea, swirling far below the bottom of the gardens was a swishing roaring mass for the wind, but nowhere near the monster it became in a storm. I allowed the views to soothe me, even as the breeze flung salt into my face.

'It's so beautiful up here,' I whispered. 'I have missed this view, this past dreary year!'

'This will be your home now, you need never leave, if you don't wish to.'

'I never shall,' I said, but then shivered as a particularly sharp burst of late summer rain began. Bastian pulled off his coat and wrapped it about me. 'You need to reacclimatise!' he said, laughing as he rubbed my goose-fleshed arms.

'I do!'

'More so when you come to live here. You've not spent much time here at night but I assure you, it gets cold indeed – and noisy when the wind whips about the old bricks.

'I remember it well from those times I have, but I will have you next to me to wrap about me, when I lie abed.'

'Always! Like this…'

He stood behind me, and wrapped his arms around me from behind to keep me warm with his body heat. I leaned back, allowing him to hold me as I ran my eyes over the beautiful seascape before us. There were still things which needed to be said, but I eased in slowly with a question I already knew the answer to,

'Should we not get the permission of your father, too?'

Bastian tensed, but didn't pull away. 'That will be difficult,' he replied, 'None of us know where he is.'

I nodded, 'I had heard rumours.'

'You had? Where from?'

'Monroe – I think I said, I saw Monroe in London.'

'Ah.'

'He has a private investigator working on the case of Alice's murder. He has reported your father's absence.'

Bastian was quiet for a long moment, but then he sighed. 'I promise, no more lies! Yes, Father left the day of the inquest, he never returned. For legal – financial – reasons, we have kept this fact a secret.' He paused, not releasing me but tensing up enough that I could feel the stress in his embrace. 'I take it that you have altered your previous course, about my possible guilt… about what happened to Alice?'

I pulled away gently, turning about. 'Mostly,' I whispered.

'Not completely?' he looked hurt again and inwardly I cursed at myself for spoiling such a sweet moment with this, again.

'Monroe thinks your father responsible for her death, because of the way he fled, but I just… I don't know anymore.'

'This cuts more so than anything I have ever known.'

'Then try to regard it differently,' I said, I put a cold hand up to his warm cheek – I had forgotten my gloves in the carriage and so my fingers were bare, 'Even with my doubts, even though all is clouded, I will still marry you anyway. I love you so very much that no matter what occurred, I will stick by you, my love, I…'

He cupped his fingers about mine, that spark dawning in his eyes. 'I am moved to think it,' he whispered, 'but I tell you again and I shall say it until my dying day. I did not kill Alice, and I do resent having that cast upon me. Especially by you! I will forgive it, I love you no less for it, but it hurts.'

I replied with a kiss. More than anything, I wanted to trust him but I knew I'd never be completely certain until Baron Carfax was located. Bastian's kiss was so sweet, so soft, enough to brush away all the pain and worry, just in that instant. He smiled again too as we parted and then pulled me back into his arms for a long embrace.

'I'm so overwhelmed,' he murmured, 'In just one hour you have turned my whole life upside-down again! I know we have much to talk on, to discuss, but for now shall we both agree just to plan a wedding, to work towards a future that we both now want so desperately?'

'Agreed,' I murmured.

'Good,' he said, then with one last kiss he pulled away, 'Now let me walk you home so that I might ask your Papa for you officially!'

'We already have his blessing!'

'That is a relief indeed, but I will come and make it official now,' he tucked my hand into the crease of his arm, 'Come, let us stroll down together?'

Seventeen

And so, finally, Bastian and I were wed. We wasted no time at all in it, and as soon as the banns were read, he took me up the hill to the little church which overlooked the fishermen's cove and together we stood, hand in hand before the vicar. It was cold, true – mid December and close to Bastian's birthday as well as Christmas, but the grey didn't seep in and my gaze was so filled with love that I drew out my own colour. It was a day I had never dreamed could really come to be, one which had ever only been a distant whisper of longing, never one I thought to live. Bastian was much the same as I, lost in something of a dream as he spoke his vows and then slid an arm about my back. My eyes were wet, my body quivering.

Outside, even as the vicar talked us through it, a cart was being loaded with my trunks and bags, to be taken up to The Cliff House and unpacked in wardrobes which were now mine. The ceremony was a small affair with only twenty people at the most in attendance, mostly villagers and one or two friends of Papa who could not be excluded. Angela Grippon came down for the service, and with her Mr Harrington to whom she was now apparently engaged.

'Well, nobody else was doing it for me!' she'd written with the news first, 'and he is rather charming and very rich!'

It was marvellous to see Angela again, and she in turn seemed fascinated to meet Bastian and Nora – those almost story-like figures to her known only though the gossip of the society papers. Nora seemed to like her too and the girls found a commonality in discussion of high society and fashion.

Papa and Lady Carfax stood as witness to the union of Bastian and I, and once the words were spoken, it was Lady Carfax who signed the certificate in lieu of Baron Carfax. My father too signed, his delicate hand dipping the ink and then scrawling that unintelligible doctor's scrawl. After the ceremony I walked, in somewhat of a daze, back to the house with Bastian's hand firmly holding mine. As we passed by the village, I was flattered to be showered in rice by the townsfolk who had come from their homes to wish us well as we walked past. Forgiven our past sins, I suppose, now that we had bowed to convention at last. I smiled at them, shyly happy as I turned away from the house where I'd lived all my life and made my way towards the place where I'd always felt so at home.

'You're very quiet Maddi.' Angela observed as we arrived at the gate, readying for the gusts of wind as we ascended up the slope to the house.

'I am fine.' I said, my eyes shining, 'But I feel a little as though if I try to speak too much I might burst into happy tears.'

Bastian, who had moved away from me to speak to his mother turned back at my words and gave me a grin without any shadow of unhappiness. Thank God for that smile, for his good humour that day. Angela laughed and took my arm in hers as Nora appeared on my other side, my two dearest friends.

'You were right too,' Angela said, 'he is a handsome thing, is he not?'

'He is,' I laughed, 'and now Mr Harrington for you!'

'Yes, dear you both must come to the wedding!' she said, but still, after the gossips, I knew I'd keep both my husband and my sister-in-law as far from London as long as I could!

The wedding breakfast was served shortly after our return, not that I could eat much for my nerves, and then dancing. As the clock struck nine, Bastian and I thanked the guests and, leaving them to continue to make merry on our behalf, slipped upstairs.

'Thank God that's over!' Bastian muttered as he sat himself down in a chair by the bed 'I dislike being the centre of attention like that.'

'And I.' I agreed.

'Do you like the room?' he asked, indicating around us. He'd moved us from his previous chamber where I had gone that night to lie with him, to a different suite at the back of the house, overlooking the lawns and the trees which led to the moors rather than the sea view of the front of the house. The room was very beautiful: the bed was made up with a blue and gold coverlet, the walls were pastel yellow, almost cream and the furniture was of a dark wood decorated with gold. The windows were large and hung with cream and blue drapes which looked as though they were newly sewn. There was a ship in a bottle behind the bed though and the very presence of it there made me smile – surely it must have been one of his! Maybe one of the ones we'd built together as children.

'It's beautiful.' I said, 'Less boyish than your old chamber.'

Bastian laughed, 'Nora decorated it,' he said, 'she said it was her wedding gift to you to not let me decorate.'

Finally, the knots in my stomach began to dissipate and I laughed with him, 'She might have given me the best gift I could have asked for then!' I sat down on the edge of the bed, 'I'm nervous.' I admitted.

'In truth? Even after all the times…'

I blushed, 'Yes.' I whispered. 'It's been a long time now since then, nearly two years now.'

'I suppose it has, hasn't it?' he smiled and then leaned in to kiss me.

I drank him in. His kisses were already nothing unfamiliar to me, but in anticipation of where this was to lead, it gave me a thrill more so than before. Not even the ghost of Alice who tried to rise was able to prevent me from kissing him again and again.

'No more pulling away before the moment,' he whispered as we parted, 'no more worry or anxieties. Now this is us, we are married and as my wife, it matters not if we make another baby – it is something to aspire, not to fear!'

A pang touched me, an old nostalgic pain for that tiny, wrinkled face I barely remembered. 'I want that,' I said, realising it as I said it, 'I want a baby Bas, I want a family.'

'You have a family, now,' he said, then found a smile, 'and as for making a baby…'

I chuckled too, albeit somewhat sadly for the echoed memory. His fingers caressed the stitching on my gown.

'How does one go about removing this?' he murmured, 'there seem to be laces all over the thing. When we danced after supper I was looking it over and thinking, by God, this wedding gown is more of a fortress than anything other!'

'What a thing to be thinking, before all our relatives! How very uncouth,' I said, laughing with him, then stood up. 'Here,' my voice turned husky, 'You untie the bow first,' he stood, wrapping his arms about me to do so, 'Yes, there, and then the back has clips holding the fabric.'

Bastian fumbled a moment, but then laughed again and used his hands to spin me about to unclasp them all. In my nerves about our wedding night, I never could have anticipated this laughter. Finally Bastian had the gown undone, then turned me back to slide it from my form.

'Oh, and now a corset too…' he murmured, but still his eyes were laughing, still his lips pulled into a smile.

And so it went on.

When at last we were both nude, he pulled me by my hand, leading me to the bed – our bed at last and there he gently lowered me to the softness. Once more came the magical feeling of two energies combining, even before our bodies followed suit. That oneness which can only be felt with skin upon skin, breath mingling on parted lips. Unlike most newlyweds who had to come to know one-another, Bastian and I were already a well-oiled machine as we lay on the pillows, touching, kissing, teasing, and then at last joining again to lock together in that sweetest of bliss. He murmured, and I let out a gasp of pleasure too. His body moved, mine joined it in a fusion of slickness, sweat and saliva. As he moved, as he slipped into a rhythm my body knew so well, I allowed my head to fall back onto the pillows, letting the moment take me to that sweetest release. And then, at the final moment, was no sudden loss of contact, no withdrawing to spill onto my belly but only more of that same closeness, intensified as our bodies gave out together into that final release.

It took me almost a month to settle into the idea that I really was married. Bastian and I had no honeymoon and so were thrust straight into our roles as a married couple. A role I went at with relish! I was given some responsibilities by Lady Carfax, who laughingly said that one day I would be mistress of the house and therefore should learn to manage it. She sat beside me and patiently went over the accounts, showing me what each column meant and how to amend them in a manner that Baron Carfax's accountant and solicitor would understand. He would likely want to go over it all himself, she added, once he returned "From his business trip", as was the official word. I was also given care and management of the servants, although Lady Carfax agreed to keep the basics of the day to day housekeeping for herself.

    Bastian and I were blissful in those early days. Both of us walking around as though we were in a dream. When we were both done with our individual duties, me about the house and him out on the lands, we took to riding together again as we had when we were younger, racing each other across the fields and taking picnics deep into the countryside where we could steal an afternoon alone. Sometimes we were even daring, recapturing the excitement of our youthful affair by secreting ourselves away in our chamber and locking the door. Nora too claimed much of my attention, and when Bastian was busy all the day, or when Nora began to complain that she never saw her brother, we spent long lazy afternoons drinking tea with her. It was a wonderful time, blissful and happy, the happiest I had ever been. I had not a care in the world and I was happy for the world to see it.

Of course, such happiness never does last.

It must have been some ten weeks or so after my marriage that I was called urgently from Fiveham down to my father's house in the village by a message from Nell. I went at once, Bastian at my side, on foot across the fields and down the cliff path. Once in the village I all but ran up the hill, reliving terrible memories of the last time I had done such, as a girl with Mama laid dead in the house on the hill. A strange merging of two days, especially when it would turn out that they would be so very similar in nature.

Appalled and frightened as I burst into the house and up to the dark chamber where my darling Papa lay covered in soft woollen blankets. He seemed so small, so helpless. His skin was almost grey and whilst his eyes were open he seemed somewhat lost in a daze. His lip pulled down on the left side of his face and that side of his body seemed somehow floppy and infirm.

'What is it, what ails him?' I panted, shocked to my core.

'I am not certain,' Nell said, 'He was like this when I came in with his orange juice this morning.'

'It's a stroke,' Bastian said gently, coming in behind me and putting his arm about me. 'Grandmother had one in her final days and was much the same, he has had a stroke, my love.'

I swallowed several times, my mouth instantly dry and sticky, and for a moment I felt weak, faint and devastated. I trembled and my lip quivered, my whole body wavered as though a faint were to come upon me.

'Steady now, it'll be all right,' Bastian murmured, his arm about me, but I gently pushed away. I could not faulter just yet! I had to ensure all was in place.

'Nell, go and rouse somebody who can take a message up to Fiveham as to what has happened,' I said, 'And we will.. will need a doctor…' my voice wavered on the last word.

Bastian interrupted, 'Go to Cattersley,' he said, 'Dr Langton is retired but he is a good man, he'll come! We don't have time to wait for somebody from Camborne!'

With everything I could think of done, I just stood, aghast, in Papa's chamber. 'Here, come sit beside him,' Bastian ordered but my heart began to pound, those were the very same words that Papa had used when Mama was dying. Feeling more fearful, I obeyed and sat myself down. As I looked down on Papa's weakened and frail frame, I was reminded so vividly of that terrible day when Mama had died. It begged, internally, for this not to be another day like that!

'Oh, Papa,' I whispered. I lifted the fingers of his good hand and was shocked to feel his squeeze. I glanced down to see him looking up at me, his eyes shining.

'Maddi…' he managed, an odd, strangled word. Even as he spoke, I felt Bastian leave so that I was alone with him.

'Papa, hush, don't try to talk!' I whispered.

He obeyed and fell back to silence and so for close on an hour, we simply sat still. Me holding his hand and him grasping me with all the strength he had left. Finally, the echo of the door came and then I heard Nora's voice behind me.

'My darling, oh – Dr Chilcott, oh, don't you look poorly but never fear dear thing, I have brought Dr Langdon to see you, he'll see you right!'

Dr Langdon was filled in on what had happened by Bastian whilst I sat next to Papa's bed feeling a little lost. Once fully up to date, he came and put a gentle hand on my shoulder.

'Could I have a moment alone with Papa?' he said, 'I might need to remove his shirt and such.'

I nodded silently and stood up. Nora's arm came about me and I felt her fingers caress my arm as she led me from the room. Tiredly, I walked to my own old bedchamber, I wanted to be close by if I was needed and the stairs seemed unsurmountable. For a moment, Nora paused at the door, and then murmured that she would go and see about making sure all of our servants knew what was going on.

'Indeed,' Bastian agreed, sitting down at my dressing table and touching the old white lace cloth where once my clutter of skin lotions had stood, 'You do that, I'll stay with Maddi. Can you go and update Mama too?'

'Of course. Be strong my loves, he will be well!'

I sat on the edge of my bed, biting my bottom lip to stop it from trembling. My husband watched me and then shuffled over to sit at my side and take my hand. 'My darling, can I get you anything?' he asked. 'A glass of water or…'

'Brandy, please. Papa's decanter is in the library.'

Bastian nodded and was gone, returning moments later with a heavy glass of the burning liquid. I took a few sips and then set it down on my dresser. Bastian sat beside me on the bed and put his hand in mine somewhat tentatively.

'Is Papa dying in there?'

Bastian did not comfort me with lies. 'I honestly don't know sweetheart. He's comfortable though and in good hands!'

I nodded, still in that strange trance. In a daze, I reached out my trembling hand for my brandy glass and Bastian handed it to me. We were both silent, both on edge, waiting. It seemed like an eternity before I heard the sound of the latch on Papa's door and then the creak of the door opening. I was on my feet.

'Papa is awake now,' Dr Langton said to me. 'You should go and speak to him, he's asking for you. I will wait out here until you are ready.'

'Thank you, Doctor,' Bastian nodded, urging me from my chamber and into Papa's.

Papa was lying still with his eyes closed. I was unsure of how to proceed – the doctor had said he was awake but he did not seem so. For a moment, Bastian stood by my side, he also unsure as to what to do, then he kissed the top of my head and turned towards the door. 'I am going to speak to the doctor,' he said. 'I want to know exactly what we're facing here. Do you want to come?'

I shook my head, my eyes were brimming with tears and I knew that if I was forced to listen to the doctor's prognosis I would break down. Instead, I took Papa's hand and sat down beside him again. Bastian nodded and then left the room, telling me to call if I needed him. I listened closely for the voices in the hallway but I couldn't hear them, either they spoke too quietly or they had retreated from outside the door. Once more I looked down at Papa and saw he was smiling at me at best he could, his old blue eyes open.

'Papa,' I said, squeezing his hand. 'Oh Papa, I did not know you were awake, you were so quiet there.' I wiped my eyes lest he saw the tears and smiled the brightest smile I could muster.

'Maddi,' he managed again, 'I fear I'm... I'm not doing very well.'

'You will be well,' I whispered.

'Are you... happy?'

'I am, but hush, no farewells, you will be well! I promise!'

He managed that odd half-smile again and pressed my hand with his as best he could. I ran a hand through his white hair, much like mine in softness.

Bastian came to the door then, and beckoned me. I kissed Papa's hand and moved to my husband.

'Dr Langton says he is very poorly. I suggest we stay here for the time being to remain close, should anything happen...'

I nodded, that way I would be able to nurse him too, something I needed desperately to do. We were interrupted though, by the doctor's white face showing at the door,

'Mrs Carfax, I'm afraid your father is failing despite my best efforts. Did you want to come back in?'

'F-failing?' I whispered, and then felt my husband's hand clamp about mine.

'Come,' he said. 'Let us stay close!'

And so there it was, just like Mama before him, in the very same room and almost as abruptly, I had arrived in time to see my Papa's final hour. He died not long there-after, his old hand in mine and his body seeming so fragile and ancient suddenly.

Eighteen

The two years after Papa's death brought with them a time of great transition. I settled in easily to being a wife to Bastian and to the running of Fiveham with Lady Carfax. My cousin Simon came down from London to take over the practice, fast becoming almost as trusted a doctor to the village as Papa had been. I suppose the family tie helped to win over the trust of the locals more than anything else could. When, a year and a half or so after my marriage, I finally expelled the doubts about my fertility after the traumatic birth of Lloyd and once more fell with child, it was my fair and handsome young cousin who tended me, who gave me my check-ups and who reassured me that all would be well – and so it was.

Evelyn was born then, not long after my own birthday, in the heat of one of the hottest summers I have known, and which closed my second year of marriage. A tiny bonny thing who was born just a fraction late. Bastian paced back and forth outside of the chamber all day, or so I was told, as I endured a twelve-hour labour to bring her into the world. But come she did, and in good health too with a hearty cry! Once she was brought into the world and I was assured that yes, she was healthy indeed, with a good set of lungs on her, I gave her over to her father – the proud bee that he was – and submitted to a good ten-hour sleep.

It wasn't until the following day, then, that I submitted to allow other members of the family into the room to meet the newest member. At once upon my allowance the door flew open and there was Nora! She all but ran to the bed to climb up on the bottom of it like a child, there she sat with her legs crossed and held out her arms. Bastian laughed aloud at his sister's eagerness and acted as courier to pass the baby from me to his sister.

'Oh! Would you just look at her!' she exclaimed, 'Oh Bas, Maddi! She's so perfect, so perfectly perfect – she looks like you Bas!'

'She does,' he whispered, 'Poor mite…'

'No! None of that! She is perfection and we shall teach her just as Mama taught us that the colour of her skin does not make her any less perfect!'

'We shall!' I said, firm.

The door opened again, then, much more demurely, and Bastian's mother entered. Lady Carfax smiled as she saw the scene before her and then pulled up the dresser chair to the bed. Her eyes rested almost hungrily on the baby and, perhaps seeing it too, Nora passed my daughter to her grandmother. Lady Carfax sat herself down on the chair, the tiny gurgling bundle of blankets and lace in her arms. She cooed at the baby a moment, talking in babble to her, then looked over at us. Bastian had moved back to the position of being half behind me so that I rested on him as well as the pillows, his arm about me, and Nora sat like a child on the end of the bed. Suddenly I was overwhelmed by a sense of something I had never had: family. Lady Carfax ran an eye over us all, then looked down again at the baby.

'Does she have a name?'

'Not yet,' I said, 'but I was thinking Evie?'

'After Grandmother?' Nora said at once.

'Yes. I only met your grandmother once, but she had a profound influence on me. I…' I glanced up at Bastian, 'I'd not yet brought it up, though!'

'It's perfect,' he said, 'Evie it is! Evelyn Henrietta Carfax?'

Of course, he would want to acknowledge his true father, Henri Lloyd. Didn't he always? I nodded, though, I minded it not.

'Hello Evie, welcome to the family,' Lady Carfax whispered, 'And aren't you just a spit of your Papa when he was your age!' she looked up at us and a strange small smile brushed her lips, 'I remember how beautiful you both were when you were born,' she added, 'even if my heart did drop to see the deep hue of your skin, how you both sported that fine black hair. Not because it was any less beautiful, but because I knew then how difficult your lives could be, in the wrong circumstances.'

'I suppose then everybody knew too, that we were not *his…?*' Bastian said. Lady Carfax looked down again at my baby, booping her little nose with one finger.

'Indeed.'

'Quite a surprise, I suppose,' Nora laughed.

'I suppose, yes, that too, although it was no surprise to me. With Bastian, I was with child before Carfax ever laid a finger on me and by the time Nora came along, intimacies of such a nature were so sparce between Carfax and I that I knew the timing was wrong. Besides, I don't think he is capable of fathering a child. Never in the years since we left have I even suspected a child.'

'Tell me a little of my real father?' Bastian asked, 'you are so closed about it all and Nora and I know so little of him.'

'It was safter to be that way. Your father – by that I mean Carfax – liked not to be reminded of it all. Henri was… is, I suppose, a decent man, a good man. He had a heart which loved unconditionally. On the island, he was well respected for his kindness, his generosity. There is a terrible prejudice there, as much as there is here really, but somehow he managed to circumvent both worlds. I adored him completely.'

'Why did you not marry him, then?' Bastian asked.

'My father, mainly. He was a captain in the Royal Navy, and he'd taken me to be stationed with him on the islands as he knew he was going to be there for some time. My father was... he suffered an affliction of melancholia just like his grandson does,' he nodded to Bastian but there was no unkindness in her words, 'at least when I was with him, he was brighter and softer. My own mother died in childbirth so ever it was just the two of us. I loved my father and I have already told you, Maddi, of how we lost him and how difficult that was, but he was not without fault. I think though years as a Navy man, he was somewhat intolerant of the natives, of any way of life that was not entirely British. He tolerated Henri as a local businessman, but when he realised we'd grown close – I just a girl still of seventeen or eighteen then too – he was furious. He threatened to have Henri whipped in the streets like the... like the beast he said he was.'

'How awful,' I murmured but Lady Carfax simply bumped little Evie on her knee and murmured to her again. Then she glanced back at me. 'Like you Maddi, I found myself in a predicament. Henri and I... we made our plans, but my father discovered us, discovered my condition and so he married me at once to one of his friends. Carfax had all but grown up on the island,' her eyes turned to Bastian and Nora, 'the Barony was not his birth-right and only came to him by a series of unfortunate deaths, it was in fact bestowed at first to his brother and it was only by chance it came to him. The rest of the family had their money tied into sugar and slaves – this you know already I suppose. The timing worked out, then, that just as I was in need of a husband, word was spreading that Carfax was to inherit the barony. My father was swift in his arrangements and I did not argue, I knew that Carfax was likely to remain on the islands for longer than my father and so there was more chance of staying closer to Henri for longer.'

'I suppose you knew not what he was, then, when you married him?' Nora asked.

'Of course not! If I had known his nature, how he beat and mutilated his slaves… he has no more sympathy for his fellow man than a wasp does! When he told me that we had to flee the islands and come home, it was the very worst day of my life.' She broke off suddenly and smiled at us, 'Hark at me dwelling in the past though,' she said, 'when I have the future of this family in my arms.'

'It is good to know your story though,' I said, 'that one day we might pass it on to her too.'

'Indeed, I suppose it so.'

Bastian shuffled sitting up a little more so to support me as Lady Carfax handed me back my child. He straightened the lace of the baby's coverlet, but then looked back to his mother.

'Do you know where Father is?' he asked, 'Why he left?'

'Of that, you have as much an idea as I do,' she sighed. 'He has not withdrawn our finances, but he has left no word of himself either. I presume he had something to do with what happened to Alice, though, and is in hiding. He's not in the Caribbean, as far as I can ascertain and so goodness knows. The further he stays from us though, the better.'

'I agree,' I whispered.

With this in mind though, once I was recovered enough to leave my bed and sit at my desk, I penned a letter to Monroe, asking him for any updates on his investigations. In return he sent me an address in the Caribbean.

"This is your husband's family", he had written, "You or he might want to make contact."

I stared in shock, my hand shaking. I'd never even thought of it but suddenly that seemed a strange deviation. I wondered if Bastian knew this address, if he'd sat and pondered writing to his real father – he certainly admired the memory of him well enough! I glanced over to where he sat across the room, our daughter in his arms. He'd been too enraptured by her to pay too much mind to what I was doing. I liked not to conceal anything from him but I also knew that if we were to write and they did not respond he'd be heart-broken all over again. I folded the letter and sat back in my chair to watch my husband play with our daughter. She was still so very tiny, perfection incarnate! Her little eyes had just started to focus properly and her little gargles were more emotive than her shrill. Of course, she was but a week and a half old and so all that could have been my fancy. Bastian looked up as I watched him and smiled.

'I know she should go to the nurse,' he said, apologetic, 'I just can't seem to bear to put her down!'

'Here. Pass her to me,' I commanded, smiling, 'you have business to attend!'

'She is my business!'

I chuckled, 'I doubt your tenants would agree, Bas…'

He smiled indulgently, then kissed his daughter's head and brought her to me. I took the gurgling bundle of lace and wool from him and then happily accepted his kiss to my brow.

'Go,' I whispered, 'We'll still be here when you return!'

Once Bastian was gone I spent a half hour or so tending my daughter, and then handed her over to the young lass we'd hired to help care for her, Olive. With this done, I went back to the letter. I wet my lips, pondered about a moment longer, and then dipped my pen.

In the end I did not write very much, I simply stated my name and who I was, explained that Mr Lloyd now had a biological granddaughter, and asked if they would be open to correspondence from us. I paused, and then added that I hoped they minded not that Monroe had given me their details, and that I was saddened at the rift between us, especially due to how much my husband seemed to revere his biological father in the few memories he had of him.

In reply, I received not just a letter, but a package from the Caribbean. I managed to secret it from Bastian into my little corner of the study and then, when Bastian was out in the village on estate business, I sat and opened it up. There was a letter, and with it a bundle of the newspapers. These were sent in their entirety, and the first two were yellowed with age. I checked the dates, the first two were dated 1840 and the newer one for 1846. They were all of the same press, *The Argus*. I looked over these again but then picked up the letter and broke the unfamiliar seal on the envelope.

To my dearest Niece by Law,
(It began)
Mrs Carfax, what a wonder to hear from you after all these years. I think the family had rather given up on the very idea of any communication from my poor brother's lost children. I am in your debt for your letter and I would ask you, with true gratitude, to yes please give our details over to your husband and his sister that they might write to me too, and to their grandparents. I am afraid though, to bear the saddest tidings, for your plan to reunite the children to their father is undone. My brother died, you see, many years ago. The newspapers I have included will give you the most of the tale for it saddens us much to think upon it, but I issue you now a warning that if the man named Carfax lives still, and is of your household, then you live with a murderer, for it was he who hastened my brother's departure from this world and sent him back to God in heaven. Perhaps too bright a soul for this world was he, for he was so very good, but that is not of a mind to soothe my parents in their early loss of him from their lives.

    Poor Henri! He vanished, you see, in the night and for five or more years he was gone until a body was found and identified as him, sunk into a cave in the cliffs. I blame Carfax, for it is true that Henri vanished the very night that Carfax and his wife fled with our babies. We can offer no proof but the timing, and yet surely this could not be coincidence? I will let you read the grim details for yourself.

    I have spoken upon receipt of your letter to my own parents, and they beg that young Bastian write to them. He was barely thirteen years old when they saw him last but still he is remembered fondly by them. Little Nora too, so often described as a cherub of a child. My mother, now aged and infirm, has a great desire to lay her eyes upon them both just one more time in her life, and thereby claim them by name, just the once, as her grandchildren – for she never was able before. I too would give much to be able to finally whisper in truth to my family of the bond we share, revelations once firmly forbidden.

Once more, I thank you from the very bottom of my heart for your letter, and I look forward to further correspondence. Yours with affection

Maria Lloyd

I read and reread this letter several times, then folded it up and sat back in my chair with the papers. The newspaper articles did not give much more detail. The first outlined the night that he vanished, stating but not connecting the sudden removal of the Carfax family the same night. Lloyd had gone out, it stated, close on eight in the evening and had never come home. The second newspaper spoke of how he was still missing, giving some ponderance to his location. Carfax and family were not mentioned at all. The final paper, the newer one, spoke of a body having been found a week previous, dead in a cave on the shore, and reduced to ought but a skeleton by the salt. The opening of the cave was above, rather than one that could be walked into, and it was surmised that there he had fallen, although none could give any reason why he might have been down on the beach either way. He'd been identified by his possessions and clothing due to quick decomposition out in the wilds there, with the salt water lapping about him and the crabs nibbling away his flesh. I folded the papers carefully and laid them down, pondering how to proceed. Lord Carfax was now doubly a murderer in my mind, and the not knowing of his location was even more troubling with this new revelation. I should tell Bastian, I knew that, and maybe Reginald too, he'd be eager to hear from me.

Thus decided, I put the papers into my drawer and turned the key. It wasn't often I had much to hide, but this I wanted to mull and then to handle in my own way, before too much came to light of it. I quickly wrote first to Monroe and with that done, I folded the letter and stamped it with the Carfax seal. I wanted not to simply drop it into the post basket though, and so I decided to take the trek myself. Nora was in the conservatory as I slipped past with my bonnet in hand and my letter in my pocket.

'You might want to come and see this,' she said.

I went at once to the window and there raised an eyebrow, there was a pillar of smoke rising up from beyond the far side of the village, just viewable around the coast.

'What do you suppose that is?'

'I have no idea!'

We watched for a few more moments, horror-struck as the smoke seemed to spread rapidly.

'Upstairs,' Nora said, 'We'll be able to see better!'

And so we piled up and looked out to a fiendish hellscape! The moors were alight! For what looked like miles upon miles from our vantage point.

'Oh dear God!' Nora exclaimed. 'The moors are alight!'

'A gorse fire for sure,' I agreed, tight-lipped and grim.

Gorse fires – where the dry brittle plants went up in a pillar of smoke – are rare indeed in our little corner of the country. Indeed the foliage itself generally makes it too damp an environment but then it had been an incredibly warm few weeks!

'So it would seem. We need to get to the village! Where is Mama?'

'I don't know, I think she went out earlier. Bastian?'

'He went into the village earlier, he had to speak to some tenants about repairs!'

'Come, then, let us go and see if we can be of use!'

I agreed and ran to kiss my baby and to give Olive an instruction to feed her if need be – a wet nurse is a useful thing to have in such a situation! – and then headed out with Nora.

Down in the village there was already chaos! Mama Carfax was ordering the villagers about, her packages of shopping waylaid at the door of my father's old house. She was the one most in charge, and was arranging the vats of water for drinking – the stream would do to feed the bucket chain – whilst seemingly to simultaneously have most of the girls of the village rushing about making tea for the men who were working on fighting the fire.

'Where is Bas?' I gasped, embracing her quickly.

'In the thick of it, of course!'

Well yes, of course he would be! I strained my eyes to see him but I could not.

'Surely it is too dangerous?'

'No – it's just smoke here and he is well covered about his mouth – more dangerous to allow it to come in and touch the village!

'Can we go? Help?'

'It's too dangerous for us womenfolk,' she said with a shake of her head, 'He comes back intermittently but us women are forbidden until the flames are closer to tame!'

Unable to be useful in my panic, I took to pacing until I caught a glimpse of my love coming out of the smoke.

'Maddi!' he gasped. His eyes were red-raw and he was covered from head to toe in soot, his clothing I already knew was ruined as was the thick scarf over his lips.

'What can I do?' I gasped.

'Just for now, help Mama,' he said, taking the scarf off and coughing, then wetting it in the bucket. 'I need to get back – don't be afraid, there are no flames here now, just smoke! We are wetting and pulling up the gorse here around the edge of the village – further back it will likely burn for days but here is safe!'

I nodded, 'be careful in there my love!'

'I promise! We have a rope between us so nobody is lost in the smoke – it's clearing now!'

With that he paused to take a beaker of water from the barrel, glugging it down, and then gave me his cheeky smile and pulled the wet scarf back up over his face.

Nineteen

The fire burned for three days straight and blacked miles upon miles of gorse right down as far as the coast. It had, I was to find, had started near the cottage which Bastian and I had once used to shelter from a storm. It had caught quickly and had begun to spread into the surrounding trees before one of the farmers had heard the crackling around his house and had run to the village for help. Bastian was riding out to the church to speak with the curate about something, when the panicked man had approached him.

After the worst of it was out, Bastian gave leave for Nora and I to join in the dampening effort, lugging pails of water from the stream about a mile south of the last of the blaze and wetting the earth there in case the fire started back up. I was terrified. I have always been a little afraid of being caught in a fire and was frightened that the wind would rekindle it, push it towards us. Eventually though, the panic died away and the work became more monotonous.

On the morning of the third day, Nora and I were allowed further in again, and made our way to where Bastian was exploring the damage to what I considered our cottage. It was burnt right out, the roof half-caved in and the whole place stained with soot. Some of the men were doing a circuit of the old building, pulling up any undergrowth or weeds which were still hot to touch to try to stop the fire sparking up again. It wasn't so much the old, abandoned cottage that was a worry, but the vegetation about it. As the flames had been extinguished though, the morale of the people fighting them had turned to cheer. There would be celebrations about the village far into the week, I surmised.

I looked over to see Bastian giving out some orders. He was covered in soot again, from head to toe, and his hair was sticking up at all angles despite that I'd forced him into a bath the night before and the one before that! I bit back a smile – we'd all be smelling the stink of the fire for days to come yet, I surmised. Nora didn't look much better and I bemoaned the state of her once pretty purple woollen skirts and jacket. A glance to myself showed me I was not much better. Before I could speak though, Bastian approached us.

'This is the last job now and then we're calling this a success. There is still fire further out but it's low and almost gone completely. I've volunteered to go inside the cottage and make sure the fire there is completely out. It's safe though, you have my word! Most of the thatch is already fallen inside so as long as I have a care…'

'Oh, do be careful Bas!' Nora said, her eyes widening.

'I promise, but we have to ensure everything is fully soaked and not likely to flare back up.'

'If you think it safe, I trust you,' I said, 'but do go in with caution.'

Bastian stepped forward and cupped my cheek in his hand, his eyes met mine and then he pressed his lips to mine, 'I will be very much on alert,' he promised, 'I have you and our beautiful daughter to think of now, five minutes, and then we can go home!'

I nodded and let him go. The men milled about and I joined them as Bastian took up another bucket and then wrapped his cravat up over his nose again – a sight I had become used to in the days preceding.

'Have a care, milord, for the thatch on the floor,' Jonas Grover – one of the local fishermen – spoke up, 'It's the most like to be cradling flames beneath!

'Noted,' Bastian said, then called out, 'Simon, can I have you close, just in case?'

My cousin moved closer at once but the very idea that he – a doctor – might be needed troubled me more so. My gut contracted. Simon patted my arm as he passed me, perhaps seeing my strain. Simon looked a little like Papa about the face. He was taller than me, very thin and had fair floppy hair. At one and thirty he was late to be married but seemed in no hurry to make that bond, seeming more content to simply settle as a young village doctor in Papa's old house which he rented from Bastian and I. He patted me gently, but then moved to the door.

I followed.

I could barely stand it and already I could feel the heat resonating. Somebody passed me a bucket and I took it, ready to pass into Bastian as I heard the splash of his own spilling. Simon took the bucket from me and passed out the empty, ready to be filled at the stream. I passed it back and then took hold of the next. At least the cottage was small, I told myself, at least it would only take minutes to explore. Bastian seemed to pause within though, another splash and then once more the buckets were exchanged. I glanced over at Nora who was in turn looking up at the roof of the cottage. If any more of it fell in then Bastian risked injury, we both knew that. Then I heard Bastian's voice:

'What the devil?'

'What, what is it?' I asked, trying to push in but I suppose Simon had picked up on the urgency in Bastian's voice and held me back.

'I...' a silence and then, 'Oh... God!'

'What?' Nora was behind me too now, pushing forward so that Simon and I were nearly pushed inside. Inside, Bastian was knelt looking at something on the ground in amongst the smoke, his head shot up to the door and for a moment all I could see of him was shock, worry.

'What is it?' I demanded again.

'Maddi, Nora, go back outside please!' he said, his voice very calm, 'now…'

I was reluctant but Nora pulled me back, obedient.

'Simon, I know it is dangerous, but can I borrow you, my man?' Bastian said, his voice still very tight, 'There appears to be a body under this broken beam!'

The world reeled. Nothing seemed to be right or true and my ears rang with tinnitus as Simon and Bastian worked quickly to remove the body from the ruins. I sat with pressed lips on the old stump without, my hands shaking with fear not just of what had been found – we knew not yet who it was – but also for the prolonged time Bastian now had to be within. At last though, they managed to pull the body from the smouldering thatch and beam and set it onto the floor.

'Should we not leave it for the coroner?' Nora asked, as Simon collected a blanket from the pile to wrap the body and bring it out. Bastian too emerged, he was slick with sweat, filthy and his features looked pinched.

'The risk that the fire will restart is too high,' he said, 'Maddi, Nora, a word please?'

I stood on shaking legs and joined Bastian and Simon by the door. Some of the locals seemed keen to listen in but for the most part we ignored them.

'Nora,' Bastian said, 'Put a hand to Maddi, there, good. Now, I have to tell you something very shocking.'

Nora nodded, steeling herself.

'Good, Maddi too, this will be a shock, are you prepared?'

I nodded too. Bastian pulled in a deep breath, there was a slight wheeze to his chest which worried me but that was pushed hard from my mind with his next words.

'The body is in quite a state of decay and has been damaged too for the fire so we cannot be sure but... but I think it might be Father – Baron Carfax.'

Nora let out a little squeak and staggered, I caught her and pulled her to me. Bastian swallowed again.

'I can't be sure,' he said, but then pulled something from his pocket to show it to us. It was badly burned and tarnished with soot but it was obvious at once what the item was. Baron Carfax had loved that watch, had worn it every day that I knew him.

'I... I will send for the constable,' I managed, then turned away and began to stagger towards the village, taking Nora with me.

Two constables arrived at the house just hours later. An inspector from Truro and a sergeant with whom Bastian had spoken the day before. I had been expecting them. By then, we'd brought the body home, wrapped in blankets in the cold parlour whilst we awaited the arrival of a coffin that was due any day. It was a grim houseguest indeed.

'How do you do?' I asked, greeting the man as he entered through the main entrance slightly out of puff for the walk up the slope. The sergeant seemed less so but then he was a younger man.

'Lady Carfax?' he asked but I shook my head, not quite realising that this *was* now my title.

'Just Mrs,' I said with a smile. 'Lady Carfax is my mother-in-law.'

The man smiled but his eyes were filled with something I could not name. 'Mrs Carfax. My name is Landre, this is my man Parker.'

'How do you do?'

'Good, thank you, and I am sorry for your family's loss.'

'Thank you. Can I help you?'

'Well, yes. It looks like there might be more to the events of today than we originally thought. I need to speak to your family. Could you gather them?'

'Of course,' I said but my voice wobbled as I led the detective into the house and rang the service bell.

'Gather the family. We will be in the parlour,' I said to the maid who nodded and then disappeared. As I led Landre and his man into the parlour, they made no effort to make idle chitchat and again my gut clenched.

Once everyone was gathered, Nora looking curious, her Mama tired and my husband grave, the officer spoke. 'Please steel yourselves, for I have serious news.'

Bastian and his Mama looked worriedly at each other, Nora and I linked hands.

'What is it?' Bastian said. 'Come man, out with it.'

'The body you found is showing signs of injury, likely put upon him prior to the fire,' he said, straight to the point.

'A… a murder with intent, then?' Nora asked.

'I – we – believe so, yes…'

Bastian nodded, then swallowed deeply and sat himself down in the chair opposite the inspector. His lips were pressed together and his hands shook, his father's watch between them as it had been several times since he'd found it. I suppose there were several explanations, the kindest being that Bastian was still processing that the man who had abused him for so long was dead, the worst, the thing I dreaded, that he held onto it of guilt, or to pretend a remorse he did not feel!

'So my father was murdered,' he said, 'You are certain? No inquests and the like, but straight to a murder investigation?'

'Oh! Oh my!' Lady Carfax said, fanning herself miserably, 'Not this again!'

'I'm afraid so, son. The coroner will hold a gathering but we are certain it is murder. My Lady, you know this must lead to the past being uncovered again. Are you sure there is nothing we need to know? Nothing we've not already been told?'

'No. There is nothing.' Bastian said, sharp.

Nora's gaze moved from one to the other as they spoke, shocked, I reached over to take her hand. She smiled a ghost of a smile at me for a second before her eyes glazed over again.

I turned to Bastian and there saw only steely determination on his features. It was obvious to everyone in the room that he feared an inquest more than he mourned the loss.

'I'll take Mama to bed,' Nora said. 'It's been a terrible shock.'

Lady Carfax nodded and stood, she seemed wobbly on her feet, distraught. Another odd reaction but then who was I, who had grown up in comfort and love, to judge those an abuser left in his wake?

'Is there anything else we need to know?' I asked when Lady Carfax and Nora were gone, the man looked apologetic.

'I simply cannot tell you. We will begin our investigations now. I will need to see the body before he is buried, as well as the coroner, and then you can go ahead and have your funeral.'

'Thank you, I think we all need the closure,' I said, 'I'll have somebody take you to the Baron's body now.'

Landre nodded and stood. 'I truly am sorry to be the bringer of such news,' he said. 'Take my card. If you have any need of me, I can be contacted at this address.'

Feeling more than a little fazed, I walked the inspector from the room, closed the door and turned to face my husband. If ever I had doubted his guilt, if ever I had convinced myself he was not capable, now I knew that those doubts were gone. I was strangely dazed, not wanting to flee and yet now convinced I had married a murderer, borne his child. Who else could it possibly be? Who else had such motive?

'Oh Bastian,' I whispered, terrified. 'What have you done?'

His face drained of all colour and as I watched, a tic developed in the corner of his left eye.

'You claim *I* have had something to do with this?'

I stayed at my position, hands folded behind my back as I leaned against the door. For a moment, I watched his expression dissolving into anguish at my words, his features looked so sincere but then he had already fooled me once before that he'd not harmed Alice either, and I was once again convinced that he had been a party to her death if not entirely responsible.

'Surely, yes.' I whispered, willing him not to tell me a lie.

He swallowed again, wetting his lips and seemingly trying to order his words. 'Maddi, I cannot believe that you would…' he paused and anger sparked on his normally so calm features. '…and I suppose I, with my insatiable appetite for killing, murdered Alice in cold blood too? Are we back to that?'

I did not reply but stood very still. He stared at me, his eyes widening even more.

'Oh God, that is what you are going to claim, isn't it?'

'What do you mean, claim?'

'When they question you?'

'What are you asking me?' I asked, 'why would they question me? Why do you think I'd say that even if I thought it?'

Bastian watched me with a careful gaze and then spoke words I'd not even in my wildest dreams expected to hear. 'To save yourself? Maddi, I know you killed Alice…'

I staggered in shock. There are no words, nothing. Blind shock. 'Because I... What?'

'You were seen, my love,' he whispered.

I shook my head, my breath tight in my chest,

'Seen?'

'Yes, seen! Up on the cliffs with Alice that night!'

'Whoever told you that, they lied! I was at home with Papa... drinking cocoa!'

'Maddi don't lie to me.' he murmured, 'I won't turn you in! Haven't I protected you this long?'

Stunned, I could not reply, choked with emotion which bubbled in my gut. I don't think ever, in my entire life, I have felt such confusion. With a sudden movement, I threw open the door and fled up the stairs to my chamber. I heard Bastian's voice calling me as I went but he did not follow. Upstairs, I threw myself down on the soft four poster bed that I shared with Bastian and tried to think. My hands grasped the soft pillows and I pulled them about me, making for myself a nest of sorts.

Darkness began to settle in about the house. I heard the sound of more footsteps at the stair and recognised them as Nora's delicate tread. I hoped she would just pass and go to bed, I was in no mood for her clear cut, emotionless common sense.

Predictably, I heard her knock at the door though. 'Maddi,' she called. 'Can we talk?'

'Not now, Nora, I am not in the right frame of mind for discussing this.'

I heard the rattle of the door handle but at least I had thought to lock the old door.

Nora sighed from outside. 'Have your way then, stubborn creature, I'm here if you need me,' and then I heard her footsteps retreating from the door, leaving me to return to my world of quiet contemplation.

As the darkness closed in further around me, I heard movement again and then 'Maddi, for God's sake!' It was Bastian's voice.

'Go away,' I replied, somewhat harshly.

The crash of the door flying open took me by surprise, a screaming crash of splinters as the old, half rotten frame gave in under the weight of my husband. I shrieked aloud, my heart pounding and I suppose for the first time in my life truly knowing fear. As Bastian strode towards me, I felt almost faint with trepidation and put my hands up to defend myself. His fingers were not rough though as he knelt beside me and took my hands in his own. Tenderly he moved my hands away and stroked the side of my face; his own a mask of sorrow and anguish. Looking straight into my sore tired eyes with his own red-rimmed and bloodshot ones he spoke.

'Maddi, I will not forsake you! I promise!'

'Bastian! Please!'

'Listen to me! I know you are afraid but I promise you I will hide your crime! Just tell me what happened so that I know what I am hiding this time!'

'I don't understand why you are saying these things!' I said, 'I didn't hurt Alice! And even if I did, I would never have left you to take the flack! Whoever said they saw me saw wrong... Unless this is your defence? To try to blame *me* for *your* crimes?'

'I have no crime! We both know I did not kill Alice! I am a good man,' he said, almost as though to himself. 'A good man Maddi, I have never willingly done wrong in my life. Why is it that everybody seems to think I am some monster who goes through life killing anybody who stands in my way?'

I felt the tears begin to fall. 'You know that I would stand by you through anything, Bastian,' I all but whispered.

'You speak as though I am already proven guilty of a crime you of all people know wasn't me! For God's sake! Tell me what happened! Trust me!'

'I do trust you!'

'No you don't!' he stated, suddenly angry. 'Not a whit!' He pulled away and the strain in his voice made me look at him sharply. 'You *never* have trusted me,' he continued, 'Never. You let me stand almost on trial for killing Alice and still you kept your leave! You kept me away for years, despite that you knew how you hurt me! You flirted with others, went up to London, God, you even considered marrying somebody else despite how I protected you! How I perjured myself to protect you! I love you, Maddi, but I'm starting to wonder how much you love me?'

'I love you infinitely,' I whispered.

'Do you?'

'You know I do...'

His eyes welled up again, his hands still holding my head, one on either side. 'Maybe that's... that's not enough?' he whispered. 'You say you love me and yet even still you hold your secrets to your chest even if it means I might be tried for murder. I'd protect you till the end of eternity but you won't do the same! You'd as soon throw me to the wolves. I never did anything to deserve this Maddi.'

'Who is it who told you the things?' I asked, 'who said that had seen me?'

'Does it matter?'

'Yes! Because you believe them over me!'

'Somebody I trust,' he said, 'Somebody who loves you too!'

'Nora?'

'No and I'll not have you drag her into this!' he said softly.

'Please Bas... I do not know what I am supposed to have done nor what you have done but together we can fight any charges they bring against you! Please stop this, you are... You are raving, you are beyond rational thought! Are you so far without reason that you would put your guilt into me? Your crimes?'

Bastian pulled away. He eyed me with all the anguish and pain I'd ever seen in those beautiful brown eyes. He thought me a murderer and I him. At that moment in time, I don't suppose either of us considered it might have been somebody else. Didn't we have the most motive? Still, I stood and tried to take his hand but it was his turn to throw me off.

'I'm going out,' he whispered, suddenly so pale. 'I won't be very long but I'm... I need to walk...'

'Bastian...'

But he was gone, leaving the shattered frame of the door hanging behind him.

I sat crying for what must have been nearly an hour. In the distance, I could hear my baby crying but I did not even have it in me to go and check on her. Nora came again to check on me, exclaiming about the door but I roared at her to be gone. She went, but not in anger, and with sympathy on her features. I wondered madly what she thought, if she believed Bastian guilty or indeed if she was the liar, filling his mind with these strange ideas about me but I had it not in me to call her back. I could not believe things had become so desolate. I felt numb and lifeless, unable even to find the strength to go looking for my husband, to comfort my daughter. My desperation was broken though, by the appearance of Lady Carfax in the now door-less frame.

'Maddi, come quickly!'

'What?' I asked, sniffing and wiping my eyes with my kerchief.

'It's Bastian…'

'Oh God!' I gasped, the panic reigniting. 'What has he done now?'

'I don't know for certain, but he's not in the house and just now whilst I was getting ready for bed I happened to glance out of the window and I thought… well I thought I saw a light up on the cliffs… near where… where they think Alice went in!'

'Oh! Oh God!'

'He was in something of a state when he left too!'

'He is delusional, I think,' I confused it, 'He is blaming these killings on *me*! He says I killed Alice but… but surely I think it must have been…' still I could not voice it, even to his Mama, '… somebody else…'

'Oh by the love of God, he's worse than I thought then!' she gasped, 'come on! We have to get him to Simon… perhaps an asylum is for the best but first we must apprehend him before he hurts himself or anybody else!'

I jumped to my feet. Lady Carfax looked as distressed as I did, she knew as well as I what depths her son's despair could take him down to.

'Oh God, let him be all right!' I gasped, pulling on my boots.

Lady Carfax and I walked the distance briskly and in silence, I was almost running but frightened to chance the crumbling cliff-edge too quickly. I prayed we were in time, in truth I felt as though I were walking to my destiny – I suppose in a way that was true. I knew that for Bastian to be safe we had to get to him quickly, he would not falter any more at the top of the cliff than he had when he put the bottle to his lips so many years earlier and I guessed Lady Carfax realised the same. I had no illusions, we were on route to save my husband's life – and we were probably too late. As we approached the cliff we were forced to walk single-file due to the narrowness of the path.

'Come, I know a shortcut,' she said, 'It leads down to the beach eventually. He went there too, before!'

I nodded, then opened up my lungs to call for my husband.

'Shush! Don't!'

'What? Why not?'

'If he is suicidal again, the sound of your voice might hurry him on with it!'

'Oh... oh God, I didn't even think...' I whispered.

'Here, follow me, be quiet so we don't startle him into anything rash!'

'Where are we going?' I asked, stumbling a little on the unfamiliar path and by then perilously close to the edge of the cliff face.

'Just trust me,' Lady Carfax said, 'I used to play down here as a girl and I suspect Bastian and Nora did too. It's a bit rocky but it's definitely a shortcut!'

'Hardly a shortcut when one has to slow this much to keep their footing,' I grumbled, but then stopped dead. Just before me, the path simply dropped away. If once it had been a shortcut, it wasn't any more. The path was about three foot wide, with a sheer drop on one side, and the built up cliff on the other. The drop before me was at least 50 foot, maybe slightly more as we were on the curve where the cliffs raised up again after the drop close to Fiveham. Essentially, I was stood on a three foot square of crumbly rock with no way to go aside from back. At first though, I still didn't see the danger.

'Oh, it drops off here!' I murmured, turning, 'We'll have to go the other way!'

Lady Carfax stood blocking the path, she was looking out over the ocean with a wistful expression on her features.

'It's so calm here, isn't it?' she said.

'I… yes, but now is not really the time for…'

'It seems such a shame, really,' she interrupted.

'I don't understand. Where is Bastian?'

'Oh, I'm sure he's off somewhere walking and sulking and trying to come to terms with knowing his wife is a murderer and does not even trust him enough to confess it – that's right, isn't it? That's what he said?'

'W-what? …Mother, let us go back up?'

'Of course still love him though, isn't that how the best of tragedy works? Your letter, when he arrives home, will show him beyond a doubt that you would have done anything for him.'

'I… what? I didn't leave a letter!'

'Oh, but you did! A letter in which you outline it all – your hatred of Alice in your youth, how she pushed you down and you lost your baby, your need to have Bastian at any cost. *Any* cost! And then when his father tried to intervene, having suspected you, how he too was suddenly in your path, but how you lured him away to your special place – that cottage on the moors where baby Lloyd was conceived. How you hit him over the head with a metal rod you had stashed there… It was what he deserved, for years of abuse and violence towards your husband, you see…'

Suddenly the drop behind me was dizzying, the ledge seemed smaller.

'And… and why would I… I pen such a horrendous letter?'

'I'm sure you wouldn't,' she smiled, 'and yet, it exists. Your confession.'

'Bastian will know my handwriting!'

'Will he, in his grief at finding you gone?'

My heart sped up and my vison seemed suddenly very clear, my hands a little shaky.

'It was you…' I suddenly realised. 'You who said you'd seen me? You planned this?'

'I needed to plant a seed, just in case of this eventuality – even then it seemed sensible to pass the blame on to you. I knew my son would protect you so I did what I had to and told him that I had seen you that night on the cliffs with Alice. It was I who told Bastian to lie at the inquest.'

'Why are you… why have you…'

'With reluctance. I do care deeply for you my dear but as I see it, there are but four suspects in this: myself, my children, or you. As fond as I am of you, it's an easy decision. Anything you say now, anything else that you know, is a danger to me, to us. Your death, along with your confession, will free us all.'

'Because you killed your husband?' suddenly it clicked into place, 'and because *you* killed Alice?'

'Oh yes, and Henri before them, but I am sure you'd have realised that too, had I left you alone to think long enough.

'But… but why?'

Her eyes ran over me, bright even in the darkness. She sighed. 'Henri because he meddled in things he should not have, financial troubles. He would have ruined us completely,' she said, 'he tried to stop us from leaving and cause trouble because he was angry that I chose to stay with my husband. He even threatened to take the children... And then Alice because Bastian was so very miserable and I knew that he deserved better. Edward – the Baron – I killed because he threatened to speak out against me when Alice died – you see he knew about Henri, so it was all much of a tangle.'

'I knew nothing of any of this,' I said, well, it was almost the truth!

'I know you've been corresponding with the Lloyd family, spying on us for Monroe too. I know how close you are to the truth but you are too foolish to put the pieces together. If you told these things to that detective, however…'

'Nobody is going to believe this fable you have orchestrated against me!'

'Oh, they will.'

I shook my head, trembling, 'No! Nobody will believe I could have killed Baron Carfax even if they believe I could have killed Alice! Even physically, he is – was – a big man and I was barely past girlhood. If you… if you don't come clean, the blame will fall on Bastian, no matter what you do to me!'

She shook her head. 'What proof? What proof is there that he did anything at all? We will have your full confession, and he will of course testify that your previous alibi for her death was false: that lie not selfless to protect him, but to protect yourself!'

A tear spilled, 'you know they won't accept that. He was almost arrested when you… when Alice… Nobody could ever think… '

'Even my son, who loves you so dearly believed it,' she shrugged, 'it's not so very difficult to plant these seeds, if the truth be told!'

I trembled, the realisation painful in my gut, but I wasn't done yet, despite how she'd stepped forward, starting to walk me right up to the edge, I put a hand on the crumbling cliff beside me, and changed my tactic.

'Bas-Bastian won't survive this,' I whispered, 'He loves me so much! If you are correct and he believes me a killer then that just proves the depth of his love! Just .. just what happened on his wedding night to Alice… you might save his being arrested but you risk his sanity!'

'He has his daughter to care for now, she will be his comfort in the pain, his reason to go on.'

'He's not strong! He…' I paused, was that footsteps? Thank God! 'He is… he will crumble, he is already starting to crumble, tonight!'

Lady Carfax opened up her lips to speak but then, blessed miracle, I heard my husband calling my name.

'Maddi? Maddi! Please! Answer me!'

Bastian's voice echoing out in the night was strained beyond belief. The sound came from towards Fiveham, and so I guessed he'd got home already and read the letter – not out on the beach after-all as we'd suspected! I did not dare respond, the moment was too tense. He was somewhere above though and I hoped he'd at least hear our voices, come and investigate.

Lady Carfax stepped forward another step, only her eyes showing that she'd heard Bastian's call, brighter and more panicked than they had been.

'Alice would have drowned,' she stated, her voice quieter. 'If I'd just thrown her in, the coroner said that – her lungs would have filled with water as her skirts dragged her under, that's why they ruled that she died before she went in – I put the bottle to her lips myself to ensure she was dead! Death by drowning must be painful and terrifying… I did not wish that kind of death upon even her and especially not you Maddi…'

'Please no,' I whispered, my bladder felt like it was relaxing in my terror, my heart so loud I could hear it above the whisper of the waves.

'However, it would seem I am out of time…' she concluded, 'I truly am sorry for this Maddi.'

'Please, don't!' and then I could not help myself, I screamed out 'Bastian! Bastian help me!'

'Maddi!' he cried again, 'Maddi! Where are you?'

I could hear that he was at least close from the sound of his voice. I wondered if I could knock Lady Carfax down whilst she was distracted and decided it was probably my best chance at survival to try. I was on the verge of making a lunge for her when I saw Bastian's frame appear at the top of the path, running towards me, towards us.

'No!' Lady Carfax cried out as her son appeared. I screamed as she leapt forward and then time slowed. Lady Carfax turned to me in a frenzy and before I even realised what she intended I felt both of her hands hit me squarely in my chest.

Twenty

I stood for a moment trying to catch my balance as I swayed. I saw Bastian's face fall into a mask of horror as he tried to run to me but Lady Carfax turned and fled up the path as I fell, knocking her son to one side, and almost toppling him too. It didn't seem real at all, the moment drawn out and long as I let a scream bubble, felt the sea reach out for me. Bastian screamed my name, his hands coming out to catch me but too far, too far even to touch fingertips. My scrabbling fingers grasped a root which was sticking out of the cliff beside me but it came away in my hand. I screamed again and tried to grab at the ragged edge which was now somehow above me but I was far too late to grasp it. My heart pounded as it realised the truth - I was falling. I heard Bastian scream my name again as I went down, then nothing but the roar of the waves.

Eternity beckoned me as I was dragged below the water, the blackness of oblivion but then I felt the pain of my body smashing into the violent waves, the jutting rocks. My stomach hit a sharp spike and I roared in pain, then a wave took me and crashed my form into the rocks of the cliff-face, crunching my back, hitting my head violently. The sea water was sharp salt, spilling into my lips as I coughed and choked on it. I even swallowed a piece of seaweed, or something similar. I went under again quickly, my arms flailing around to try to get myself back up to the surface. I gasped in another mouthful of foul-tasting salt water but suddenly I was back up to the surface of the waves. The pain was immense, I reached my hand around and found that the back of my head was bleeding.

Up above, not the worst distance but enough that already I knew it was unclimbable, I heard my husband's screams. His anger and pain roared even over the rush of the waves. I was already fumbling, trying to get out of my skirts which seemed to suck to my legs, adding weight to pull me down. The waters lapped, a frenzied caress, but in those first instants I was more shocked than anything, not just that she'd pushed me, but shocked to be alive too. Shocked that the rocks beneath the waves had not broken me into pieces. I suppose despite that it had riled the waves to fury, the storm was somewhat in my favour as it meant the sea was higher, more to cushion before the sharp and jagged rocks.

There was a brief respite, but then the wind moaned a long growl and then suddenly the tide was ferocious again. I gripped for a rock but my hand slipped as I was thrown around like a ragdoll for a few moments. My heavy skirts were dragging me down still but I forced my freezing fingers to work, to keep me above water, trying to remember swimming techniques that I had learned as a girl. With a sudden burst of energy, I tore open the clasp of my skirts and wriggled out of the heavy petticoats, watching them float away. Somewhat lighter attired, I felt I could swim a little but still my dress was heavy and I was tiring quickly, the pain in my head causing my whole body to throb as the salt water caressed the wound. I put my hand up to my head again and cried out in shock to see the amount of blood I was spilling.

Then I heard it – the splash of somebody else hitting the water. Bastian! The fool had leapt in after me. I tried to call for him, trying to find him. Then I saw the patch of red and my gut clenched. So much blood. God! Surely he must have hit a rock? Cracked his skull?

Then I saw his body rise back up, his eyes were open! Conscious! I screamed for him and he seemed to shake the daze just as I had, swimming as best he could with one arm – he must have injured the other!

'Bastian…!'

'Maddi,' he gasped, one strong arm coming to grasp me, the other hanging limply at his side. I felt stronger just for him being there, together we could encourage each other to get back to shore.

'Are you hurt?'

'My head,' I moaned, clinging to him. 'It's bleeding! Your arm?'

'Hurt!' he managed through the swirling waters. A wave tried to take us but Bastian kicked against a rock, steadying us. I wanted to sob on his shoulder, feeling a bout of nausea start up in my stomach, but a particularly vicious wave caught me and tore me from his hands again. I screamed as I was tossed into a sharp rock, pain flooding my back where I was struck again.

'Maddi!' Bastian's voice was bordering on panic but I was winded and the waves were dragging me down. Then I felt his hand on my arm again, pulling me back up. I clung to him frantically, terrified that I'd be lost, or that I would lose him, and heard his hiss of pain as I grabbed at his injured arm. I released him at once and was dragged away again. I began to make little cries of panic, terror for the idea that there was a good chance I might never leave the water alive.

'Bastian… If I don't make it…' I shouted above the rowdy waves as he swam for me again and grasped me tightly to him.

'Stop it! You will!'

Another wave took me even as he spoke and once more, I was thrown into the rocks. I gasped as I felt my skin tear again, so fragile in the hands of such an attacker.

'Bastian…' I cried as he grabbed me yet again, crying a little with fear and tiredness.

'Maddi! Hold on!' he said, then moved so that I was held grappled on his back. I clutched him, just holding on as he began to swim one-handed towards a large outcrop which could not have been more than four or five foot above us. It was arduous work against the tide and twice again we almost lost the battle. The waves were lapping the outcrop but if we could get up, it was safer at least. Seeing his destination, I slid back down and swam too, taking some of the pressure from him. As we arrived, it was I who found it easier to climb, then turned back to grip his hand in mine and half pull him up. Bastian gave a grunt and then lay still. It wasn't until that moment that I realised the extent of his injury, the slash in his arm which ran from the back of his hand to his elbow, the arm seemed to be broken too, from the shape of it, but thankfully the bone was not protruding.

'Oh God!' I gasped, 'your arm!'

Bastian said nothing, but pulled his body back, towards the cliff where our outcrop met it.

Safe.

Bastian looked grey with effort and pain though. Despite that I'd shed my petticoats, I still had my skirt and, using a rough edge of the ledge, I tore the hem to several long strips and then moved back to Bastian.

'Hold your arm above your head,' I said, ever the doctor's daughter. 'Above your heart! It will slow the bleeding!' He obeyed. I gripped the wound in my hands and held the pressure on until the bleeding at least slowed, and then used my torn skirts to bandage. As I pulled it tight, he screamed, but then it was done.

'Keep it raised!' I ordered, tying a sling of sorts with my sodden skirt material, then scuffled back to the edge to survey the situation.

It was dire enough a view. The tide would be turning soon, I knew, but as it was we were completely surrounded by water aside from the sheer cliff-face behind us. From out at sea the wind still ripped by, roaring as it did so and turning the edges of the waves to brightest white horses dancing as they fell forward to crash about us. There was no route back to the village from here, not at high tide, and it was not swimmable. I glanced back at where Bastian lay so still and pale against the rocks. How long could we last in such conditions? Already I was shivering to a point that I felt I would never be warm again and I was relatively uninjured in comparison to Bastian. At the thought I put my hand up to my hair, sticky still, but no longer wet with blood! Good!

'Maddi…' Bastian's voice was thick and choked in pain. Carefully I made my way back to him across the slippery shelf.

'Bas, my love, I know you are in pain but…'

He shook his head, using his good hand to rub away tears. '*Mama?*' he whispered. 'Did Mama really…. Do this?'

I'd not even begun on that chain of thought yet! 'I know, my love, I know! She did but… but we will get through it!'

'She killed Alice?'

'Yes.'

'And… and Carfax?'

'Him too,' I whispered, I did not mention that other yet – her confession that she'd killed his natural father too, that would have finished him off, I think. I put my hand into Bastian's – it was like ice! He was shivering uncontrollably, his whole body juddering. I put my arms about him, hoping that my own form – drenched as it was – would give him body heat rather than sap his.

'I'm… I'm sorry…' he whispered at last, 'I'm sorry that I said – that I believed – what I did.'

'And I too. We were so convinced it was one of us. Both… but…but did you really think it was *me?*'

He nodded, then shuffled and since again, 'I did… Mama was… was convincing,' he was shivering again, his whole body trembling, I bit down on panic and in an attempt to keep him talking and awake, I spoke again:

'And I thought it was you! What a pair we are!'

'W-who w-would ever h-have believed it was Mama?' he asked through shivers. I pulled him closer, trying to warm him.

'I-is Nora safe?' he asked.

'I don't know!'

'She c-can look after herself, I a-am sure, and Evie. Mama would n-never hurt Evie... would she?'

The bead of panic inside me tried to bloom again but I quashed it, 'no, I don't believe she would,' I managed, 'but then I never thought she'd hurt me, either.'

Bastian let out a strange growl and laid his head back against the cliff behind us. His eyes were already raw from both crying and the pain.

'How long until the tide dips?' I asked, he knew the waters better than I.

'Two, three hours.' The stutter from shivering was lessened, I noticed. My body, cold as it was, was warming him at least a little. He no longer seemed so fazed either, despite that I could feel his body juddering beside me. I was cold too but I suppose my adrenaline was still keeping me alert then.

'So long!' I whispered.

'It will pass,' he murmured, 'We will be fine, I promise, just a bit cold and... and sore but...'

I said nothing but laid my head down on his shoulder, it was going to be a long wait. The water's swish and roar was almost hypnotic. Bastian and I sat huddled together, shivering and in the end even words dried up, so that we sat together in silence just holding each other. At about an hour in, I finally heard a sound above us, the sound of footsteps. At once I was on my feet.

'Hello!' I shouted, 'Hello is somebody there?'

'Maddi?' Nora's voice. 'Heavens rejoice!'

'Nora! Thank goodness!'

'What, where are you?' she called down.

'On the ledge, just below!'

And then her dear face peering over. 'Oh! Goodness! What is happening? Mama came in all of a flutter and said you were... oh God! She said you were dead from a fall and that Bas... Bas was... Bas are you down there too?'

'I'm here,' he managed to call up, 'closer in towards the wall. I'm injured but alive.'

'Oh thank goodness!'
'Where is my daughter?' I called up.
'Well, in her nursery of course...'
'And Mama?'
'Mama went back out, she was in a panic! She said she was going to town for a doctor but that was over an hour ago and I got scared and...'

Bastian had closed his eyes again, the sudden removal of my form from him had set him shivering again too. I had to do something.

'Nora. We need your help! Go to the village and get us some blankets and an arm sling from Simon? We're freezing and trapped until the tide turns properly. Don't trust your mother though!'

'Don't trust Mama?'

'She... she pushed me...' I managed it, 'She's come unhinged and needs a doctor but for now it's more pressing that I get a blanket because your brother is in mild hypothermia and a sling because he has a badly broken arm.'

Nora seemed engulfed with panic again for another moment, but then cried down and affirmative and sped off into the night.

After that, the fear of us dying down there lessened. Nora was back within fifteen minutes laden with blankets and in the company of my cousin, Simon, who called down all sorts of medical questions at us. The boats couldn't come for us as I had suspected, due to the storm, but with the use of a rope to lower things down, they could at least keep us comfortable as the tides turned. The blankets they lowered down first and at once I wrapped them about Bastian, tearing up a little as he clenched his teeth against the pain. They lowered down too a bottle of rich warming brandy, clinking and clacking against the cliffs as it came down to us.

'Here,' I ordered, holding the bottle up to my husband and with gratitude he drank the dulling spirit. Nora remained up above us throughout, then, whilst the rest of the party moved away to gather at the beach edge, waiting for the waters to part enough to rescue us.

What a long night that was! And yet, all things must end and so did that terrible long dark wait. Eventually, the waters began to recede and with the ropes which Nora threw down from above, we were able to lower Bastian down into the by then waist-high water, and then myself. It was difficult to walk for the current and the shifting sands under my feet but Simon and some other men from the village met us about halfway and they wrapped us at once in blankets, helping to lift Bastian up and carry him where his strength was failing. All at once, I felt weaker too, the strength I was holding onto somehow vanishing when the responsibility was off me. Simon put an arm about me, holding me up and urging me on, just a step, and then another. The rest is a blur.

Twenty-One

And so I bring this tale to an end, and with it those final fine details of what actually had happened. This is pieced together bit by bit wherever possible, from various sources which I have gathered over the years to try to explain it all. Of what had happened in the Caribbean, details were more shaded. Baron Carfax had been facing bankruptcy and so the stories about his embezzlement were indeed true. He'd stolen and diverted money to himself and then had been about to flee. Hearing of it, Henri Lloyd had gone out to speak with them, and to take custody of his children, if he could. Whatever had happened, the detail is shrouded in mystery even still, it had ended with Lady Carfax shoving him so that he fell into the cave where his poor body had lain for years, unfound. Despite that he'd not witnessed the murder, one of the Carfaxes had suspected that Monroe might have realised what had happened, and so the bribery had begun. Them to Monroe, not the other way around! Monroe, in writing to me, claimed no knowledge of the murder but I suppose I shall never really know.

The rest was more straightforward. Lady Carfax had decided to remove Alice from the picture, mainly due to her son's attachment to me, his suicide attempt, and increasing pressure of the annulment. Alice's death she had set up to look like a suicide, with me as the scapegoat should it have been needed. In a moment of foresight, she'd told Bastian she'd seen me on the cliffs and thereby had – as she so succinctly put it - planted a seed. Baron Carfax, however, had buckled, for whatever reason – most likely fear in his wife's behaviour – and so had threatened to talk. This we could only surmise from Lady Carfax's words to me before she'd pushed me. Somehow she'd lured him away and killed him out on the moors. There she'd somehow laid him out in the cottage – another pointer to my guilt.

And so then, to what happened afterwards. Lady Carfax was never brought to justice. Many people, Nora included, believe her to be alive somewhere, absconded and hiding, but Bastian and I both saw her face as she fled, and neither of us believe that is the case at all. If you want my view, I think she probably went into the water too, afterwards, but managed to elude being found as the people worked to rescue Bastian and I. I hope so. I don't like to think she's still out there, somewhere, watching!

Bastian was, of course, well after a fashion. He was very weak at first but with the care of his sister and I, he soon began to regain his old strength. His broken arm has given him odd aches and pains his whole life but he bares them with a smile, knowing as well as I do that it could have been so much worse. We are forever thankful to be alive, always, and in our close encounter with the hooded one, we both appreciate every moment more so.

Bastian and I took a trip a year later, leaving Evie with her aunt for care, and so Bastian was able to reconnect once again with his paternal grandmother. Nora went out alone several months after that and she never came home, finding there a family and a young man who was to become her husband where here was still so raw for her. Now that I am delivered of my third child, three beautiful girls, and there are years between us and those days of anguish and fear, I think we too might follow Nora, and have this draughty old house packed away and made ready for a tenant. Nobody can deny now, that there is little for us here, but back there in the Caribbean there is a family and a life filled with warm sunshine to be had. We just have to reach out and take it!

Author's note.

Whilst this novel is not an early one in terms of publication in my career, it is so in terms of when it was written. The House Above the Waves (THATW) was actually only my third novel, and was written back in 2005! THATW is also the first novel I wrote which contained no supernatural or fantasy elements, just a simple love story with a gothic-style murder mystery twist. Over the years, it has sat quietly in my "done" folder but never actually felt quite "done". Last year I opened it up again and began a read through which resulted in a full text revision. Since I had written it, the Black Lives Matter movement had been blown up into visibility here in the UK as well as in the states, and alongside this came a boom in understanding of some of the terrible ways in which POC were treated historically. Combined with this is the recent movement to a richer representation of POC in historical drama, with this small minority being finally recognised in a very white-washed medium. Suddenly, as I read and edited, it felt like this was the right time for a novel such as this one. Interestingly, in the feedback I received from my ARC readers, one of the things one of them said was how shocked they were at some of the language, especially the slurs that Alice uses in relation to Bastian. It made them feel uncomfortable. This, I explained, was actually done intentionally, as were using outdated terms and concepts as well as scenes like the heartbreaking realisation that Nora powered her skin to try to pale her complexion and the scenes where Bastian pities his daughter for looking "like him". I really wanted THATW to tell a story more than just the fictional adventures of Maddi and Bastian. I wanted it to paint a picture of what life really would have been like for somebody like Bastian (or indeed Nora!). I do apologise to anybody who found this to be hurtful or uncomfortable. I left that scene in because I am a firm believer that for progress in equality to continue, it is important that uncomfortable history needs to be not just remembered, but remembered without being romanticised.

Please see below for other novels I have written:

Fantasy

The Rostalis Trilogy:
The King's Idiot
The Queen's Dragon
The Dragon's Heir

Supernatural Romance

The Blood of the Poppies
The Man Who Painted a Fairy

The Haverleigh Trilogy:
Ella's Memoirs
The Black Marshes
Donor

Printed in Great Britain
by Amazon